THE MEDICO OF PAINTED SPRINGS

THE MEDICO OF PAINTED SPRINGS

JAMES L. RUBEL

ISBN-13: 978-1-957868-83-7

Published by
Cutting Edge Books
PO Box 8212
Calabasas, CA 91372
www.cuttingedgebooks.com

TABLE OF CONTENTS

Chapter One: First Blood 1
Chapter Two: The Warning 12
Chapter Three: Death Stalks. 22
Chapter Four: Gangrene 34
Chapter Five: The Reaper Rides 43
Chapter Six: The Gunhawk Deals 53
Chapter Seven: Ruin Rides the Mesa 63
Chapter Eight: Pieces of Glass 74
Chapter Nine: Gun Smoke 82
Chapter Ten: The Unknown Stranger 93
Chapter Eleven: Doc Deals a Hand 103
Chapter Twelve: Cloudburst 113
Chapter Thirteen: Feathers for the Doc 123
Chapter Fourteen: Puff Runs Wild 134
Chapter Fifteen: The Medico Lets Loose 143
Chapter Sixteen: Murder at the Circle Bar T 154
Chapter Seventeen: Maw Handles the Sharps 163
Chapter Eighteen: Escape 174
Chapter Nineteen: The Finger of Suspicion 184
Chapter Twenty: Morphine Instead of Bullets. 194
Chapter Twenty-One: Doc Keeps His Promise 204
Chapter Twenty-Two: Peace Comes to Painted Springs 214

CHAPTER ONE
FIRST BLOOD

Painted Springs!

Cliff Monroe had to grin as his gray eyes took in the row of weather-beaten, paintless, frame buildings that lined both sides of the dusty street.

The vehicle that had brought him from Tombstone slid to a creaking, squealing halt in front of the town's hostelry. The young physician, the ink hardly dry on his medical diploma, unkinked his long legs from their cramped position, and stepped down to the street. He smacked his broad shoulders with the flat of his hand to unload some of Arizona's surplus real estate, took off his Stetson, wiped the dust from his face, and got his first close-up of his new home.

The street was deserted except for two men watching each other gravely from opposite sides of the street. The populace had apparently gravitated to cooler spots. The scene was almost too peaceful.

Cliff turned to accept his baggage from the driver. That individual let out an unexpected yell, dropped the baggage on his passenger's head, and came tumbling after it. He grabbed Cliff by the arm and without ceremony or explanation dragged the medico to a position of safety in the rear of the vehicle.

The action was swift, unexpected. Now noting the man's actions, Cliff too peered around the rear of the stage. There was no need to question the man's strange behavior. The answer glared back at him from the actions of the two men he had lately noted eyeing each other.

They were now half way across the street and obviously goading each other with caustic remarks, their hands hanging perilously close to their six-guns. Cliff saw the man nearest to him suddenly take three strides and pass the center of the street. Almost simultaneously came the sharp bark of two .45s. The young medico had seen the hand of the man on the opposite side flow smoothly to his waist, had seen the spurt of bluish-red flame that leaped from his hand.

For just a moment, the man who had taken the steps stood rocking on his heels. Then his knees seemed to give way beneath him. The six-gun dropped to the street. Cliff saw one hand clutch spasmodically at his chest as he slumped over and collapsed in a heap. The other man holstered his gun, turned on his heel, and without even a backward glance at the huddled figure in the street, disappeared through the doors of the Lone Deuce Gambling Palace.

The medico had an immediate desire to go to the aid of the wounded man, but his early training had taught him that it was not always healthy to mix into something that didn't concern him. Instead, he followed the driver from behind their shelter.

"You're the new medico, ain't you, Bud?"

A bulky figure of a man stood facing him, his mild blue eyes peering into his with just the faintest suggestion of a twinkle. A long black frock coat hung loosely from his heavy shoulders. The stag butts of a pair of six-guns protruded from the tails of the clerical garment. A sheriff's star was pinned to his checkered shirt. His grizzled hair was only partially covered by the broad-brimmed black felt hat.

Cliff grinned and nodded. "I'm Dr. Cliff Monroe, yes." He motioned toward the huddled figure in the street. "Is that my first patient?"

The sheriff extended a bony hand. "Glad to know you, son. My name is Dorr Plum. I'm the sheriff of this county. I reckon that is your first patient if he ain't dead. Maybe we better take a look. I ain't layin' any bets. That Puff Gordon is a smart hombre with his iron. He don't usually miss a vital spot at that range."

Cliff got his medical kit and followed the sheriff to the center of the street, wondering why the law made no effort to apprehend the killer. Men began to appear from all sides. They gathered around as Cliff kneeled down and made a hasty examination. He found the man still breathing but getting weaker from loss of blood. He straightened up and spoke directly to the sheriff.

"He isn't dead yet by any means, but he's getting close to the border. There's a chance of pulling him through if I can find the bullet."

This information was greeted by curses from the men behind him and by sneering laughs from the men in front of the Lone Deuce. Such ribaldry was out of place and Cliff glanced sharply at the offenders. The man the sheriff had called Puff Gordon was standing in the doorway of the saloon, his lips set in a contemptuous grin. The medico had a momentary view of a pair of dark, venomous eyes flashing a veiled warning to him, then the sheriff's curt commands to carry the wounded into the hotel broke the spell.

The proprietor of the hotel chased the curious away, called loudly for his wife to bring hot water, and led the men with their burden to a room on the ground floor. Cliff unpacked his shining new instruments, rolled up his sleeves, and set to work. While the gray-eyed medico perspired over his first patient, the garrulous law officer explained the shooting.

"This is a right likely spot you picked to set up a practice, Doc. The sheepmen and the cowmen is up in arms. There's a range war goin' on that's likely to give you more patients than you know what to do with. It got so bad here 'bout three weeks ago I was scairt the governor might take a hand, so I called a conference and declared a truce. The center of that street is the dead line. The sheepmen stay on the other side, the cattlemen over here." He chuckled and mopped his forehead with a bandana. "It was a toss-up to see which side would get the Lone Deuce, that bein' the oasis in the county, but the sheepmen won. Course, at that it's an even break. The cattlemen got the only eatin' place in town. If a cowhand gets thirsty for a drop of red-eye he's just plain out of luck unless he wants to take a chance on mixin' it with lead on the way across. It's the same with them wooly tenders. If they gets hungry for some of Maw Blane's beaten biscuits, there's only one way to get it. Come a gunnin'."

"Do you mean to tell me that any man who crosses that line takes his life in his hands?" Cliff was astonished.

"That's the deal, Doc. That there Puff Gordon is a killer and ought to be swinging from the nearest cottonwood, but I agreed to keep my hands off as long as they stayed on their own sides. That's what happened to Pim here. Gordon can claim self defense 'cause Pim was the first to cross the street."

"Yes, and it's a down right shame." An elderly woman came into the room carrying a kettle full of steaming water.

"Hello, Maw!" the sheriff greeted her. "This here is Doctor Cliff Monroe, the new county health officer. Doc, this is Maw Blane. Her old man runs the Mansion House, but it's Maw's biscuits that brings in the business."

Cliff acknowledged the introduction with a nod, took the kettle of water from her, and in a moment was absorbed in his probing operations. Finally he straightened up and displayed a small chunk of lead gripped in his forceps. "Got it all right. There's a good chance now. If he pulls through the night, he ought to be as good as ever in a few weeks."

Maw Blane said, "It's a crying shame. What can I do, Doctor?"

Cliff got his first good look at her as he finished bandaging the patient. She could have passed for sixty, for her hair was iron gray, her face seamed with lines, but then the frontier makes old women fast. Beneath the rough exterior and homespun dress Cliff knew lay a heart as big as all out of doors. She was that type. It shone from her eyes and radiated from her like magnetic force.

"We'll just have to keep him quiet for a spell, Mrs. Blane." He saw tears of compassion in her eyes and hastened to add, "There is no cause for worry yet. There doesn't seem to be much fever. The bullet grazed his right lung and lodged close to the rib. If you can look after him for a bit, I'd like to get settled and unpacked."

The sheriff chuckled. "He ain't even had time to wash his face, Maw. All you got to do, Doc, to get patients is just to goad 'em into crossin' the street. You might come out on the veranda after supper and chaw some of Maw's biscuits. That's likely to bring some of the sheepmen over. If that don't work, you can cross over to the Lone Deuce and stand out in front with a quart of that snake pizen Tim Roney sells. That 'll sure start a massacre. Most of these cowhands has got swollen tongues they been dry so long."

Cliff grinned at the sheriff's humor and shook his head. "I guess that won't be necessary. If you'll show me where my headquarters are to be, I'll get cleaned up and unpacked."

The sheriff stood up and moved toward the door. "We got a right nice set of rooms waitin' for you, Doc. It's right over my office. I figured the law and health ought to be close together."

The medico found his rooms to be pleasant and comfortable. He was soon back to see his first patient. Pim was sleeping as well as could be expected considering the shock to his system.

Maw questioned him. "Where are you from, Doctor? I understood the sheriff to say you hailed from Texas."

Cliff nodded. "I was raised on a Texas ranch, Mrs. Blane. My father, John Monroe, owned the Bar Lazy X. Dad sold out some years ago and we moved to Fort Worth. He always had a sneaking respect for the medical profession and I entered medical school more to please him than anything else. After I got into it I found that I liked it."

"Whatever made you pick out this den of iniquity? If it wasn't for Paw ownin' this rat-trap of a place, I'd move out tomorrow, bag and baggage. There's the hardest-headed bunch of no-accounts in this county I ever laid eyes on. Take this crazy range war that's ragin'. It's just plain nonsense. There's plenty of room for both sheep and cattle to graze, but no—the cattlemen got to have it all and the wooly herders feel the same way. I can't blame the ranchers much, havin' been raised in Texas myself. After all they was the first on the ground and them sheep certainly make the free grazin' ground unfit for any other animal that wears horns."

Cliff smiled. "I understood you leaned toward the leather rather than the wool, Mrs. Blane. I probably would too, having been raised a cowman, only I have to remain neutral. My job here is to succor the sick."

Cliff soon had his office arranged and his shingle hung out. He was proud of that sign. It had been made by an expert sign painter in Fort Worth when he had accepted the position of County Health Officer for Brant County, Arizona. It made the sheriff's weather-beaten sign and those nearby look like the work of amateurs which they were.

His first patient, Percy Pim, the owner of the Circle Bar T, and the leader of the cowmen, was on the road to rapid recovery. His success with Pim, on which there had been odds bet that the man would never recover, increased his prestige, and patients began to flock in on him with all manner of ailments. The sudden flare-up of the range war ending in the shooting of Pim, had died down and the county was at peace, at least temporarily.

The sheriff had assured Cliff that the line in the street applied neither to the law nor to the health officer. Tim Roney, the bartender of the Lone Deuce, had been one of his first patients, calling to him to come over. Tim was suffering from a carbuncle which was making his ordinarily excellent humor exceedingly bad. As Tim was quite definitely aligned with the sheepmen, they being his only customers, he dared not come to Cliff's office for treatment. Consequently, the medico made almost daily trips to the Lone Deuce to treat him.

Several times while on these trips he saw Puff Gordon and his cronies lined up at the bar. Conversation immediately ceased when Cliff came through the doors. Finally Puff barred his way one day, planting himself squarely in front of him, his jaw thrust out belligerently, his dark eyes hard and unfriendly. Tim had started for his room, his temper already on edge from a sleepless night. The bartender turned and saw what had happened and came back.

Puff grunted, "Which side of this war are you on, Doc?"

Cliff had disliked the sheepman's looks from the first day when he had seen Puff swagger off after the shooting. The man's present attitude didn't contribute anything in his favor. His own eyes became a trifle grayer, a bit icier. He said:

"You seem to forget, Mr. Gordon, that I am a doctor and neither a sheepman nor a cattleman."

Tim interrupted at this point. He was getting tired of waiting. He pushed Puff roughly aside. "Come on, Doc. Let's get this over." He glared at the sheepman and taking hold of Cliff's arm piloted him to the rear of the gambling palace.

"You don't pack a gun, do you, Doc?" he questioned, as Cliff completed the painful lancing of the carbuncle and was bandaging it.

"Certainly not, Tim." He chuckled. "It isn't considered good ethics for a physician to carry firearms."

"Well, I'd feel a lot safer if I was you carryin' one. I ain't liked the talk that's been buzzin' around here lately. Since you pulled Pim back from the great divide, these sheepmen have about decided you're a cattleman. Puff Gordon has been doin' a lot of talkin' about runnin' you out of the county."

Cliff shrugged and repacked his kit. "Probably just talk, Tim. I hardly think he'd try anything like that."

Tim shook his head and lowered his voice. "Maybe not, but just the same I'd pack an iron if I was you. There's somethin' dang funny about this range war. If somebody 'ud throw down on Puff and put him out of business, I betcha there wouldn't be no war. He goes hightailin' it over into the next county every once in awhile to meet somebody, and every time he comes back the trouble starts again."

Tim followed Cliff past the bar. The same men were still there. One of them stuck out his foot as the doctor came within reach. The medico had to grab hold of the bar to keep from sprawling.

He didn't see the action behind him, but he heard the thud and crash of glass as the bartender brought a bottle down viciously on the sheepman's head. He turned in time to see his assailant sink to the floor. Then he heard Tim yell:

"Holster that iron, Puff, or I'll salivate you."

The gunman muttered something under his breath, scowled at the prone figure on the floor, and raised his eyes finally to meet Cliff's. "Yuh better not cross that line again, Doc," he snarled. "The sheepmen don't cotton overmuch to meddlin' medicos, especially vets that bring mangy mavericks back to life."

Tim raised his voice angrily. "Get out of here and stay, you ornery buzzards. The doc comes as often as he likes. This is my bailiwick and no gunhawk is givin' orders."

Puff backed to the door with his cronies at his heels. As he reached it he growled, "I'm givin' orders on this side, Doc. If yuh want to stay healthy yuh better stick to yore cattle friends on the other side."

Cliff wondered about the bartender's suspicions when he got back to his office. From all the reports he had heard, Burke Starweather was the real leader of the sheepmen and Puff his hired killer. Yet if Starweather was really the boss, why would Puff make periodical trips into the next county? Even Maw Blane had said that first night as they worked over Pim, that if Puff was removed from the scene, the range war would die out. And why should Puff single him out to make threats against his life? He had done nothing to incur the enmity of the sheepman outside of saving the rancher Pim's life. No, there was some other reason.

Cliff was in his office the next day and was suddenly drawn to the window by the thud of hoofs and the loud cries of the sheriff. A big black stallion was cavorting in the center of the street, on his back a young woman who was laughing, while the sheriff was endeavoring to hang on to the bridle of the frisky animal and lead him to the Mansion House hitching rail. Several of the cowmen were standing on the hotel porch, laughing, and yelling advice.

But by the time Cliff got down the stairs to see the fun, the animal was safely tethered to the rail and now stood quietly while his owner dismounted. He heard the girl say:

"He's just naturally a smart sheep horse, Sheriff. He's not accustomed to being hitched to a cow rail."

Cliff got a good look at the newcomer as she came from behind the stallion. He knew who she was immediately. The descriptions he had had of Nancy Starweather were not overdrawn. She was prettier even than the verbal paintings he had heard. He had a glimpse of bright corn-colored hair framing an oval face tanned to a golden color by the hot winds of the mesa. Her slender figure was encased in doe-skin riding breeches and topped with a flaming yellow shirt. He stopped short and stared.

The girl apparently felt that scrutiny for her eyes engaged his. She looked him over with a coolness that brought the red to his face. The sheriff came to the rescue.

"Hello, Doc!" he grinned. "Come over here and meet the pride of the county. Nancy this is Cliff Monroe, the new medico. Next time your old man gets one of them gout attacks call on Cliff here."

The girl acknowledged the introduction with just a slight lift of her eyebrows. Cliff, still red from the coolness of her stare, managed a bow. Nancy vanished inside the Mansion House followed by the sheriff.

The medico vaguely wondered as he retraced his steps to his offices, if the girl was really as big-hearted as the tales told of her. She was undeniably pretty. Much prettier than anything he had expected to meet in Painted Springs. What had been the color of those eyes? Were they violet or blue? He was busy going over in his mind the girl's fine points, when he heard steps on his stairs. A moment later he heard the tap of high-heeled boots in his reception room. He looked out.

"Hello, Cliff, you old buzzard! Just thought I'd drop in and see if you was the same ornery critter I used to chase around the Bar Lazy X."

"Kentucky Landers!" Cliff gripped his hand and grinned from ear to ear. "What are you doing out here in Arizona?"

"I'm ramrod out at the Circle Bar T. When Pim told me who the new doc was, I come hightailin' it for town. How's old spike chin and the missus? I moved out here right after your dad sold out and went to Fort Worth."

For a time they talked of their old days together when Kentucky had been a cowhand on his father's ranch. Finally the cowboy lowered his voice and leaned closer.

"I understand you can cross that there dead line, Cliff. Would you mind doin' a favor for an old pal?" His manner was most mysterious. He got up and glanced across the street, licked his lips, at last coming back to face Cliff. "Next time you cross over, get me a bottle of red-eye, will yuh? I ain't had a drink of real liquor since this fool war started, and my tongue is just about dried up to the size of a gopher's."

Cliff chuckled. "I thought there was something like that in the wind." He shook his head. "Nothing doing, Kentucky. No drinks until the war is over."

The cowhand frowned. "Say which side of the fence are you on, Cliff?"

The medico shook his head. "Neither, old timer, I'm neutral. I've got to be. My job as county health officer makes it imperative that I visit both sides. All that concerns me is sickness. I'd as soon doctor a sick sheepherder as a cowpoke."

Kentucky's forehead wrinkled. "I was sort of hopin' you might be on the right side, but—" He put his hand on Cliff's shoulder and his eyes looked troubled—"you better watch out for that Puff Gordon. I hear he's threatening to run you out of town. If you need any help, you can just bet the boys'll back you up."

CHAPTER TWO
THE WARNING

News traveled with lightning speed in Brant County. Cliff's success with his first patient, the relief he administered to the ailing, gave him tremendous prestige. Unfortunately for the medico, the majority of the cases were charitable ones, there were few who could afford to pay him for his services, but Cliff didn't mind. He felt that he was making headway, gaining a practice, and learning from experience. Many of the sick couldn't come to his office, so the medico purchased a horse from Percy Pim, a fine big roan, and from that time on, Cliff and his horse, which he named Snort after the animal's peculiar habit of breathing, were familiar sights from one end of the county to the other.

Finding it necessary to rise at an early hour in order to reach some ailing member of a sheepherder's tribe at a remote corner of the county, Cliff began to appreciate the reasons for the naming of Painted Springs. The spring itself was now nothing more than a few drops of water oozing from its underground source, but the surrounding terrain where the water spread, was lush with bright green grass, waving willows, and hosts of wild flowers. Directly in back of the spring rose a red sandstone cliff, its sides patterned into myriad formations by the spring rains. In the early morning, when the sun was just beginning to cut through the sea of swirling mist that covered the mesa, or in the late afternoon, these turrets, embattlements, and peaks of jagged rock reflected a riot of tones.

In the background stood the jigsaw line of hills, the higher peaks of the range, and the hollows with their reservoirs of color.

The mesa itself, dry now, was covered with gray-green cholla, while beyond it and at the limits of the county, the saffron-hued desert began. Here were Apache plumes, dry and desiccated, shriveled greasewood, parched mesquite, and waving plumes of ocotillo.

Many a morning as he crossed the mesa and cut into the water-gutted arroyos, the face of Nancy Starweather appeared in front of him like a mirage, setting him to wondering. It was the color of her eyes that had bothered him the most. He had only seen her that day she dismounted in front of the Mansion House. Each morning as he mounted Snort for his almost daily trips to his patients, he lived in the hope that he might cross her path in some unseen section of the range, stop and talk to her, or ride side by side until he could obtain the answers to the questions that assailed him.

But if Nancy was abroad, Cliff saw no sign of her. No matter how close he came to the Starweather ranch with its large flocks of sheep, he never got close enough to as much as catch a distant glimpse of her. Several times he did see mysterious horsemen from afar who quite apparently had no desire to meet him. They would vanish mysteriously into gullies leaving no trace. He questioned some of his patients as to these riders, but without success. The inevitable reply would come from the Mexican sheepherder, "Quién sabe?"

Occasionally he would find a small band of sheep, separated from the larger flock, and would ride closer to investigate. What he usually found sickened him and proved that the range war was by no means finished. What he had thought were live sheep, proved to be dead ones, shot from ambush by some unseen attacker.

The same proved true of stray herds of cattle. Some mysterious rider would cut them out from the larger herd, drive them into some arroyo or gully, and there butcher them with a six-gun. He said nothing of these discoveries to either the sheepmen or the cattlemen, but he often discussed them with Dorr Plum. The sheriff would look his disgust.

"Keep that to yourself, Doc. I know it's been goin' on, but it's just like we was sittin' on a powder keg waitin' for the fuse to get to her. Let them crazy loons find it out for themselves. You can't knock no sense into their thick skulls."

Cliff left the sheriff and started across the street to see how Tim's carbuncle was getting along. He had just reached the swinging doors of the Lone Deuce when Puff Gordon emerged and barred his way. His eyes were bloodshot from an overdose of red-eye, and Cliff realized that the man was in an ugly mood. He tried to ignore him, and push on past, but Puff had no such ideas. He shoved Cliff back.

"This here is sheepmen's territory, Doc. You better hightail it back across the street. I thought I told you once I was givin' orders on this side."

Cliff liked neither the tone of the bully's voice nor his manner of approach, but he held his temper. He replied, evenly, "I thought we had settled that, Mr. Gordon. Again you seem to forget that I am the county health officer and not aligned with either side. Tim Roney happens to be in need of my services and I'm going in to visit him."

Puff's eyes narrowed. "You're a goin' back across the street, and you're not a goin' to come back here again, unless—" His hand went menacingly toward the six-gun—"you'd like to be carried back horizontal." The joke seemed to please him and his thin lips split into an unpleasant grin.

Cliff's eyes changed suddenly from a light gray to the color of slate. "I'm not looking for any trouble, Mr. Gordon, but since you asked for it, here goes." Very slowly he set his medical kit on the plank boards of the Lone Deuce's veranda, straightened, and his fists clenched. "Do I have to knock you out of the way or will you get out of the way."

The sheepman guffawed. "Listen to what's talkin'!"

If he hadn't laughed, he might have seen the fist that rose upward from Cliff's side and caught him on the jaw, sending him reeling backwards. As it was, the blow coming so unexpectedly, wiped the smile from his leering face. His high-heeled boots caught on a crack and he sprawled, hands clutching for support, spreading his length on the boards.

He scrambled to his feet with his hand reaching for his holster. Cliff saw the six-gun spring into his palm, saw the killer look in his eyes, expected any moment to see the stab of blue flame, and to feel the impact of the lead.

"You damned lousy maverick!" the sheepman snarled. "There's goin' to be a new medico in this county and right soon."

If Puff hadn't withheld the pressure of his finger on the trigger to curse his opponent, he would have made good his boast. If his eyes hadn't been blind to everything but Cliff, he would have seen the frock-coated figure that had in several strides reached the center of the street. There came the sudden blast of a six-gun. Puff let out a cry of pain as his iron went spinning from his hand. Cliff heard the sheriff's voice booming from behind him.

"Next time you throw down on the health officer of this county, Puff, I'll just naturally let daylight into you. If you aim to back up them orders of yours, you better use your paws. Appears to me like the doc was willin' to give you all you want. Hop to it, Cliff."

The bark of the gun had brought the curious from their duties. Two sheepmen and the bartender appeared at the door of the saloon. On the opposite side of the street, Paw Blane and a rancher were now staring at the scene.

But Cliff was hardly aware of them. He was watching his opponent. Puff rubbed his injured hand for an instant. Suddenly he mouthed a curse and made a dive for the medico, arms flailing. Cliff met the attack with a short left jab to the sheepman's midriff, followed it with a right to the bully's head, jarring the man to his heels. Puff staggered back, rallied, and again sailed in, but this time with more caution. His fist connected with the side of Cliff's head. It sent lights dancing before the medico's eyes.

"Sock him, Puff," came from one of the sheepman's cronies.

Cliff stepped nimbly aside as his opponent swung viciously at him again, sparred for a moment waiting for his head to clear. Suddenly his fist lashed out with the speed of a rattlesnake's strike, landing with a loud smack on the sheepman's jaw. Puff reeled backwards. Again one of those fists of the broad shouldered medico came sailing at him. He dodged and tried to guard himself, but Cliff's fists were like a swarm of angry hornets buzzing about his head.

Paw Blane was leaping up and down on the hotel veranda, yelling at the top of his lungs. There were no longer any cheers coming from the Lone Deuce. There was no doubt in the minds of any of the bystanders as to who was getting the worst of it. Even Puff realized this quite suddenly. Somehow he managed to elude the medico's flying fists, to back off, and gather his scattered forces.

His horse was directly behind him. The sheepman decided that he had had enough. He turned, made a desperate leap for the saddle as if the devil himself was on his tail, and dug his spurs into the animal viciously. The horse whirled and with a thunder of hoofs carried Puff out of town and out of sight in a cloud of dust.

The sheriff slapped Cliff on the back. "Son," he said, admiringly, "you sure pack a mean wallop in them paws of yours. It's just too bad you studied to be a medico. You'd made a powerful good fighter. That's one time when that no-account skunk got what was comin' to him." He frowned suddenly and shook his head. "But it's bad, Doc. That wooly nurse is liable to take a pot shot at you some day when you're ridin' them hills."

Cliff picked up his kit. "I don't think he'd stoop to such tactics, Sheriff. I'm much obliged though for your timely arrival. I was expecting any moment to see that cannon go off. The barrel looked as big as a hogshead."

For the next few days Cliff was greeted with more friendliness at the cattle ranches, but at the sheepman's it was decidedly cold. They accepted his ministrations because there was no other doctor within fifty miles. Yet they showed very plainly that they considered him definitely in the opposing camp. Even the Mexican herders, who had greeted him warmly before, were now unfriendly.

Several days later he came into the Mansion House for lunch to find Nancy Starweather sitting at the table deep in conversation with Maw Blane. She nodded to him as he sat down in the chair beside her. Maw got up to get him a plate and the girl turned to face him.

"I hear you are something of a fighter as well as a doctor. Is that part of a physician's training, Doctor Monroe?"

Cliff reddened and laughed to hide his embarrassment. He was more than pleased to find this girl sitting by his side, but he didn't like the mockery in her voice. He said stiffly, "That's rather unfair, isn't it, Miss Starweather. Even a doctor has to defend himself at times, especially in a country like this where there are so many demented persons."

Nancy's eyebrows arched. "Meaning, I suppose, that you think we are all more or less crazy." She laughed. "I guess you are right, Doctor."

Cliff shook his head. "I was referring to the maniacs who insist on keeping this range war alive. By the way, Miss Starweather, how is your father? I understand he has had another one of his gout attacks."

She nodded. "Father is limping around the house and making life miserable for everyone."

Cliff was unconsciously studying her eyes as she spoke. "That's queer. I'd have sworn your eyes were violet, but they aren't. They are really a turquoise blue."

"Do you think so, Doctor?" There was a good deal of the coquette in Nancy and the smile she gave him was devastating.

"What a pretty compliment! I see you are also a flatterer. You are really quite a remarkable young man. Physician, fighter, flatterer, and rather nice looking—" She cocked her head on one side and regarded him impishly—"in a rough way. It's too bad you have to be aligned with the enemies of my father."

Cliff frowned. "Please get that notion out of your head. I cannot afford to align myself with either side. I am neutral."

Her face clouded over suddenly. "Tell me. How is Manuel's little boy? Do you think he is better?"

"Much better, Miss Starweather. It was just a case of malnutrition. If they will just continue to feed the little fellow properly, in another month or so, he'll be as fit as a fiddle."

She then questioned him about his other patients. Cliff was astonished at her information. She seemed to know each one of the ailing intimately and to have visited them. He wondered why he hadn't crossed her path in the hills. Had she avoided him deliberately?

Lunch over, she professed an interest in his office. He explained his remedies, showed her his modern equipment. He even prevailed on her to listen while he diagnosed and prescribed for two patients. When the last one had gone she said:

"You love your work, don't you?"

"Most assuredly. I feel that I'm doing some good in the world, even though the reward is slight."

"I think it is splendid. If I were a man I think I should like to be a physician."

They reached the hotel's hitching rail. As he was saying good-bye he saw Puff come out of the Lone Deuce and stand there watching them, his eyes narrowed. Nancy saw him, smiled at Cliff, turned the stallion, and trotted him across the street. Puff came to the edge of the porch and stood there puffing on a cigarette while he talked to her. Cliff went back to his office.

There was no longer any question in his mind as to his feelings toward Nancy Starweather. He was deeply in love; in love with a girl who was miles out of his reach at the present moment. The sheepmen had definitely placed him in the opposing camp. Even if the girl did by any chance return his love, her father would put his foot down on such a romance.

Cliff had never seen Burke Starweather, but his mind held a vivid picture of the old man. A dozen individuals in Painted Springs had painted the sheep baron to him as a scoundrel, a hard-headed old fighter, and a man who would stop at nothing to attain his ends. The medico didn't believe all he heard and now that he knew Nancy better, he was inclined to take some of the information with a grain of salt. He couldn't quite picture Nancy's father as being as bad as he was painted. No doubt the man had been goaded into doing things because of the cattlemen's enmity toward him and his wooly animals.

It was late the next afternoon when Cliff, tired from a day's hard riding to distant patients, started back for Painted Springs. He had covered half the distance and had just dropped into the Arroyo Espectro, a deep cañon that separated the sheep ranch of Mullaby from the free grazing ground to the south, when the sound of gunfire, three quick shots, startled him. A moment later there came to his ears the pounding of hoofs, then silence.

Cliff urged the roan forward. At the end of the cañon he found what he had expected. Three wooly bodies were bunched in a mass. His horse shied away from the corpses, but the medico urged him closer to get a better look. A groan from the nearby brush as his horse's hoofs tapped on the shale floor brought Cliff to attention. He dismounted, led the roan around the dead animals and peered into the mesquite. A man lay there, his face and hair matted with blood.

Cliff made a swift examination. The herder was a stranger to him. The bullet had undoubtedly done its work. It was only a miracle that the man was still alive. Cliff washed his face, forced a drop of liquor between his lips, and made him as comfortable as possible. It was all he could do. The man's life was ebbing fast.

The herder opened his eyes finally and stared at the doctor. He tried to speak. Cliff leaned closer, listening intently. The gasping and choking words from the man's frothing lips were barely distinguishable. Cliff's eyes hardened.

"You say it was a sheepman? What did he look like?" Cliff held the wounded man by the shoulders.

The herder tried to speak. It was useless. The tiny spark of life had burned out. His body went limp in Cliff's hands.

As Cliff again mounted and topped the rise that led to the mesa and town, he saw a horseman coming towards him at a steady lope that would cross his path. Soon he recognized the rider. It was Puff Gordon. The man reined in and came to a stop directly in front of Cliff.

"I just thought I'd give you a warnin', medico," he snarled. "This country ain't big enough to hold us two. If I was you, I'd pack my carpet bag and hightail it for a healthier climate."

"Meaning what?" Cliff regarded the other steadily.

"Meanin' that us sheepmen ain't got no use for a vet, especially one who pokes his nose into things what don't concern him. I'd hate to see such a nice young fella rid out o' town on a rail." He grinned unpleasantly.

"You're pretty handy at making threats, aren't you, Gordon? As yet I don't know why you object to my presence—" He placed the accent on the 'yet'—"but you might as well get this straight. It will take more than threats to run me out of the county."

Puff's eyes narrowed even as his face turned a shade redder under its bronze coat. "I'm givin' yuh two days, understand?" he growled. "If yuh ain't out of the county by then, us sheepmen knows a good way to send yuh out." With that he wheeled his horse and spurred him.

Cliff jogged along as the sheepman vanished into a gully and was hidden from view. The meager information he had gleaned from the now dead herder had pointed the finger of suspicion at Puff Gordon. He was convinced that there was something more behind this range war than just a bunch of disgruntled ranchers. Puff, he knew, was an employee of Starweather, but was he also an employee of some one else? Was Puff playing both ends against the middle? Had he deliberately shot that herder and butchered the sheep with the hope that the sheepman would retaliate and do the same thing to some cowhand and his steers?

He found the sheriff in his office when he got to town. He told him of the dead herder and the sheep. He also told him of Puff's threats.

"I sure wish you'd pack an iron, Cliff." The sheriff shook his head. "I don't like the looks of things. He's a tough hombre, that Puff Gordon, and a killer if I ever see'd one. Things is goin' to bust wide open 'round here, one of these days. They can't go on butcherin' each other's cattle and sheep without it endin' up in a free for all. I wish I could keep the news of this herder's murder to myself, but I can't. Just as sure as hell, some cowpoke is goin' to get his. When he does, then the war is on with a vengeance."

"Well, I'm convinced that Puff Gordon is at the bottom of it, Dorr, even though I can't prove it. It's just as Maw Blane said, if you'd remove him the range war would die out. It's a darned shame the law lets a man like that loose."

"Ain't it? But he's smart, Cliff. Puff is nobody's fool, and I just don't savvy the play yet."

Cliff grinned. "Neither do I, Dorr, but sooner or later that maverick is going to show his hand. In the meanwhile don't worry about me. Puff isn't fool enough to try any shananigans with the county health officer. It wouldn't be healthy."

CHAPTER THREE
DEATH STALKS

Nancy had heard Puff talking to her father the next morning about the finding of the dead herder, and knew that retaliation in some form was planned, but her father was suffering untold agonies with his gout, and she thought the wisest move was not to mention the affair to him or try to get additional information.

"Why don't you let me call Dr. Monroe, Dad?" she asked. "I'm sure he could help you."

Burke Starweather grunted. "That hoof and mouth specialist? You want me to call in a man who's in the other camp? I'd rather suffer the tortures of the damned."

"Don't be childish, Dad. I know he is definitely lined up with the cattlemen, but you're getting impossible to live with. You've got to have medical attention and Dr. Monroe is the only physician within fifty miles. Whether you like it or not, I'm going to ride in and ask him to come out."

Starweather groaned. "Damn this achin' hoof, anyhow!"

"That settles it." Nancy squared her shoulders. "I'm not going to see you suffer when there's a doctor handy, even if he is perhaps a horse doctor."

There were none of the hands at the corral, which was strange for that hour in the morning, but she guessed that they were at the scene of the crime, so looped and saddled the black stallion herself, mounted, and headed for town. She found Cliff in his office busy with several patients and was forced to await her turn.

"This is a pleasant surprise, Miss Starweather," he greeted her. "Is this a social call or medical?"

Nancy smiled, but it was more or less frosty, and Cliff felt it. "I wanted you to come out to the ranch, Dr. Monroe and see Dad. His gout is ruining his good disposition and making him impossible to live with."

"Of course I'll come. I have another call to make at Manuel's anyhow and that is right on the way."

Cliff got his roan from the livery stable and stirrup to stirrup they headed across the mesa toward the S Bar 8. Cliff tried his best to keep up the conversation, but the girl was taciturn and decidedly cool. She answered his inquiries stiffly and seemed to prefer silence. The medico had to give up at last. His companion was not in a sociable mood.

Reaching the S Bar 8, Nancy unsaddled the stallion, while Cliff got his medical kit from the saddle bag and tied the roan to the corral poles. He followed her silently to the house. They found Burke Starweather sitting on the porch, his leg swathed in bandages and his foot propped up on a chair for more comfort. He was apparently relieved to get medical attention, but far from friendly. Cliff had his first chance to size the man up.

The sheepman was a large man with grizzled moustache and a beard trimmed to a point. His eyes, which were a slate color, were now racked with pain from his pulsating foot. He winced and said, "Damnit," in a gruff, quarrelsome voice when Cliff began to unwrap the bandages to make the examination.

Cliff touched several sore spots. "Pretty bad foot, Starweather, but I think we can ease the pain up some. Then if you'll follow directions, in a week's time or more, you should be able to walk on it. You perhaps won't agree with me, but proper diet is about the only thing that will do you any good. It is caused principally by too much uric acid in the blood stream. You'll have to cut out meat in every form, stop drinking, and go on a strict diet of vegetables."

Starweather grunted. "That's cattle food."

Cliff laughed. "Hardly that, Starweather. Sheep and cattle are about the only animals that have sense enough to eat nothing but greens, but even they won't eat the kind of vegetables I want you to eat. What you need is starches. Potatoes, plenty of bread, mixed with any of the other greens such as beans, cauliflower, lettuce, and so forth."

"You're a hell of a doctor. I can't live on that kind of stuff."

Cliff was getting a better insight into the character of Nancy's parent. The old man was undoubtedly stubborn, tenacious, and inclined to doubt anyone else's judgment. He produced a bottle of pills from his kit, wrote out instructions about their use and handed it to Nancy.

"This is about all I can do for you, Starweather. Use some hot poultices on the foot and take this as prescribed."

"Say, what are you, Doc?" the sheepman blurted out suddenly. "Which side of the fence are you on? You appear like a pretty sensible sort of a cuss."

Cliff welcomed the opportunity. He grinned. "Seems like everybody around here is determined to get me into this range war whether I want to or not. You all forget that I'm the health officer of the county." He shook his head. "Just as I've told everyone else in this district, I'm neutral. It's my business to tend the sick. It makes no difference to me which side they're on. You ought to realize that. I think I can truthfully say that I saved Percy Pim's life, while on the other hand here I am trying to ease your pain."

Starweather snorted and his brows contracted. "That polecat Pim! Too darned bad the onery critter didn't die. It 'ud be good riddance. This country ain't big enough to hold us both and some day he's goin' to find it out."

Nancy put a hand on his shoulder soothingly. "Now, Dad, don't get yourself all worked up. It's bad for your gout."

"Shucks! If it wasn't for the pesky disease I'd be right with the boys now, takin' a pot shot—" He stopped suddenly, realizing that he had almost said too much.

But Cliff appeared not to notice the slip. He stood up, putting his kit under his arm. "I'll have to run along now. I'll drop in and see you in a few days. Good day, sir."

Cliff went for his horse. What had Starweather meant by that remark? Were the sheepmen planning a raid in retaliation for the killing of the herder? Two of the S Bar 8 boys rode in as Cliff was packing his kit into the saddle bag. He overheard part of their conversation, noticed their surprised glances in his direction, observed that their conversation was cut short immediately. They scowled at him. Cliff just gave them a friendly grin, mounted, and rode off without even a backward glance.

Starweather's remark, the little he had overheard, and his own knowledge of what to expect, he pieced together into a framework. But had he any right to interfere in this range war? He decided he had. It was up to him to warn the Circle Bar T. They ought to at least have a fighting chance, particularly as he was sure that it was no cattleman who was responsible for the death of the herder.

The shortest way to Pim's spread was through the Arroyo Espectro and Cliff took it at an easy lope. He did not wish to appear hurried in case he ran into some of the S Bar 8 boys. He noted as he passed the scene of the killing, that the dead sheep had been stripped of their hides and flesh by the nightly prowlers of the cañon, also that the herder had been given a decent burial.

Topping a rise he ran into three of the sheepmen doing guard duty. Far below lay the fertile range of the Circle Bar T, and the sight of the three men convinced Cliff that trouble was in the immediate offing. They all greeted him in a surly fashion, eyeing him suspiciously.

"Where yuh headin' for, Doc?" one of them asked as Cliff reined in to pass them.

A faint flicker of light came into the medico's eyes, but was gone instantly. These were the men who kept the range war alive. Hard-fisted, fish-eyed, hired gunmen. Many of them with prison records and a lot that should have had them. Cliff despised them as he would a rattlesnake. He stopped the roan, reached for the makings, and coolly rolled a cigarette before replying. When the smoke was going properly to suit him, his eyes met those of the man who had questioned him.

"I'm on my way to the Circle Bar T. Have to take one last look at Pim's wound, then I'm coming back this way to see Manuel Geosta's boy. Why?"

The man's eyes narrowed and he frowned. "Where yuh been?"

"I don't know that it's any of your business, but I don't mind telling you. I just came from the S Bar 8, having attempted to relieve the pain of Starweather's gouty member. If there aren't any more questions, suppose you three get out of the way. I've a lot of riding to do before the day is over."

"He does too damn much noseyin' around, if you'd ask me," one of the others spat out.

The first sheepman looked suspiciously at the medico sitting unconcernedly on his horse. "I reckon yuh didn't hear nothin' up there now, did yuh?"

Cliff looked at the tough face and fishy eyes with perfect innocence. He shook his head and grinned. "About all I heard was the groans of my patient and his fluent curses. Should I have heard something?"

The man's eyes dropped and he turned away, shaking his head. Cliff went on down the slope at an easy pace, but as soon as he was out of sight and into cattle country, he urged the roan ahead in swift flight. Reaching the corral of the Circle Bar T, he dropped lightly to the ground and made for the ranchhouse. He found Pim and his hands busy tackling their lunch. They greeted him and urged him to join them. Cliff sat down, passed a few remarks about the dryness of the country, and tackled his food.

He saw Kentucky Landers finish and rise to go. Cliff stopped him with, "Wait, Kentucky. I've got some news for you."

It was not the words, but the way he said it, that made all hands turn towards him. For a moment you could have heard a pin drop. Cliff pushed back his chair. The noise of the scraping legs on the bare floor seemed to make men even tenser.

Cliff said, "There's trouble brewing over in the other camp. I didn't get enough to give you men any real straight dope, but I did hear enough to convince me that the sheepmen are planning a raid of some kind on the Circle Bar T, because of that herder who was killed."

It was like the explosion of a bomb in their midst. Chairs were pushed back hurriedly, but Pim stopped them with a quick command. "Let's hear it, Doc. We all know now that you're a cattleman."

Cliff frowned. That was just what he didn't want them to think. "Don't get me wrong, Pim," he said. "I'm no cattleman and I'm no sheepman. I'm the health officer of this county. I didn't bring over this warning because of any love for the ranchers. I just happen to be sure that it wasn't a cattleman who killed that sheepherder. I don't want to see any of your boys killed for something they didn't do."

"Thanks just the same, Doc." Pim fidgeted in his chair. "Just what did yuh hear."

"I didn't hear much, but I guessed plenty, and I think you're going to see a raid on your property from the direction of the Arroyo Espectro. I noticed that you had quite a herd of nice shorthorns close to that pass. I passed three of the sheepmen's hired gunmen doing guard duty at the top of the rise. My advice is to put some men out there."

It was enough information to satisfy the owner of the Circle Bar T. "The damned wooly nurses," he growled. "Get goin', waddies. We'll give them dirty killers a right nice dose of lead."

Cliff decided that it would be unwise now to try and visit Manuel at the edge of the desert. There was no telling when or where the battle would take place, and he wanted to advise Dorr

Plum as well. As he mounted his horse, one of the Circle Bar T cowboys called to him:

"Better stick around, Doc. There's likely to be plenty holes to plug up. We're aimin' to fill yore office with patients."

The medico was to recall that remark later, but now he had more pressing things to think of. He urged the roan at top speed back towards Painted Springs, located the sheriff and imparted the news of the pending engagement to him. The sheriff cursed fluently.

"I was sure scared of that, Cliff. I don't place much stock in my ability as a peace officer in this damned county, but I'm a goin' out there anyways and try and stop 'em. That Percy Pim is sure a spitfire for a gent with a name like he's carryin'."

Dinner hour at the Mansion House that night was a quiet affair. The word of the coming clash had reached the ears of the Blanes, as well as the neighboring ranches. Maw's well-filled table was almost deserted. What few customers there were ate quietly and soon vanished from sight. Cliff rolled a cigarette and sat down on the broad veranda of the hotel to wait. In spite of the clarity of the night, with a crescent moon squatting over the distant peaks, and the sky sprinkled with flickering stars, there was a distinct chill in the air. Painted Springs was silent. Even the Lone Deuce which ordinarily was the scene of ribald music and hoarse laughter, was now ominously quiet.

Cliff was the first to hear the thud of a hard-driven horse's shod hoofs coming into town, and a moment later Dorr Plum dismounted and hitched his mount to the rail. Cliff, anxious for news, called to him, grimly, "Has the battle started yet, Dorr?"

The sheriff shuffled over and spread his big frame in a rocker. His black frock coat was gray with dust. He grunted, "The mangy ornery bunch of lunatics! I tried to argue with Pim, but it weren't no use. He's got thirty of his boys strung up there at the pass, and if them woollies come down it's sure goin' to be a slaughter pen. I'm plumb disgusted, Doc. They don't need a sheriff in this county, they need an army."

Cliff agreed, looking thoughtfully toward the distant hills, where even now the men might be at each other's throats. They were too far from the scene of carnage to hear the gunfire. All they could do was sit and wait. The sheriff's hands were tied. He couldn't lay the blame on the ranchers. If the sheepmen chose to put their heads in a noose by crossing into enemy territory, it was their own funeral. Cliff, too, was powerless to interfere. All either of them could do was to hope that the casualties would not be too severe.

It was past midnight, when Cliff was awakened by a cavalcade that came steaming into Painted Springs. He heard the sheriff's deep voice, followed by the clump of high-heeled boots climbing to his rooms and office. He quickly struck a light.

Two of the Circle Bar T men came in carrying one of their own men. Cliff recognized the wounded man as the one who had yelled at him that afternoon. Kentucky Landers was at their heels. They stretched the man out on Cliff's cot, and while the medico set to work, Kentucky told him of the fight.

Len Frame, the wounded cowboy, had been riding guard close to the pass. His nearest companion was some three hundred yards south of him. Suddenly and unexpectedly the sheepmen had started through the pass. Len had let loose with his six-gun, but had been shot down before help could reach him. The blast of his gun, however, had been warning enough for Pim and his ranchers. They met the sheepmen in force and drove them back with minor casualties on both sides.

Len opened his eyes and stared up at Cliff. A faint grin crossed his face. "I told yuh, Doc, yuh should 'ave stuck around, but I wasn't aimin' to be one o' yore patients."

Cliff shook his head. "I know you weren't, Len, and I'm afraid there isn't much I can do for you, but I'll do the best I can."

"Sure yuh will, Doc. Somethin' tells me this is the last round-up for Len Frame. I reckon I'm lightin' a shuck for the happy huntin' ground." His face suddenly contorted with pain, his teeth clenched, a barely perceptible groan came from his blue lips.

Cliff looked at Kentucky and shook his head. "It may be a minute and it may be an hour. It's a miracle he lived long enough to be brought here."

Several days later, Cliff again crossed the mesas on his way to see Manuel's boy. He found his patient to be making remarkable progress and he congratulated the Mexican and his black-eyed wife. On his way back through Ghost Cañon at an easy lope, he rounded a pile of boulders and scrub pine to see Nancy, sitting on the ground, her clothes disheveled. There was no sign of the black stallion. Cliff reined in quickly.

"Taking a siesta, Miss Starweather?" he grinned. Then he noticed a deep cut on her forehead and her paleness. He dropped off the roan hurriedly and reached her side. "What happened? Are you hurt?" He couldn't have kept the concern out of his voice if he had wanted to.

She showed her displeasure at meeting him. "I'm perfectly all right, thank you." Her voice was brittle. She stood up, let out a little cry of pain and dismay, and but for Cliff's quick action would have collapsed.

The medico picked her up in his arms and carried her to a patch of grama. He tied the roan to a scrub pine, got out his kit, and dropped to his knees beside her. Very gently he removed her riding boot and made a swift examination of her foot. She winced as his hands touched the injured member, but compressed her lips and managed to hold back the cry of pain.

"Just a sprain, Nancy. I'll bind it up, then I'll have a look at that head of yours. Looks like rather a nasty cut. What happened to Midnight?"

Her eyes met his momentarily and a faint smile crossed her face. "He had his way at last," she answered, ruefully. "He caught me off my guard, shied at something back there in the mesquite. My foot caught in the stirrup and he dragged me a bit."

Cliff grinned. "I guessed as much. He's a beautiful animal, but no horse for even a cowgirl to ride." With deft hands he bound her ankle and placed a plaster over the cut on her forehead. "You'll have to ride Snort back to the S Bar 8. It's a cinch you can't walk on that foot."

He brought the roan over to her side, picked her up, and placed her in the saddle. The close contact brought the red to his face. It had been all he could do to fight down the desire to kiss those full red lips. Nancy sensed it, and her own face glowed with twin spots of color. But she made no offer of riding double, although the medico had expected it. Instead she took up the reins and started the roan up the cañon at a slow walk, Cliff following.

She was again the same silent, taciturn girl, who had ridden with him to the S Bar 8. Cliff plodded steadily along at her side, his long legs keeping pace easily with the roan's stride. Once he looked up at her and said, "Does the ankle hurt much?"

She answered with a shake of her head, "No." But he was distinctly conscious of her eyes appraising him.

They reached the Starweather ranch at last. Her father saw them, growled under his breath, and made a move to hobble on his cane to meet them.

"Keep your seat, Starweather," Cliff called to him. "I'll bring her in." He stood by the roan's side, arms extended and waiting.

Again those twin spots of color burned in the girl's golden cheeks. She looked helplessly at her father, realized that he was a cripple, and at last swung herself into the medico's arms. She could feel the pounding of his heart against her breast, as he carried her up the steps and placed her on the sofa.

"Thanks," she said, trying to make her voice impersonal. "I'll be all right now."

Starweather had managed to hobble into the living room after them. He glared menacingly at Cliff. "You damned sneakin' medico," he growled. "What are you doin' on the S Bar 8. This here is sheep country and we don't hold no love for cattle folks."

Cliff reddened to the roots of his hair and his eyes narrowed, the pupils gleaming black in their gray setting. The muscles in his neck tightened. "Meaning what, Starweather? I found your daughter with a sprained ankle in Cañon Espectro. What would you have me do, leave her there?"

"You're damned right. Better to leave her there and rot rather than accept help from the likes of you. You seem to think you can doctor both sides and carry tales back and forth. Well, you can't. You was the one who warned the Circle Bar T, otherwise we'd 'ave had a successful raid."

Cliff's temper couldn't be controlled any longer. He was sick of being baited and accused of being first on one side and then the other. His jaw tightened and he flared back, "You're damned right, I warned them, and I'd do the same thing for the sheepmen if some cowhand took it into his head to murder a cowhand and point the signs toward the other camp. You men are the biggest bunch of lunatics I've ever hoped to see. That herder wasn't killed by any cattleman."

"Then who killed him? You seem to know so all-fired much about that murder. Tell me who killed him. I'll nail his hide to a barn door."

Cliff realized that he had said too much. There were no means of proving his assertions. The little the herder had hinted to him before he died had been only enough to point the finger of suspicion toward some sheepman. Furthermore, the success or failure of his suit for Nancy's hand hinged on keeping the goodwill of the S Bar 8 owner. As long as Starweather merely suffered his presence, the better were his chances of winning the lovely blonde girl who as yet had given no sign that she even liked him.

The spurt of anger died. He said, with a shrug, "If I knew, Starweather, you wouldn't get the chance to touch his hide. We have a sheriff in this county and a good one. I'm not taking offense at your remarks, because undoubtedly in your own mind you are justified. I shall continue to do my duty as I see it. Good-bye, Nancy. Take good care of that foot and keep off of it as much as possible. Hot water with epsom salts will help to alleviate the pain."

Nancy's eyes followed him to the door. In them was something that would have pleased the medico, if he could have but seen it. She sighed and looked at her glowering, heavy browed parent.

"There's something about that young man that I like, Dad," she said a little wistfully. "I wish he was more of a sheepman and less of a cattleman."

Her parent merely grunted and hobbled back to his chair.

CHAPTER FOUR
GANGRENE

Cliff had ample time to reflect upon the inconsistency of women as he rode back towards Painted Springs. There seemed to be only one answer to Nancy's coldness and that was his apparent close association with the cattlemen. He couldn't quite bring himself to believe that the girl disliked him personally. She had been too friendly, too enthusiastic about his work, that first day when he had explained the secrets of his profession. But how had Starweather discovered that it was he who had warned the ranchers of the raid? Had some cowhand on the opposing side announced it during the battle?

Suddenly he remembered Puff Gordon and his threats and a grim smile crossed his face. His two days grace were up according to the gunhawk. Where was Puff? He remembered that he hadn't seen the bully in his accustomed haunts. Was the man again away on one of his mysterious missions to the adjoining county? Now that he looked back to that night of the raid, he realized that the Lone Deuce had been unusually silent of late. It had been several nights since he had been awakened in the early morning by drunken loud voices.

He questioned the sheriff as to Puff's whereabouts, but that individual merely shook his head. "Haven't seen him, Cliff. Why did you ask? You ain't spoilin' for another set-to?"

Cliff grinned, but shook his head. "That part is forgotten, Dorr. No, I was curious, that's all. I just realized that I've been able to sleep several nights without interruption. The town has been unusually peaceful lately. Haven't you noticed?"

The sheriff nodded thoughtfully. "Now that you mention it, I reckon it has been sort of quiet like. Them Circle Bar T boys might 'ave learned 'em a lesson. I heard that they got three of the sheepmen. Leastways, that's what they claim, but I ain't seen no new tombstones in my travels. I reckon they're just layin' low and lickin' their wounds. Them gunhawks of Starweather's is like a pack of mangy coyotes anyhow. Lord, I wish this damned range war 'ud fold up."

Cliff reached the S Bar 8 several days later just at noon. He found both of his patients hobbling around with the aid of canes. Nancy greeted him with words that were outwardly cordial, but with a certain aloofness that convinced the medico he was still considered as an enemy. However, she graciously invited him to stay and partake of the noonday meal. Having looked over both patients thoroughly and being satisfied that they were both much improved, they sat down to lunch. Cliff kept the conversation away from the range war and led it into more pleasant channels, regaling his host and hostess with humorous anecdotes of his years in medical school.

Both of them seemed to brighten up as the meal progressed and Cliff was just congratulating himself on having leaped one hurdle in his race towards his goal, when the luncheon was interrupted by the arrival of a party of horsemen. Starweather got clumsily to his feet and hobbled to the front door.

Cliff heard the sheepman say, "Bring him right in here, boys. The doc's here now."

Cliff made a grimace at Nancy. "It's a hard life, young lady. Don't ever marry a doctor. We can't even eat our meals in peace."

The way he said it brought a heightening of color to her cheeks. She followed him into the living room. Cliff knew now why Puff Gordon hadn't been in his accustomed haunts. The man was stretched out on the sofa, a dirty rag bound around his forehead, his arms hanging limply at his sides, and his face the color of gray chalk.

Nancy gave a little cry of pity as she saw him. "Dad, what happened? Is he dead?"

Starweather shook his head. "Not yet, I reckon, but it's a good thing they brought him in. He don't look far from it to me."

One of the men who had brought him in was the same fish-eyed individual who had stopped Cliff that day. He now glared at Cliff and snarled, "All right, Doc. It looks like yore turn, and yuh better not let him cash in." His hand touched the butt of his six-gun meaningly.

Puff opened his eyes and stared into the face of the medico, his thin lips twisting into a sardonic grin. "I got you to thank for this, you—" He choked and his voice ended in a gasp of pain.

Cliff didn't bother to answer the gunhawk. "Get some boiling water quick, Nancy. Got a spare bed, Starweather? Two of you men carry him there, while I sterilize my instruments."

"God Awmighty!" The gunhawk was staring at the medico's sharp knives and instruments of torture. "You ain't goin' to stick Puff with them things, yuh murderin' coyote." With that he shoved the muzzle of his six-gun into Cliff's ribs.

There was no time to argue. Cliff's fist came upward from his waist as he felt the cold steel pressed into his side. It landed with a smack, glazed the eyes of the gunhawk, and tumbled him backward into a senseless hulk. Cliff hadn't even stopped to consider the consequences to himself if the man had side-stepped that blow. Puff's life depended on swift action.

Nancy came in with a pail of scalding water. She saw the man stretched on the floor and looked at him questioningly. Cliff shrugged and pointed to the gun, all the time busy cleaning his instruments, which he laid out carefully in a handy position on the kit.

"The fool tried to throw-down on me," he said. "Can you stand the sight of blood, Nancy? I'm going to need help."

Her face paled, but she nodded in acquiescence. Cliff handed her the kit of instruments, picked up the pail of water and followed her to the room.

"Get out everybody," the medico commanded. "Miss Nancy and I will handle this alone."

Puff opened his eyes and winced as Cliff gave him a hypodermic. Then his eyes caught the sheen of Nancy's golden hair and he smiled at her. Nancy found his hand and pressed it. Cliff saw the action and his heart dropped a notch. It was the first time he had ever seen any look in the sheepman's eyes but one of murder. Now they were regarding the girl with adoration. Cliff jabbed the needle in again, unconsciously venting his wrath on the wounded man. Puff scowled.

And so while Cliff, a deep hurt in his heart from Nancy's fondling of the patient, worked swiftly, steadily, and silently, the girl stood pale but determined, her eyes following every movement of the surgeon's deft hand. She held the tray of instruments in front of him, her one hand unfaltering, while the other pressed Puff's hand in encouragement each time he groaned.

At last Cliff stood up, wiped his face on the sleeve of his shirt, and gave Nancy a grin. "That's about all we can do for the present," he said. "It's pretty bad but it could be worse. He'll have to be watched constantly now for the next forty-eight hours until the poison gets out of his system. Could you put an extra cot or something in here for me? I dare not leave him even for a minute."

"You think he'll live, Cliff?"

She had used his first name mechanically and the medico thought it had never sounded so sweet although he sensed her apprehension and interest. Puff was dangerously ill from lack of care. It was too soon to predict whether the man's vitality, weakened from exposure, could throw off the gangrene and poison that was flooding his system.

"There's a fighting chance, Nancy. If he had been brought to me when first shot, the wound wouldn't have been serious, but gangrene is like a prairie fire. Those poultices must be changed hourly. If we can keep the poison to a minimum for forty-eight hours, there's an excellent chance for full and complete recovery. Otherwise it means—" He hesitated—"the loss of his leg at the hip."

He had been watching the face of the girl so earnestly that he did not realize that his patient had recovered sufficiently to hear every word. His first intimation was a growl from the gunman.

"If I lose my leg, Doc, yuh better hightail it pronto. That'll shore show which side of the fence yo're on. Yuh saved that maverick Pim's life and I'm warnin' yuh, yuh better save my leg." The man's face was contorted with anger and pain. "It ain't goin' to be healthy for the medico 'round here if yuh don't."

Cliff's face flushed and his eyes deepened in color. "Just keep your shirt on, old timer. I'll do the best I can. Don't worry about that. A patient is a patient whether he's a sheepman, a cowman, or a sick dog. There's no doubt in my mind that this county would be considerably better off without you, but nevertheless I'm going to try my darnedest to save your life, worthless as I think it is. But remember, you've got to help. I can't do it without your cooperation. Nancy, tell this fat-headed sheepman that he's got to have rest and quiet."

Unconsciously Cliff had wanted to try her out and so while Nancy begged Puff to follow the doctor's orders, Cliff was watching every change in her facial expression, every flicker in her blue eyes. Yet when Puff had closed his in resignation, Cliff was still at sea as to her feelings toward the sheepman. There was no doubt in his mind as to the wounded man's feelings towards her. That accounted in part for his enmity, but not for all of it. There was some other reason and Cliff thought he had discovered it. Puff was afraid of what the medico might uncover while visiting the sheepherders.

Starweather had a cot brought into the room for him, and Cliff sat by the hour watching his patient with hawklike eyes. The poultices on the gaping wound were changed regularly, but if the wounded man was aware of it, he gave no sign, other than to occasionally open his eyes and to stare thoughtfully at the figure of the medico. Nancy brought Cliff his dinner, but stayed only long enough to inquire after the patient.

But before the forty-eight hours were up, Puff was on the road to recovery. The fever had abated, and the wound was beginning to clean itself preparatory to healing. Already the torn and scarred tissue was turning to a brighter red. And so that night just before he left, Cliff had a chance to visit for a few moments with Nancy.

"You've been splendid, Cliff," she praised.

"Then you no longer think that I am aligned with the cattlemen?"

"That would be unfair to think that now after what you've done."

Cliff was tired, but not too tired to welcome this opportunity to talk to Nancy. "Can you tell me why," he questioned, suddenly, "these sheepmen and ranchers hate each other so deeply? It all seems so futile. There is range enough for both. Two men have been killed since my arrival and several wounded. Sooner or later there will be more deaths. We're sitting on a keg of dynamite. Any moment the thing may blow up. Why can't it be stopped?"

The girl's lips compressed into tight little lines. Her eyes, so soft and lovely, became brittle in remembrance. "Dad will never give up the fight, Cliff. I don't want him to. We have a score to settle with Percy Pim. It was eight years ago when we moved into the Hawk valley. My brother Jim. He was ten years older than I and I adored him. He was a fine figure of a man then. Just twenty-four, loveable, curly black hair, full of fun and always ready to fight back if offended. That was his worst trait. He was quick-tempered." She stopped and her eyes scanned the distant hills, over which the scimitar moon was just displaying its topmost point, coating the sandstone peaks with silver.

Cliff relaxed in his chair, appreciating the stillness of the night air, waiting for her to go on.

"We were sheep folks then, born and raised to them," she went on. "Percy Pim was ramrod for the Block H, and one night some of our sheep strayed from the flock and wandered on to his range." Her voice broke momentarily. "Pim met my brother that night in Landow, they had words. They brought Jim home in our buckboard. He died before morning. The shock killed my mother. Dad couldn't stand the sight of the place after that and we sold out and came here only to find that Pim was now the owner of the Circle Bar T through the death of his uncle. It didn't take Pim long to discover us. For a time he played every conceivable trick on us, until Dad organized the sheepmen."

Cliff shook his head thoughtfully. "Vengeance! It's a terrible word, Nancy. I can see now why your father hates Pim, but what good is all this range war going to do? It doesn't bring back your brother Jim nor your mother. Your animals are being slaughtered and your herders killed. There is plenty of range for all. It is all so senseless, this continual bloodshed."

She turned her head and looked full at him. "What would you have us do? Forget? No, Cliff. One never forgets things of that sort. Perhaps Jim was killed in a fair fight, but still it was murder. Pim is noted for his quickness of hand. Jim was only a kid. He never even had the chance to fire his gun. Pim killed him before he could get it out of its holster."

Cliff argued further. "But can't you see the outcome? The longer this lasts, the worst off the country will be. Why don't you use your influence to help settle it? I'm sure Pim and the other cattlemen would listen to reason. They're sick of it. At least most of them are."

Nancy laughed mockingly and stood up abruptly. "I see you are still a cattleman at heart, Dr. Monroe. You want us to give in now, when victory is almost within our grasp." Her words were cold and brittle. "Did Pim suggest that you approach me?"

Cliff put a restraining hand on her arm. "Please, Nancy! That isn't fair. It's just that I see the futility of it all. No one's life is safe in this community any longer. These hired gunmen that both sides have brought in are ruthless. Their very existence depends on keeping the range in an uproar. They're a merciless, cruel band of cutthroats, who will stop at nothing. Houses, barns, will be burned. Even women and children aren't safe while the county is overrun with such criminals."

The girl disengaged his arm. Her eyes now were twin points of flame in the darkness of the veranda. "If I were you, Dr. Monroe, I wouldn't mix into something that doesn't concern me. The sheepmen can take care of themselves. I suppose you will be out tomorrow to visit your patient. Good night!"

Cliff saddled the roan, frisky after his long rest, and cantered toward town. He had thought the girl was big enough of heart to overlook such a thing as vengeance. Yet he could see her side of it, could picture that night when the stalwart son had been brought home in a creaking cart, his body riddled with slugs.

Dorr met him at the livery stable. He too had just come in from a ride to a neighboring ranch. "Where in tarnation you been, Cliff? I was just about to go lookin' for your carcass, thinkin' maybe that bully Puff had drilled you."

Together they walked to the Lone Deuce for a nightcap. Cliff told the sheriff of the wounded Puff. Dorr Plum shook his head. "Too dang bad the critter didn't cash in his chips, but at least we'll have peace for a spell. With old Starweather too gouty to walk and Puff flat on his back, I reckon it'll be sort a quiet 'round here. One thing sure, Cliff, he can't run you out of town like he threatened. Least ways not for a spell."

"What do you know about Percy Pim?" Cliff asked suddenly as they walked back across the street.

"Not much, Cliff. I understand he used to be ramrod for some outfit down in New Mexico. This here Circle Bar T belonged to his uncle."

"Did you know that he killed Starweather's son?"

"God Awmighty no! When and where did he do that?"

"Back there in New Mexico." Then Cliff told him of his conversation with Nancy.

When he had finished the sheriff said, "Well, that accounts for a lot that's been botherin' me, but it don't help none. It just means them mangy lunatics 'll stay at each other's throats 'til hell freezes over. Shucks! I'm getting plumb disgusted with this here country."

CHAPTER FIVE
THE REAPER RIDES

With Starweather crippled and his chief gunman flat on his back, peace again descended upon Painted Springs, at least as far as open warfare was concerned. The Lone Deuce Gambling Palace, scene of many a fracas, still disgorged its tipsy patrons in the early hours of the morning, but they were all sheepmen or gunhawks of the sheep contingency. With their leader absent, the sheepmen contented themselves with jibing their cowmen adversaries from the opposite side of the street, while the cattlemen contented themselves with boasting of the flakiness of Maw Blane's biscuits, and inviting them to cross the street for a real home cooked meal.

Whenever the remarks became too caustic, the sheriff would stick in his oar, chase the woolly tenders back into the Lone Deuce, and drive the cowhands inside the Mansion House. This was not appreciated by the cattlemen for the word of Puff's injury had been broadcast and there were a number of the more belligerent ones who counseled immediate warfare to wipe the sheepmen from the county.

Pim was one of these and Cliff saw him discoursing at some length one day on the veranda of the hotel as the medico jogged in from an outlying patient. He stopped short as Cliff dismounted and strode toward his office, his cold eyes following the medico's broad back.

"If it hadn't been for Doc," he grumbled, "that polecat 'ud have cashed in his checks. He'd be wieldin' a pitchfork and heapin' coals on the devil's fire."

Maw Blane arrived at the threshold of the hotel's front door in time to hear it. "And if you weren't all such a bunch of darned fools, there wouldn't be no range war. Doc only did his duty, Perk Pim. Now I suppose you're all figgerin' that Doc is a sheepman. That 'ud be just about as much brains as you pinheads 'ud show."

Pim's face creased into a sour grin. "Nobody but a sheepman would 'ave helped that snake. No, I reckon yo're wrong, Maw. Cliff has just naturally fallen for mutton. He's gettin' sweet on Nancy and it sure looks like he was growin' a crop of nice white wool. Course I don't blame him none for cottonin' to that gal, but he's wastin' his good time, 'cause that mangy pa of hers 'll never let her marry no man that was raised with a steer for a playmate, such as Cliff was." He shook his head. "I just can't understand a man like that havin' anythin' to do with them woollies."

Maw snorted. "That's cause you ain't got a lick of gray matter in that thick skull of yours. Cliff's only doin' his duty as the health officer of this county, same as the sheriff is tryin' to do his. You don't get sore, I notice, when Dorr tries to argue the sheepmen out of battlin' with you."

Pim glanced up the row of shaded porches that lined the street and saw the medico hit the boards with a bound and in a few long strides reach his roan. He began to feverishly pack his saddle bags. "You men better get back to your ranches, Pim," Cliff called to them. "Hell's let loose in this county. Will you throw some grub together for me, Maw? I may have to be gone for a few days."

The rancher had gotten quickly to his feet, his gun-hand dropping automatically to the holster tied down at his side. "What's worryin' you, Doc? Is the woollies on the prod again?"

Cliff shook his head. "This is one deal where a six-gun won't help any. It's something you can't fight with a gun. I wish to heaven we could. It's smallpox."

"Aw shucks!" Pim sank back into his chair with a grunt of disgust. "That ain't nothin' to be scared of. I had it when I was a kid. It ain't near as bad as it's painted."

"I observed that from the looks of your face," Cliff answered ironically. "However if you're smart you'll follow my instructions. Keep away from those Mexican herders and if any of the boys get sick, call me immediately. Smallpox is worse than a tidal wave."

Cliff got the grub from Maw, finished his packing hurriedly, and went across the street to the Lone Deuce. To Tim Roney he gave the same warning. Without a moment's hesitation the bartender drove his customers outside, locked his doors, and notified all his patrons that the saloon was closed indefinitely.

The sheriff next came jogging in and Cliff gave him the news. "One of them is in my office now, Dorr. That's how I found out. He's likely to spread the disease all over town, but it can't be helped now. I'm hoping that he came direct to my office. I'd be much obliged if you'd stand guard or put somebody there to watch my office until I get back. Don't let the herder out and don't let anyone in."

The medico leaped to the roan's broad back and set a swift pace for the first of the herder's huts at the edge of the range. He found the disease to be spreading rapidly in spite of the great distances that separated the herders from their neighbors. There were already a dozen cases in the pustule stage, their faces and bodies broken out with sores. At least another dozen were vomiting and running a high fever. The medico did what he could, urging the roan from one cabin to another, until horse and rider were a mass of sweat and dust. They were an ignorant lot and Cliff felt that it was almost a hopeless task. His supply of the new cowpox serum was limited and it would require several days to get more from the nearest railroad. Still he rode on, managing to reach all but the furthest of the Mexican herders.

It was almost midnight when he returned to Painted Springs to find the sheriff propped up in a chair by the steps leading to his office, his six-gun across his lap.

The sheriff grinned as Cliff dragged his weary limbs towards him. "You sure look like you'd been rollin' in alkali, Cliff. How does it look?"

"Pretty bad, Dorr. I've got to get a man off pronto for the nearest railroad. I've used every drop of serum I had. Know anybody around here I can send?"

"Sure, son. Just give me the dope and I'll have one on his way quick as you can wink yore eye."

The medico wrote the information out hurriedly, handed it to the sheriff, and climbed the stairs to his rooms. One look at his patient, whom he had left stretched on his couch convinced him that the man was beyond help. As soon as the sheriff returned, together they dragged and carried the body to the local graveyard, and buried it without ceremony. Cliff disinfected his clothes, burned the coverings of the couch, and went to sleep.

At the crack of dawn, he was again astride the roan, stopping first at the S Bar 8 to give the warning there. He found Puff on his feet and hobbling around with a cane. The sheepman greeted Cliff with his usual unfriendliness, which the medico ignored. He examined the wound, found it well healed, and told Puff to use it as much as possible. Starweather too, seemed much improved, but Cliff's announcement of the smallpox epidemic was like a bombshell.

"Jehosaphat!" he exclaimed.

The gunman merely shrugged. Disease meant nothing to him. He had never been sick a day in his life except from bullet wounds. "What's that to be scairt of?" he growled. "Besides it's only a herd of greasers. There's plenty more to be had over the border."

"Yes," Cliff snapped back at him, "but don't forget it's a white man's disease. If I had enough serum I'd vaccinate everyone in the county. Smallpox is just about as contagious as anything known to medical science. We don't know who these herders have been associating with. We don't know where it will strike next."

"Where what will strike?" Nancy had heard his voice and had come to the door. "Oh, good morning, Cliff!" Cliff smiled. She was a picture framed there in the doorway, her corn-colored hair twisted into a lump at the base of her head, her eyes bright and sleepless. "I've just brought some bad news, Nancy. An epidemic of smallpox has broken out among the herders."

"How awful! Can I help? Is there anything I can do?"

Cliff shook his head. "The safest thing for you to do is to stay right here at the ranch. You'll have to stop your visits to the herders. I don't want to see anyone here at the S Bar 8 contract it."

The girl's eyes narrowed. "And you really think I'll follow those orders? Hardly, Cliff. Puff, you can ride, can't you?" Then—"Saddle the stallion and your sorrel. We're going with Dr. Monroe."

"But, Nancy—" Cliff was delighted at the prospect of having her with him, but the danger she ran made him shudder. Just the thought of that golden cheeked girl sick, nauseated him. "It's dangerous. I can't let you."

Her slender shoulders squared. She raised her head defiantly. "I'm going whether you like it or not. Get the horses, Puff."

The gunman chuckled. "That's one order yuh can't enforce, Doc. Nancy and I'll give yuh a hand, won't we, Nancy?"

And Cliff had to leave it at that. The girl was adamant. Further argument he soon found was useless. Puff brought up the horses and the three rode off towards the desert's edge, passing through the cañon Espectro, on past the gray-green fields of cholla, and up through the foothills to the cactus-studded waste beyond.

The sheepman rode his sorrel with the skill of a top-hand, setting a fast pace, his narrow waist and broad shoulders swinging easily with each pound of the horse's hoofs. The black stallion was close beside him, while Cliff had to content himself with dropping a little behind. The roan was not as fast as the other two mounts, and the gunman seemed to take delight in keeping the medico just far enough behind so that he couldn't join in in their conversation. Nancy's laughter mingled with the deep throaty voice of the sheepman, came floating back to the medico as he urged the roan forward.

Cliff found himself hating the sheepman for his easy camaraderie with Starweather's daughter. He was sorry now that he had stopped at the S Bar 8 to give the warning. He didn't relish the companionship of the gunman. Yet he knew that Puff had welcomed the chance to ride with Nancy and to be of service.

They reached the first herder's mud covered hovel, and now it was Cliff's turn to shine. Puff had to stand in the background, simply being of service when called, while the medico mixed concoctions for his patients. Nancy was like an angel in disguise. Unafraid of the dread disease, fearless of the consequences, she administered to the sick, and lightened the medico's task.

Cliff got his breaks when some patient died and required immediate burial. At such times, Puff was forced to return for extra help. These periods came with all too frequent regularity. The serum had not yet arrived and the herders were dying like flies, wiping out entire families. It was a miracle that they managed to save Manuel Geosta, his pretty black-eyed wife, and the ailing boy. Nancy had a great deal to do with that. She gave the little family especial care, bringing them choice bits of food, making steaming mutton broth for them, and helping them to conserve their strength.

Finally the serum arrived by stage. The sick ones were easy to handle as far as the vaccination was concerned. It was those who were still healthy who were difficult to handle. Many times it was only the presence of the bully Puff and his hired fish-eyed gunhawks, that convinced them that the slight prick of the needle and scratching of their arms was preferable to painless death by gunfire.

Day after day, the triumvirate rode the mesa and the hills, burning, disinfecting, nursing, and bringing the sick back from the door of death. Cliff found himself treating the sheepman with more respect. Puff too, seemed to have forgotten his animosity toward the medico. All enmity had been swallowed up in the giving of service. Each was trying to outdo the other; each was striving unconsciously to be the hero of the drama, to win the heart of the fair-haired girl who shared their tribulations and trials.

Then at last came the day when success was in sight. There were no new cases, no new deaths, and the sick were recovering rapidly. They stopped for lunch in a grove of scrub pine, Nancy doing the honors for the two men.

"We should be sitting down to a ten course banquet," she laughed. "You're sure the worst is over, Cliff?"

"Positive," he grinned back at her. "The fire is simmering out now. That serum came in the nick of time. Are you tired, Nancy? You look pretty fagged out. Better take a day off and sleep tomorrow. I can handle it alone from now on, unless Puff wants to continue." He glanced at the dark face beside him. "You two have been bricks. I'm afraid the county health officer would have been a failure without you."

The sheepman reddened and shook his head. "I got other business to attend to." A sly grin wrinkled the corners of his eyes. His eyes traveled to the distant green mesa, where herds of cattle grazed, then back towards the dividing line where the flocks of sheep were bunched in gray masses.

Cliff read the meaning in his eyes. The chief gunhawk was well. With the epidemic stamped out, it would be the signal for more warfare. Even now the sheepman was laying his plans.

But Cliff found the gunman waiting for him in Cañon Espectro the next morning. The medico was surprised, yet he welcomed the chance to talk with him alone. He said:

"Puff, why don't you and I bury the hatchet? You know that I'm neither a sheepman nor a cowman. Let's forget that little trouble we had a ways back. What do you say?"

The sheepman looked sullen. "This here country ain't big enough to hold us both, Doc. You know it and I know it. Sooner or later we're goin' to tangle. I jist don't like the way yuh straddle the fence. I ain't never said nothin' before, but I knowed it was you what squealed on us before. Yuh ain't goin' to get another chance. We'd a run them mavericks clear out o' the county that night if yuh hadn't wised 'em up."

"I admit that, Puff. What's more I admit it wasn't any of my business, but it wasn't a cowman who murdered that herder in the cañon."

"No?" the gunman snarled. "Then if yo're so damned smart, who was it?"

Cliff looked him full in the eyes. "It was a sheepman. One of your hired gunhawks."

The bully pulled his horse to a walk suddenly and leaned closer to Cliff, his eyes cold and narrowed. "Do yuh know that for certain, Doc?"

"If I did, that gunman would have been in the sheriff's hands a long time ago." He shrugged. "It's just a guess, but I think it's a damned good one."

Puff seemed to breathe easier. His hands relaxed and he managed a grin. "Jist a guess and a damned poor one, I'd say."

Cliff had seen the change in the gunman's expression, and guessed what it meant. Puff knew who had killed that herder and was exceedingly anxious that no one else knew. Somewhere behind all this range war, a strong hand was guiding it, a hand that knew no mercy, that would stop at nothing. In some way Puff was the hired killer of that guiding spirit. But who was it? Was it the grizzled old sheepman Starweather with his hatred of Pim? That didn't seem possible. God knows the sheepman had reason enough to despise the owner of the Circle Bar T, yet Cliff couldn't quite picture Nancy's father as the ruthless killer, a man who would slaughter one of his neighbor's herders for the sake of creating open warfare. The two didn't fit together. With all his gruffness, his stubbornness, and his tenacity of purpose, he was sure that Starweather wouldn't stoop to murder.

Puff left Cliff late in the afternoon and struck off south, while Cliff headed for the S Bar 8, where he had been invited to dine. Nancy, cool and refreshed from her rest, her slim figure clothed in a gay colored print, greeted him as he rode up. Cliff washed and cleaned himself as best he could, then came back and sat down beside her on the porch.

He answered her eager questions about the patients. "I tried to bury the hatchet with Puff today, Nancy, but I'm afraid I wasn't very successful. He turned me down rather coldly." He glanced toward her. "I hope when the time comes, that you won't turn me down quite so frigidly."

Again those twin spots of color burned in her cheeks. "Do you think the time will ever come, Cliff? I doubt it."

"I hope so," he answered softly. "That's about the only thing that keeps me going. I know I haven't any right to say it, but—"

The clump of Starweather's heavy boots on the floor of the living room stopped him. He shook hands with the sheepman and almost immediately dinner was announced. Nor did he have another opportunity to speak with Nancy alone. Starweather made himself obnoxious the entire evening questioning Cliff about the country, the ravages of the epidemic, and other matters of interest to him.

When he finally got back to Painted Springs, he found a group of cowmen congregated on the veranda of the Mansion House. They all showed their unfriendliness toward the medico. Even Kentucky Landers failed to give him more than a surly nod.

Ordinarily the doctor wouldn't have riled at the cool reception, but at that particular moment he was boiling inwardly from the events of the day. Puff's curt refusal to bury the hatchet, his inability to express his feelings toward the girl he loved, and now this sort of a reception from men whom he had thought were at least friends, lighted the fuse of his anger.

"Come here, Kentucky," he called, as that individual turned his back and started to get out of sight.

The puncher hesitated, then finally turned and faced him, but keeping his eyes averted from the medico's deep gray ones.

"What's the matter with all you men?" Cliff fumed.

Kentucky's brows furrowed into a scowl. "Yo're a sheepman. Yuh made your bed. Now yuh can lie in it."

Cliff snorted, "I thought it was some fool notion like that. You bunch of lunatics! Did you think I came here to doctor people or just to sit on the side lines and watch? I've tried to treat sheep-men and cattlemen alike. I saved Pim's life and Puff Gordon's. That makes it a horse a piece. There might be a few more fools congregated into some other county, but I doubt it."

The puncher's feet shifted uneasily. "Kind of on the prod tonight, ain't yuh, Cliff?"

"Call it what you like, but I don't mind admitting that I'm thoroughly disgusted with the intelligence of my neighbors. Can't you men get it through your thick heads that I'm straddling the fence?" He laughed harshly. "I suppose I'll have to set up a chicken ranch to prove to you maniacs that I'm neither beef nor mutton. Have it your own way. Life's too short to argue with a parcel of fools." He turned on his heel and vanished up his office stairs.

Kentucky, red of face and considerably crestfallen, rejoined his comrades. As usual the educated physician had had the last word. Consequently as the men returned to their ranches, the puncher was forced to bear the brunt of a deal of good-natured ribbing. They were all more or less ashamed of the outbreak and proceeded to take it out on Kentucky, working him into a fine frenzy before they arrived at the Circle Bar T.

CHAPTER SIX
THE GUNHAWK DEALS

Puff Gordon passed the turret-like formation of Painted Springs after midnight. His route led him across the cholla covered mesa, through water-gutted arroyos, and past shale ridges to the arid stretch at the desert's edge. Reaching a sandy wash where a giant Joshua tree served as a landmark, he dismounted, tied the horse to one of the branches, and sat down to wait.

For a time, no sound broke the eerie stillness of the night, but the distant throaty howl of some coyote or the padded thud of his mount's shod feet. Only the glowing end of his cigarette distinguished the faint outline of the man.

At last there came to Puff's keen ears the ring of shod hoofs on gravel. His body straightened and tensed. In a few quick strides he reached the horse and his fingers clamped over the animal's nostrils. Puff could make out dimly now the silhouette of a lone rider following the hard bed of the wash. His six-gun flowed from its holster. In a sharp voice he challenged the rider. The reply was reassuring. The sheepman dropped the gun back into place, released his horse's nostrils and stepped into plain sight.

"Why the hell weren't you here last week, Puff?" the newcomer questioned gruffly, dropping from the back of his mount. "If you think I ride fifty miles to sit in this place waitin' all night for you, you're just gettin' plain loco."

"Keep your shirt on, Carl," Puff shrugged. "I dang near didn't get here a' tall. One of them damned mavericks put a slug in my leg and if it hadn't a been for that nosey medico I'd sure cashed in my chips. We ain't got a chance to lick them punchers unless yo're ready to raise the ante."

The other chuckled. "Me and Ralph has laid out a plan that 'll sure bring them cow nurses to time. There won't be a damned cowman within fifty miles of this county when we get through with 'em. Now listen."

Then in rapid words he outlined the plan. Puff sat silently, nodding his dark head occasionally in understanding. When the man had finished, he said:

"What about Burke? Goin' to let him in on this?" The other snarled, "Hell, no! That old polecat might get uppity and afraid to soil his fingers. This here is insidious. All you got to do is just bring about two of the boys. We'll have the cattle bunched and ready to drive. We're pickin' the best ones that ain't so far gone and can travel. Don't even tell the boys the deal. Be here the night after tomorrow, but remember if any of them steers kick in on you while you're drivin' 'em, put a bullet in their heads pronto and bury 'em."

Puff met his two gunhawks sometime later. "Mansic's got fifty head of shorthorns he wants driven to the Circle Bar T night after tomorrow," he announced. "I don't know what the play is, but our job is to run 'em on to the range and let 'em mingle with the rest of the herd." His eyes darkened and he snarled, "Be sure you widemouthed idiots keep your traps closed."

Fortunately the night picked for the drive was a dark one. The small herd was bunched and ready when Puff and his gunhawks arrived. There were a few more instructions given to the sheepmen, then the herd began to slowly move towards the Circle Bar T, urged on by the grim-lipped riders. Puff waited until they were well started before circling back. He found the man who had delivered the cattle.

"Any news about that transfer of the doc?" he asked. "That hombre is rilin' me bad. If you gents don't remove him from the county right smart, my trigger finger is goin' to get over-nervous one of these days."

The man laughed. "From all I've heard, Puff, you ain't fast enough with an iron. What you need to do is go into trainin'. I understand the medico packs a right hefty wallop and ain't slow on his feet either." He shrugged and chuckled again. "Ralph couldn't get nowheres with the head physician at Tombstone. This Monroe gent it seems has some sort of a pull."

"Too cursed much pull to suit me," the sheepman exploded with anger. "He's the one that warned them cowmen of the last raid. Yuh better find some way to get him out of this county 'fore I let daylight into him."

"What's the matter, Puff?" the man questioned. "Sort of steppin' on your toes with the gal?"

But Puff had had enough ribbing for the present. "If you gents don't want yore hides nailed to a barn door, I'm warnin' yuh, yuh better get that medico out of the county. This climate ain't healthy for none of us as long as he's ridin' the mesa from sheepman to cowman. He hears too much and he knows already that it weren't no cattleman that killed that herder."

In a few minutes he had caught up with the herd, given instructions, and was riding point. The night air rang with the low of the marching cattle and the steady tattoo of their hoofs on the hard baked ground. Puff led them in a wide circle passed the little town of Painted Springs, across the furthest corner of the Mullaby sheep ranch, and on into the Cañon Espectro. Corraling them here, the steers were bunched into small herds, driven up the rocky pinion-studded sides of the ravine, and turned loose at the top to drift down the long slope toward the range and the Circle Bar T. Long before morning the entire herd had bedded down for the night and were lost in the brand of Pim's ranch.

Cliff riding the next morning toward an outlying herder's hut, observed the signs of the cattle, as he passed through the cañon. This was sheep country and he wondered what cattle were doing there. There had been no word of any pitched battle between the opposing factions since the smallpox epidemic. Both sides had been too much occupied with nursing the sick and burying their dead.

Cliff imparted his information to the sheriff when he got back to town. That individual frowned and said, "It sure looks like there was clouds comin', Cliff. Them lunatics has been too danged quiet now for almost a month. What do you suppose them steers was doin' in the cañon? Did you see any signs of sheep too? Which way was the herd movin'?"

"Near as I could figure, Dorr, it looked like they came from the direction of Mullaby's ranch. I didn't have much time to investigate because I saw one of Puff's gunmen riding guard up on the crest. I didn't want to appear nosey. I'm having enough trouble as it is. The cowmen think I'm a mutton eater and the sheepmen think I love beef. But if I were you, I'd do a little investigating on my own hook before the sign gets too old."

"That's just what I will do. It don't seem natural that a sheepman would be drivin' a herd of steers, and I'm plumb certain that no cowhand 'ud be doin' it."

Late that afternoon Cliff again met the sheriff and questioned him, but Plum was more mystified than ever.

"They came across the Mullaby ranch all right, Cliff," he grunted, "but I couldn't find no signs after that. Mullaby's got a couple of thousand sheep that just blotted out all the sign from there. It's danged mystifying, that's what it is. I ran into Puff on the way back. He seemed as happy as a two year old with a new toy. Damnit! I wish we could do somethin'. There's gunsmoke in the air. I can smell it or my name ain't Dorr Plum."

Yet in the following weeks, the county remained as peaceful as any small eastern farm. The dividing line separated the combating forces and neither side made any hostile moves. But Puff talked freely and in a way that worried both Cliff and the sheriff. His boastful remarks that within six months there wouldn't be a steer in the county, was greeted with derisive laughter by the cattlemen, yet underneath the words Cliff felt sure there was something more than just idle boasting.

Cliff found Nancy to be pleasant but cool. She always seemed genuinely glad to see him, but distant enough to prevent his making any overtures. Several times in a round about way, he tried to glean information from her as to future possible conflicts, but at the mere mention of the subject, she shut up like a clam, intimating that it would be just as well if he minded his own business.

Once he met Puff at an outlying herder's hut. Cliff harbored no doubts as to the gunman's enmity. The snarl in his eyes and tongue were unmistakable, yet with it all the bully carried himself with a cock-sureness that convinced the medico that there was something planned which boded no good for the cattlemen.

"How's the leg, Gordon?" Cliff asked as he came out of the herder's hut and saw the bully sitting with one leg across the saddle horn, while he expertly rolled the makings.

Puff scowled. "A damned sight better than a lot of other legs is goin' to be in this county, Doc. Yuh might jist as well make up yore mind to spread yore healin' salves among these greasers, 'cause there soon won't be no punchers around here and nothin' much in the way of cattle but a few milk cows."

"Meaning what?" the medico asked, innocently. "Surely the sheepmen aren't expecting to drive every rancher out of the county?"

Puff grinned. "Cripe, no! We ain't wastin' no more lead on them mavericks. We won't have to run 'em out. They'll he hightailin' of their own free will. I expect you'll have to move too, Doc, 'bout that time. You'll never make no money doctorin' these greasers."

Cliff shook his head. "You might as well get that idea out of your head, Gordon. This is my bailiwick and I expect to live here the rest of my life. But what is this holocaust that is about to descend on the poor cattlemen? I'd hardly expect you of being the one who would nurse any ideas of the Supreme Being taking a hand."

The sheepman took on a mysterious air. "I don't know no Supreme Bein' as yuh call him." Then he shrugged—"But it sure is goin' to do my heart good to see them cowmen packin' up and leavin'. I'm tellin' yuh, Doc, this country ain't goin' to be healthy for cattle folks."

With a wave of his hand the sheepman roweled his horse and vanished over the rise, leaving Cliff more mystified than ever. The sheepmen were resorting to some other tactics than open warfare; something that had made them sure that the ranchers would be glad to leave Brant County.

Cliff and the sheriff had been very careful not to disclose to any of the cowmen their discovery of the cattle tracks in Cañon Espectro. In devious ways they had nosed about and in a round about way had discovered that if any of the cattlemen had been responsible for that strange herd, they were keeping it to themselves.

After Cliff's forceful remarks to Kentucky Landers that night, nothing more had been said or intimated that the medico was on the wrong side of the fence, and as Kentucky and Cliff were old friends, he often stopped at the Circle Bar T for a chin and to pass the time of day. But things were running apparently on well oiled wheels at Pim's ranch as well as at the other neighboring ranches. Pim was expecting to make a fat shipment in the fall, there had been plenty of feed, and if any of his hands had noted the increase in the size of their herd, they no doubt laid it to natural causes.

Still the owner of the Circle Bar T took no chances with his stock. He lost many a head in the periodical warfare and now his own men guarded the range with sedulous care. Puff's boasting was common gossip and the ranchers were ever on the alert for some sign.

Kentucky said to Cliff one day, "I'll sure be glad when this range war is finished. I'd give a month's wages for one good bottle of red-eye. It's jist gettin' too danged peaceful in these parts to make life interestin'. We ain't even had a shot at one of them woolly tenders for nigh on to a month. A good scrap 'ud be right welcome to most of the boys."

"With a few more burials to follow," Cliff answered, ironically.

"Yeah! I suppose yo're right, Doc. Len Frame was a good hand." He shook his head. "Still I claim it's too funereal. If it wasn't that Pim was aimin' to make a big shipment, there'd be trouble right now. He's jist achin' to tangle with Puff Gordon again. He's a practicin' all the time with them irons of his and jist between me and you, Doc, he's faster 'n a side-winder. Another man he'd like to go gunnin' for is that polecat Starweather. I heard the other day that Starweather dropped the word that it was Pim who started that epidemic of smallpox among the herders. Maybe it's so, but I don't think it. Pim don't cotton to no lousy tricks like that."

"That's ridiculous!" the medico exploded. "I don't believe Starweather ever said such a thing. I'm sure I don't know how Pim could carry the germs and plant them on some Mexican. Of course, he's immune himself, having had the disease, but where he'd find a case is beyond me. There are carriers, but I don't believe your boss is one of them."

"Jist the same it didn't make Pim feel any kindlier toward the old reprobate. There's nothin' he'd like better than to cross shootin' irons with that sheepman. Hello, here's the old gent hisself and it looks like he was in a powerful hurry."

The rancher stopped his horse in front of the bunkhouse. His face was purple with apprehension and a mixture of anger and dismay.

"Say, Doc," he called. "Do you know anythin' about sore mouths in cattle?"

Cliff shook his head. "Not much, Pim. What's the trouble? We delved into the science of humans where I studied. The course didn't include the veterinary's art."

The rancher looked crestfallen. His head sank on to his chest. He seemed to have aged in the few moments since the question had been asked. Finally he managed to say, "All hell's broke loose out there on the range. There's a hundred head nursin' their mouths like they had the hoof and mouth disease. I told the boys to weed out all the sick ones and segregate 'em, but it sure looks like Gordon was about right. Will you come out and take a look at 'em, Doc?"

At the mention of the hoof and mouth disease, both Cliff and Kentucky had gotten to their feet. It took but a moment to reach their horses and to follow the rancher across the cholla-covered range to the sick animals. Cliff had had one experience with the dread disease while on his father's ranch, but he had been just a kid at the time.

He picked the sickest looking of the steers, had the cowhand hogtie it, and began to examine it. "You understand, Pim," he said at last, "I'm no expert on the diseases of cattle, but this looks bad. If I were you I'd get the nearest vet over here as soon as possible as well as the government cattle inspector. Keep a sharp watch on the herd and at the slightest sign of sickness, cut the infected animal out and put him in with the sick ones."

Pim's face was gray. "But, Doc, there ain't no vet closer 'an Phoenix and that's over a hundred mile. The vet in Tombstone died about two months ago and as far as I know there ain't been another one moved in. I just can't understand it. Every single one of these steers carries my brand. Where in hell could they have picked it up?"

The memory of those tell-tale tracks in Cañon Espectro flashed into Cliff's mind, but he held his peace. It was bad enough to have the county infected with the hoof and mouth disease without having bloody warfare in the bargain. Besides he had nothing but suspicion to go on. Accusing the sheepmen of such a dastardly deed would avail him nothing and only bring the wrath of both sides tumbling about his ears.

"The germ is in the earth, Pim. That's the way the cattle pick it up, through the hoofs and the mouth. I'll do the best I can, but you men 'll have to help. First I want you to send a man to Tombstone for any information, books, or leaflets, he can find on the disease. Then you send someone to the neighboring ranches to give them warning. They better round up all their strays and bring them in for examination. You know what this means?"

Pim shook his head dully. "I know it means the ruination of the Circle Bar T if many more of them critters get it."

"I didn't mean that, Pim." Cliff put his hand on the other's arm and regarded him steadily. "As far as I know there's only one way to deal with the hoof and mouth disease."

"What's that?" Pim's voice was shaking. Kentucky was listening anxiously.

"Shoot them and bury them as fast as they contract the disease."

"God Awmighty!" The words exploded from the cowboy's lips.

Pim just turned a shade grayer, and his thin lips compressed into a straight line. For a moment he didn't reply. Finally the words came choking out, "Why goddamn you, you mutton eatin' medico! Think I'm goin' to kill all my cattle on yore sayso. Get the hell off the Circle Bar T and stay off."

Cliff hadn't expected such an explosion and as the words sank in his fury mounted with the speed of a striking rattlesnake, but his voice when he spoke was as cold as the snow-capped peaks of the saw-tooth range.

"I'll be delighted to get off and stay off, don't worry about that, Pim. It's your funeral not mine, but it just happens that there are other ranchers in the neighborhood who will require my services. I'm notifying the sheriff that the Circle Bar T is under quarantine. You let one of your cattle stray off your home range and I'll see that you get a nice little rest in the calaboose. I happen to be the health officer for this county and that applies to all animals as well as humans. Never mind about sending a man to Tombstone. I'll take care of it myself."

The rancher's hand had dropped to his hip with lightning swiftness as the threat sank home. Kentucky had seen the move and quick as a cougar had pushed his horse in between them, effectively preventing any gunplay on his boss's part.

"Easy there, Boss," he grunted. "Easy now. The doc don't carry no iron, yuh know."

"It's a damned good thing he doesn't," the irate cattleman snarled. "You heard what I said, Doc. This is free grazin' range and I'm runnin' my steers here as long as I got two guns to back 'em up. You can tell that to the sheriff."

The medico's gray eyes were no longer friendly and sympathetic. There was as much fire and temper in them as in the eyes of the glaring rancher.

"I wouldn't advise you to try it, Pim, unless you want to ruin your business as well as the business of every cowman in the county. Puff Gordon boasted that you ranchers would be too yellow to stay after another six months. He told me he was savin' his lead for real vermin. Maybe he's right after all. Certainly none of you have showed any signs of having anything above the collar but a headful of steer manure. I'm not making any threats. I'm just telling you. If every last one of your steers isn't off that free range inside of a week and corralled, I'll see that you get a nice little stretch in the county jail for resisting an officer of the county. You men have run this section about long enough to suit yourselves. From now on and until the disease is definitely at an end, I'm dealing the hands. Good day!"

CHAPTER SEVEN
RUIN RIDES THE MESA

And Cliff made good his threat. The mere mention of the dread foot and mouth disease to the sheriff put that capable officer into immediate action.

"Goin' to back up his range with six-guns, is he?" Dorr hitched up his gun belt and a hard grin split his weather beaten face. "Cliff, that tough hombre ain't got enough six-guns to outface the law in Brant county. I been itchin' to face that stubborn mule with the law backin' me up, and I'm sure goin' to make him like it."

True to his word, the tight-lipped sheriff rocked into the Circle Bar T with twenty grim looking ranchers and cowhands sworn in as special deputies from outlying sections. Cliff had already mailed a letter by stage to Tombstone for all the available information on the disease with instructions that the nearest government inspector make tracks for Painted Springs.

Pim greeted the sheriff with an angry sneer on his pock marked face. "Looks like that cursed mutton eatin' medico has been shootin' off his mouth, Dorr. What do you intend to do?"

"We just aim to see that every one of them Circle Bar T cattle is corralled, Perk. Them's the orders of the health officer, until the inspector gets here."

"And what if I refuse, Dorr?"

"You'll dang well soon find out," the sheriff answered grimly. "This is one time when the law's backin' up the health officer and keep yore hands off them irons unless yo're courtin' a quick and painless end. Now do I have to use force or will you follow instructions? Some of these men are neighbors and friends of yourn. Just don't forget that you ain't the only cattleman in this section."

Pim backed down. There was nothing else for him to do. He was outnumbered and outvoted. But it hurt and inwardly he chalked up one score against the man who had saved his life that some day in the near future would have to be evened. Stubborn, determined, and seething with fury, he set his hands to work, and for a time fought a losing battle against the disease. Each day saw the death of more of his cattle and the infection of others, but still he refused to call on Cliff to aid him.

In the meanwhile Cliff had received the information he sought and for a time played a lone hand, riding from ranch to ranch, examining the cattle, and watching for fresh outbreaks. Some of the ranchers listened to him and followed his advice. The infected cattle were slaughtered and buried in deep trenches, their hides slashed to prevent anyone skinning them. Holes were dug, the cattle led to the edge and there butchered with six-gun or rifle. Where his advice was followed, the disease was stamped out, but there were a number of the cowmen besides Pim who felt as he did. Some of them looked upon the medico as a trouble maker and a friend of the sheepmen.

Cliff tried his best to get these men to kill their sick cattle without success. Consequently, by the time the government inspector arrived, there were a number of the ranches in bad shape. To John Ferris, the government man, the medico explained this, outlining what he managed to accomplish since the discovery of the disease.

Ferris was a square-jawed, agate-eyed individual, conscious of the law behind him and not afraid to use it. They went first directly to the Circle Bar T. Pim met them at the corral bristling with guns, ready to do battle for his stock. Cliff introduced them.

"If you came out here to slaughter my stock," the irate Pim snarled, "yo're goin' to get the surprise of yore life. Ain't nobody goin' to ruin my beeves with lead. I'm backin' it up with gunplay."

Ferris's face split into a broad hard grin. "Pretty tough hombre, ain't you, Pim. Well—" The words came drawling out—"you seem to forget that it's Uncle Sam yo're fightin' now. I hate to make you eat yore own words, but unless you follow orders to the letter, I'll just have to call on the governor to send troops in here. Suppose you take yore hands off them irons and lead us to them steers. Maybe it ain't the foot and mouth disease. If it ain't yo're in the clear. If it is I'm givin' orders what to do. Savvy?"

Pim stood undecided for a moment, his gray eyes glaring with hatred at the medico. Cliff returned the stare with perfect calmness. Pim was over a barrel and he had no choice but to comply unless he wished to go to war with the government. The rancher realized this finally. He called to Kentucky Landers who had been idly leaning against a corral post watching and listening intently.

"Take Mr. Ferris down to the pasture, Kentucky." With that he turned on his heel and walked stiffly towards the house, his bat-wing chaps rustling faintly like the wind through dry leaves.

"Yuh sure made the old man back down, Mr. Ferris," the cowhand admired as he forked his horse and led the way. "I been arguin' with him for a week now to call Cliff in, but the stubborn critter jist hates to have anyone tell him what to do."

Ferris made a swift examination of the sick cattle. "Yore diagnosis was correct, Doc," he said as he finished. "The damned stuff is worse 'n a fire. We'll have to act fast here or there's no tellin' where the stuff 'll spread to. See here, Kentucky." He opened the sick steer's mouth and pointed. "That there is a sure sign. They always have them vesicles on the mucous membrane and that saliva runnin' from their jaws. And notice how tender them hoofs are? You better send to Tombstone for some carbolic acid or chlorid of lime. Get yore men busy diggin' a long trench 'bout eight feet across and 'bout six foot deep. Run them cattle up to the edge and butcher 'em so they just fall in naturally. Course you can burn 'em if you think that's any easier, but it takes a right smart lot of wood to burn them critters up."

Cliff and the inspector found the owner of the Circle Bar T sulking at the ranchhouse. "I know this sounds pretty tough, Pim," the inspector said in a conciliatory tone, "but if you'd a listened to the Doc here it wouldn't been near as bad as it is. The government pays the appraised price for all cattle slaughtered under my orders, but as you didn't follow the health officer's orders, it ain't right that I should allow you full damages."

"You say the government pays for them butchered cattle?" the rancher squawked. "Why in heck didn't you say so in the first place, Doc?"

Cliff answered coldly, "If you'll look back, Pim, you'll remember why. In the first place you didn't give me a chance and in the second place I wasn't sure that they did, although I understood that they paid some sort of bounty. If I were you I'd hop to it and get those infected cattle butchered and buried. The main thing is to wipe out the disease before it gets to the rest of your herd."

"All right, Ferris," Pim acknowledged reluctantly, "I guess I've been a stubborn old fool. What do I have to do?"

Ferris outlined the procedure, explaining the best way to butcher and bury. "Then," he went on, "yuh got to disinfect yore barns and corrals. A five percent solution of carbolic acid or chlorid of lime, one pound to three gallons of water 'll do the trick. Do the same thing with the horse's hoofs and your own shoes and the men's if they go walkin' in among them steers. If yuh got any dogs or cats, yuh better kill them and put them in the same hole. They don't usually catch the disease, but they carry it around. I'll be 'round in a day or two to see how the job is comin'."

"How does a thing like this start, Ferris?" Cliff inquired as they were riding toward another ranch.

"Don't nobody know, Doc, as yet, but it's generally conceded that it comes from a specific virus. Most of it's been brought into this country from abroad." He shook his head. "It's damned funny that it 'ud start there on the Circle Bar T. There was another case of it several weeks ago below the border in Sonora, but the authorities down there caught it in time. I understand they don't pay nothin' down there for the slaughtered cattle and I hear it almost broke the cattleman that had it."

"Can sheep contract it?"

"Yeah, but it ain't as bad in sheep and they ain't as likely to get it as cattle and hogs. Why?"

Cliff told him then of the range war that had been raging and of his discovery of the cattle tracks in the sheep range.

"That 'ud be a heck of a dirty trick for even a sheepman to pull," the inspector snorted, "and nobody but a lunatic would think of tryin' it. Course, they could drive them cattle by easy stages from the border. After we get through inspectin' maybe we better take a run over to that Mullaby sheep ranch. You ain't heard of any sickness over there, have you?"

Cliff shook his head. "I haven't been over that way lately."

"Did Pim ever say anything about his herd increasin' suddenly?"

"Not a word. Of course it would be an easy matter to filter in a small herd of infected animals without notice, particularly if they were branded with the Circle Bar T brand. Pim had close to seven thousand head on the range and fifty more or less wouldn't be observed. Of course if the brand was different, they'd spot them in a hurry, but I did notice that several of the sick ones didn't look like the average run of Pim's shorthorns."

Ferris nodded. "We'll take a look at some of them sick ones tomorrow and see if there's been any runnin' irons used. Course, the government can't do much. That 'ud be a hard thing to prove, but if we could prove it, Uncle Sam would certainly lay a heavy hand on the culprits."

With the inspector on hand and now known to the ranchers, Cliff had more time and leisure to call on his human patients. The news of the cattle epidemic had increased the good humor of the sheepmen, although they were all watching the spread of the disease with some alarm. Cliff noticed particularly as he rode through Cañon Espectro that the gunhawks were taking particular pains to see that no stray cattle crossed into sheep country.

He stopped at the S Bar 8 hoping for a glimpse of Nancy and also to inquire about Starweather's gout. One of the hands made a sly remark to him about his veterinarian ability, but Cliff had been ribbed by experts and he answered it with a sharp retort that brought the red to the man's face.

Starweather was more interested in the arrival of the government inspector and the possible consequences to the cowmen than he was in having his gout inquired after. He said, with a sly grin, as he greeted the medico:

"Are they keepin' you busy, Doc, with them steers?"

Cliff's eyes narrowed slightly. The finger of suspicion was pointing towards this man, yet he couldn't bring himself to believe that Nancy's father, tenacious and vengeful as he was, would stoop to such a trick to drive the cowmen from the range.

"I think we're getting it licked now, Starweather. At least I hope so. It would just about ruin this county and the neighboring counties if we don't. By the way, you haven't had any signs of sickness among your sheep, have you?"

Starweather's face fell. "No, not yet, but we're keepin' a close watch on the line."

"Any sickness developed at Mullaby's ranch?" the medico inquired pointedly.

"Mullaby? No, I reckon not. Why Mullaby's?"

Cliff's eyes had never left the sheepman's face. Yet he saw nothing there; nothing that could be taken as suspicion. "He's the closest to the Circle Bar T. If anything broke out over here, that's the logical place for it to start."

"Yeh, maybe it is. I hear Pim wouldn't listen to you. That's jest like that polecat to be stubborn as a mule. It 'ud be too bad if you had to slaughter all his herd."

"There's no danger of that." Cliff then went on to impart the latest news, telling the sheepman in detail of the losses sustained to date by the cattlemen.

Starweather showed his pleasure at the news by the broad grin on his leathery face and the glitter in his eyes. Cliff could see that the old man was distinctly pleased at the discomfiture of his enemies. There wasn't the slightest sign of sympathy and it nettled the medico. There was no sign of Nancy and finally Cliff rode off, his mind still undecided as to the guilt or innocence of the sheepman.

The next day in company with the inspector he made a surprise visit to the Mullaby ranch. The stocky little sheep owner was not pleased to see them. Ferris grilled him at some length about his animals, rode out to the flocks, and under Mullaby's sullen eyes, made a swift examination.

From Mullaby's the two men rode toward the desert and the foothills that separated the range country from the arid waste beyond, but in spite of their careful search they could find no evidence of any cattle having been driven from that direction. The dry winds had wiped all signs clean if the cattle had come that way.

Unfortunately, Ferris was not as close lipped as the medico, and he imparted his suspicions to the spitfire Pim, probably because he felt sorry for the man. Pim had been the greatest sufferer from the disease. Consequently, when Cliff next appeared at the Circle Bar T, he found an undercurrent of hatred toward the woolly tenders that was rapidly developing in a conflagration.

From Kentucky he learned of the cause. Ferris in his remarks had dropped the hint that the foot and mouth disease had been deliberately planted. Plans were already on foot to give the sheepmen a taste of real warfare. The word had been surreptitiously passed, that as soon as the inspector gave the ranchers a clean bill of health, it was to be the signal for retaliatory measures.

Cliff knew that it wouldn't take much to fan the embers of hatred into a veritable furnace that would sweep the mesa and the county like a prairie fire, but when he approached Pim, trying to head him off, he was met with a gruff command to mind his own business.

Cliff was slow to anger, but when aroused he didn't hesitate to mince his words, and he told the rancher in no uncertain terms exactly what he thought of such stupidity.

"Killing sheepmen isn't going to bring back your slaughtered cattle, Pim. Besides you've got no kick coming. But for your own stubbornness, you wouldn't have had half the losses you did have. Let the law unearth the guilty ones and take its course. You can't destroy and murder on suspicion. Perhaps Starweather is the one behind it, although I can't believe that he is. Won't you men ever get a grain of sense into your thick skulls? This range is big enough and rich enough for both beef and mutton. There's plenty of room for all."

"It 'ud be a good thing for this county, Doc," the owner of the Circle Bar T responded icily, "if all the mutton eatin' fools was run out of it, and that's just what we aim to do. You can carry this information to yore friends on the other side, if you got a mind to. Just as soon as the inspector gives us a clean bill of health, all hell's goin' to break loose. We're a goin' to run them woolly nurses clear out of the state. Nobody can tell me that that there foot and mouth disease wasn't brought in by them stinkin' polecats to ruin us and Starweather's the head of the sheepmen, ain't he? Even a heifer could figger that out. You just better tend to yore own nittin', Doc."

Cliff saw further signs of the impending trouble as he rode from ranch to ranch in his regular duties. He saw guns and rifles being cleaned and oiled; saw the women folk tearing long strips of cloth for bandages. The stage from Tombstone delivered wrapped and disguised packages to the town of Painted Springs with increasing regularity. Men went about their regular duties grim of face and agate-eyed.

But the weeks went by and still Ferris roamed the county, slaughtering, killing, and burning or burying the infected cattle. Each calf or steer as it dropped into its last resting place seemed to make the ranchers a bit more determined to wipe out their enemies for good and all.

Cliff ran into Nancy one day as he topped a rise and passed through the straggling picket lines of the sheepmen. She was standing by her horse in a clump of piñons watching the smoke from a funeral pyre on the free range below. Unable to break the sun-baked ground and short of hands, Kentucky had chosen fire as the easiest way to rid the Circle Bar T of the last of Pim's infected cattle. The smoke was rolling up from the mesa in a thick column, and the smell of the burning hide and flesh could be detected even at that distance.

"Hello, Cliff," she said, eyes bright, as he dropped from the roan and stood beside her to gaze at the gruesome sight. "That's what I call retribution. It will take many a long month before our neighbor Pim can replace what the fire and pestilence has deprived him of."

"You're right, Nancy. This has been a bitter pill for the cattlemen to swallow. It isn't only your enemy Pim, remember. The disease has struck at the heart of the county's greatest industry. If it hadn't been for the government, a lot of those cowmen would have had to move. As it is, most of them are busted, flat broke. This would have been a prime market year. Beef is at the top now. By the time they get their herds built up, it may be a different story."

"It serves them right," the girl answered slowly. "They wanted to hog the entire range."

"Yes, but didn't the sheepmen have the same idea, Nancy? Surely you're big enough to see both sides of the fight. There's plenty of room for both. I don't know as I could lay all the blame on the cowmen. After all, they were the first. A little intelligence shown on both sides would have resulted in peace to the county."

Nancy looked at him oddly for a moment. Finally she said, a bit coolly, "Then you are a cattleman at heart."

He shrugged and shook his head, gray eyes deepening. "I didn't expect that from you, Nancy. Neither did I expect to find you standing here gloating over the misfortune of your opponents. That isn't like you."

"What do you expect me to do? Stand here and weep because the murderer of my brother is losing his shirt? I hate Pim as I have never hated any man. He deserves all the misfortune he gets." Her lips tightened. "Hanging is too good for such a scoundrel."

Suddenly she laughed and placed one foot in her mount's stirrup. With a quick spring she was in the saddle, reins held tight to hold the stallion's prancing. "Losing his earthly possessions is a much better way. I come here nearly every day to watch them slaughter. It's the grandest sight."

"Would you feel the same way, Nancy, if Ferris was condemning your father's sheep? I think not. The shoe would then be on the other foot, and yet—" His eyes engaged hers—"that is possible. The disease is not licked yet by any means. It spreads rapidly and there is a chance that it may reach the sheep. After all that might be called retribution too. When a man or a group of men start a prairie fire in order to drive their enemies to cover, they must expect trouble if the wind changes."

"Just what do you mean, Cliff? Are you insinuating that the sheepmen started the foot and mouth disease? That's ridiculous!"

"Nothing is ridiculous when two warring herds of lunatics hate each other as much as these two sides do. The fact remains that the disease does not come except from a specific virus brought in by infected cattle. The Circle Bar T is the nearest ranch to the sheep line. It wouldn't be difficult to filter in a small herd of infected cattle."

"And you think of course that my father would stoop to such tactics." The girl's blue eyes were flaming spots of color now. Her generous mouth was drawn into a straight line. Her hands were gripping the reins tightly. "I might have expected that from a—cattleman."

Cliff frowned and laid a restraining hand on her arm. "Think it over, Nancy," he said, grimly, "when the raiders swoop down on the S Bar 8 and burn your house and barn. I don't know whether your father knew anything about it, but he's the leader of the sheepmen and if he didn't he'd better find out who did it. There's a horde of ranchers, steamed up like angry hornets, that think he's responsible. The S Bar 8 is likely to be the first stopping place."

"Take your hand off my arm, Doctor Monroe." Her voice was harsh and brittle. "I always understood that you were straddling the fence. I see that you are nothing but a cowman after all and—I loathe the breed."

With a quick and vicious kick of her spurs, she whirled the stallion. Cliff had to jump back to avoid being struck by the flying shod feet of the animal.

"And that's that!" he mused aloud, as he saw her vanish over the crest. "Cliff, my boy, you're dumber than the dumbest rancher in Brant county. You've cooked your goose with the only girl that's worth having. Why don't you learn to keep a civil tongue in your head?"

CHAPTER EIGHT
PIECES OF GLASS

Cliff was in his office several days later when the sheriff burst in on him with the news that John Ferris had given the ranchers a clean bill of health. The medico knew what that meant. He quickly closed his office, followed the sheriff to their horses, and spurred toward the Circle Bar T. As usual Cliff carried no gun, but that morning he would have welcomed one, if only for the sake of trying to make the cattlemen give up their retaliatory measures. The sheriff had his customary stag handled .45s protruding from the folds of his black frock coat.

"How are you going to handle this, Dorr?" the medico asked.

"Doggoned if I know, Cliff." The sheriff scratched his head in perplexity. "There ain't no use appealin' to that maverick Pim, but I was kind of hopin' that maybe some of them other cowmen might listen to reason. I'm plumb afraid it's a wild goose chase we're on, but they can't blame a fellow for tryin'."

"When did the inspector give them the word?"

"Late last night. Riggers of the Boxed Y brought me the news this mornin'. The cowmen are congregatin' at the Circle Bar T today. The plan is to drive for the Starweather spread first and give that mutton man a taste of some real beef. I thought maybe I might talk 'em out of it, but—" He shook his head hopelessly—"I don't know."

The two riders circled the Dos Cabezos range, avoiding the sheep ranches, urged their mounts at top speed through and across the water-gutted arroyos, until they reached the level mesa of the free range, where a sea of swirling mist enveloped the landscape. The distant peaks were saffron-hued in the morning sunlight. The scene was as tranquil as any New England countryside, but the medico knew that somewhere on that vast plain of waving chaparral and grama, tight-lipped, keen-eyed, and grim-faced cowmen were gathering, armed to the teeth.

They pulled their mounts to a stop in a swirl of dry dust by the corrals of the Circle Bar T. Cliff observed the excess of buckboards and the large number of horses saddled and hitched to the fence. Men were standing about in groups, six-guns strapped to their narrow thighs, cartridge belts loaded with ammunition. Most of them regarded the sheriff in perfect friendliness, for the raw-boned officer was well liked in Brant county. A few of them spoke to Cliff, while others hung back.

"Looks like a gatherin' for a quiltin' bee," the sheriff remarked loud enough for some of them to hear. "Where's Jim Croll and Pat Zanders?"

"There both up at the house with Pim," Calico Ganz, a cowboy of the Squared X, answered.

"Thanks, Calico." The sheriff wheeled his horse and with the medico close behind went slowly toward the house.

They found Pim and the rest of the neighboring ranchers holding a council of war on the veranda. Conversation ceased abruptly as Plum and Cliff dismounted.

"Good mornin', folks!" the officer greeted the cattlemen.

Jim Croll, a good-natured hulk of bone and muscle, was the only one who showed any pleasure at seeing the sheriff and the medico. "Hello, Dorr! Hello, Doc! You two hombres are ridin' the mesa pretty early ain't you?"

Plum had tried to keep his temper in check, but the good natured greeting of the cowman and the sour looks of the others made him explode. "You ornery bunch of side-winders!" he growled. "Don't you know you can't take the law into yore own hands in this county. Are you all goin' plum loco?"

"Meanin' what, Dorr?" Pim's eyes were like twin gimlets. "This is just a friendly gatherin' of the cowmen's association. Far as I know, neither you nor the medico was invited to sit in."

"Well, I'm a sittin' just the same, you danged fool." The sheriff stood with legs spread, his bony hands resting on his hips. "You thought you could pull off some more of yore shananigans without me knowin' about it. You can't run no sandy on me, Pim."

"What you aimin' to do, Dorr?" The owner of the Circle Bar T grinned. "You can't throw down on the entire county now, can yuh? All you got behind you is a pair of six-guns and a mutton eatin' medico without an iron. You better run along and mind yore own business, you and the Doc. We ain't hankerin' after no interference."

"Now you listen, you danged fool. I know all about what you loco cowmen are figurin' on doin' and I'm here to stop you 'fore you start pickin' lead out of your carcasses. You all got the idea that Starweather started this epidemic. Well, it ain't so. Where in Sam Hill would that sheepman find any hoof and mouth disease? Besides he's got a daughter and I'm thinkin' you men ain't makin' war on the women folks."

Pat Zanders, owner of the Squared X, spoke up. "We ain't aimin' to hurt either the old man or his gal except in a material way. Least ways, that's what yuh might call it."

The sheriff snorted. "No, you'll just raid the S Bar 8, kill off a parcel of mutton, burn his barns and maybe his house. What do you think that fightin' sheepman is goin' to be a doin' while yo're performin' them deeds? Sittin' in his rockin' chair, twiddlin' his thumbs? You know danged well, he'll have his Winchester throwed down on you and somebody's goin' to get hurt."

Cliff chimed in. "The sheriff is right, men. You can't hurt Starweather materially without endangering his life and that of Nancy's too."

This was too much for Pim. He thought he could discern deflection in the ranks. Too much argument with the officer and the medico might force him to change his plans. Cliff saw the gun whip into his hand too late.

"Seein' as how you two gents know so much about our plans," he snarled, "I reckon the safest way to handle this is to place you where you can't bother us."

Pat Zanders and Jim Croll objected, but Pim shut them up with, "I'm handlin' this. Tie them two hombres up and we'll give 'em a chance to cool their heels in the fruit cellar. That 'll give us the doc handy in case of casualties."

But the sheriff stood his ground. "You know what this means, Pim? Resistin' an officer of the law is mighty ticklish business."

Pim didn't waver. "I'll take a chance on that, Sheriff."

And so with muttered imprecations, the sheriff and the medico were led to the underground chamber, their hands securely lashed with rawhide, and left to fume and fret as much as they wished. Pim's parting shot was, "I'll leave yore irons up here at the door, Sheriff. Chang 'll bring you some water and lower it down through the vent to you. Adios!"

"And now what?" Cliff asked his fellow prisoner with a wry grin. "Here we are like sardines in a can. You haven't by any chance got a can opener have you, Dorr?"

"No, doggone it! But there's goin' to be one hombre that's goin' to get bull-dogged when I get out of here. I'm a goin' to throw that stubborn-headed Pim into the calaboose and give him a taste of his own medicine."

"How are you, boys? Sittin' pretty down there?" Pim's voice came down through the vent. "I just wanted to tell you that we're forkin' our horses now for sheep country. There's a powerful lot of cleanin' up to do over in that country and I reckon there's goin' to be fewer mutton eaters in this county when we finish. Don't worry about the gal, Doc. I'll see that there ain't a hair of her pretty blonde head harmed. Course an accident might happen, if she should get uppity, but I don't look for no trouble. We just aim to let Starweather and his gal camp out on the prairie for a spell."

The medico's face set into grim lines, but he made no answer and the sheriff only grunted. They heard the trample of hoofs mingled with the voices of the cattlemen as the raiding party mounted. Finally even this sound was denied them. The sheriff said:

"Do you see any glass jars near you, Cliff? This place is darker 'n all get-out. I could use a nice jar of strawberry jam right now."

Cliff chuckled. "You had your breakfast, didn't you, Dorr?"

"I wasn't figurin' on eatin' the pizen, Doc. A piece of sharp glass makes a good cuttin' knife, providin' you can lay yore hands on it."

"Well, here's the answer to a prisoner's prayer," Cliff's voice cut through the blackness, "but I can't reach it. It's just even with my head."

"Use yore noodle then, Doc. See if you can't smack it off the shelf so's it 'll bust on the floor."

Then came the faint knocking of the medico's head against the wooden framework on the wall, coupled with his grunts and labored breathing as he pushed his head against the row of mason jars. Finally there came a muffled crash and the sound of splintering glass, followed by an exclamation of disgust.

"Help yourself, Dorr," Cliff said. "If you want a square meal, try licking my boots. Pim must use glue in his jam."

The medico heard the sheriff squirming his trussed body closer. "Glue is right, Doc. I'm goin' to have to get me a shampoo when I get out of here. Set down here with yore back to mine. If my fingers ain't lyin' I got hold of a piece of glass that's sharper than all get out or else a rattlesnake's just taken a nip at me."

Cliff tried to ease himself down slowly, but the descent ended with a dull thud as the thongs at his ankles tripped him and he sat down heavily in the mixture of broken glass and sticky preserves. Nevertheless he worked his rump backwards until he felt the sheriff's back at his.

"You might try sawing at the rawhide, Dorr," he hinted, as the sharp glass nicked his wrists.

"Well, I ain't got eyes in the back of my head," the officer retorted with a grunt. "Ain't that dang rawhide loose yet?"

The medico strained hard at the bounds, felt the thong give, and finally part. "It's okay, Dorr. Wait until I get my legs untied and I'll take care of you. Your hands are about as gentle as a clawing cat, and my rear end feels like someone had dragged me over a bed of cactus."

"That's right! Start complainin'. There ain't no pleasin' some folks."

It took Cliff but a moment to untie the sheriff's wrists and ankles, and that individual scrambled to his feet, groped for the door and hurriedly tried it. But it was one thing to be untied and another thing to get out. The cellar door had been securely padlocked and bolted on the outside. The two prisoners weren't much better off than before.

Suddenly the sheriff let out a yell, cupping his mouth close to the ventilator. "Help! Help! There's a rattlesnake down here."

"Where?" the medico hissed. "Where is it?"

"Shut up, you danged fool," Dorr whispered back to him and again his voice bellowed in entreaty through the stovepipe.

After repeated howls, they finally heard footsteps above. Then the Chinese cook's falsetto voice came down through the pipe, questioning.

"There's an ornery buzzin' rattlesnake down here, Chang." The sheriff's voice sounded fearful and loaded with entreaty. "Drop me down one of them six-guns, will you?"

This was greeted by stony silence on the part of the Oriental. Dorr begged again, interspersing his remarks with frequent howls of fear, and cries of pain. The medico jumped up and down, adding his voice to the din. Finally Chang was convinced.

"Here she come, Sheriff," his voice echoed down the pipe.

The sheriff caught the six-gun in his hat, yelled loudly and sent a bullet crashing at the padlocked front door. The reverberation of the iron in the small room was almost deafening, but a hole appeared in the splintered woodwork where the slug had gone through.

The Oriental's anxious voice piped down the vent. "Catchee buzz-buzz?"

"Sure thing," the sheriff's voice boomed back. "Much obliged, Chang."

The sheriff waited until the sound of the Oriental's slippered feet had faded, and he was sure that he was out of earshot. The six-gun blasted again, this time smashing full into the lock. Both men put their weight against the door and the sheriff fired again. The fourth shot completed the complete destruction of the lock and bolt. The sheriff ejected the empties as he peered out and quickly reloaded from his belt. Gun in hand, and with Cliff at his back, they stepped into the bright sun. Not a hand was to be seen at the Circle Bar T. Their horses had been unsaddled and turned loose in the corral. It took but a moment to catch them, saddle up, and swiftly mount.

But the Chinaman had seen them. He was sneaking towards them with a double-barreled shotgun, his yellow withered face determined to prevent escape. The sheriff's gun barked once, the slug hitting the barrel of the shotgun and spinning it from the Oriental's hands. Before the surprised cook could recover, the two men were fast vanishing over a rise in the direction of Painted Springs.

"I was expectin' something like this, Doc," the sheriff grunted, as he urged his sorrel to greater speed. "I got ten deputies waitin' in town, and we'll sure give them cattlemen a surprise. They ain't goin' to harm old Starweather and his daughter if I can help it."

"Well, I hope we're not too late," Cliff responded, his mind carrying a vivid picture of the S Bar 8 and the golden-haired girl, perhaps barricaded behind the adobe walls of their ranchhouse and fighting side by side with her gouty parent. She was that kind of a girl, he knew. She hated Pim as much as her fire-eating parent did, and she wouldn't hesitate to shoot and shoot to kill, if the rancher got into range.

The minutes and the hours dragged as the two riders spurred their mounts across the mesa, down through the washes, up the cañons, and at last into Painted Springs. The sheriff made swift work of gathering his deputies and at last with fresh mounts, they were ready to take the field.

Cliff had hurried to his office, laid in an additional supply of medicines, and was ready to join the posse, when suddenly he turned back, opened his trunk and made a quick search. His face was a bit grimmer, his eyes hardened to the color of slate as he found the object he sought. It was an old cartridge belt, a holster, and much used Colt .45.

The sheriff grinned in appreciation as he saw the armament buckled at the medico's waist. "Now yo're talkin' turkey, Cliff. That there's the only kind o' medicine to use on them varmints. Come on, boys. All hell's let loose in Brant county and there's goin' to be a lot of the boys 'll smell gun smoke and go over the road to Boothill. I aim to salivate a few myself and I ain't goin' to cry none if both them tough hombres, Perk Pim and Puff Gordon, cash in their chips."

CHAPTER NINE
GUN SMOKE

There were more than sixty men in the party that left the Circle Bar T with Pim in the lead, a motley assortment of human beings, from young fresh-faced punchers, never before baptized by gunfire, to grizzled old veterans of many a range war. The greenest of the cowhands were laughing and looking forward to the raid with keen anticipation, but the older ones, some of whom were still carrying the scars and slugs from past battles, were grim of demeanor. They knew that some of that band would never live to see another sun rise. Yet it was a chance they had to take. The sheepmen had driven them until their backs were to the wall. Brant county would never be a safe place to live and raise their progeny unless such men as Starweather and his hired gunhawks were driven from the country.

They rode in groups, each band headed by a hard-jawed veteran. Scabbards held fully loaded carbines. Each rider in addition to his rifle carried an armament of two six-guns, strapped in a variety of different ways to his thighs. Some carried the butts protruding forward, and here and there the bulge of a shirt proclaimed a shoulder holster with an extra six-gun for emergencies.

Spreading out fan-wise, they went steadily up the rise. But if they had expected to reach Cañon Espectro unobserved, they were disappointed. The sheepmen had in some way been informed of their plans and they were waiting at the crest, rifles hidden behind boulders and clumps of piñon and mesquite. It was Pim, wily old gun-hand that he was, who spotted a movement among his enemies. His carbine flashed out with deadly speed and he sent a shot crashing toward the crest. His spurs raked his mount's ribs, sending that animal charging ahead. At the same time, he let out a yell to his followers.

One party of riders broke away from the main string and went kiting to the south. Another group cut away to the north. Sporadic rifle fire now came from the crest, the men hidden, only the flash of their guns telling of their whereabouts. Horses screamed in agony as the lead tore into their tough hides, sending them to their knees.

The cattlemen were quick to seek cover. They turned their mounts loose and went forward on foot, crawling from one clump of mesquite to another, flattening themselves out as much as possible, keeping up a continuous fire on the sheepmen above them. Only an occasional howl of pain as some puncher got hit, interrupted the steady rataplan of the guns.

Grimly, relentlessly, the cowmen advanced steadily toward the crest, and finally with an exulting yell they charged. Calico Ganz, tough cowhand that he was, was the first to feel the sting of lead in his side. It felled him like a blow from an ax, sending him pitching forward in a huddled heap to the sun-baked ground, his knees striving mightily to straighten. For a time, he lay quietly, fighting the mist that swam before his eyes. Finally he propped himself on one elbow, straightened his arm and drew a bead on a clump of piñon directly ahead of him. There came the flash of a gun and at that instant the puncher's fingers clamped to the trigger. A gunhawk of the mutton clan, came out of the scrub pines like a charging bull, tripped and fell flat on his face.

"I reckon that evens the score, yuh yella skunk," Calico murmured. His face went gray. The arm that had supported him gave way. His head went forward and buried itself into the ground.

Now came another chorus of yells from the cañon, mingled with the tattoo of gunfire. The sheepmen on the crest suddenly began dodging and diving for the floor of the gulch. Most of them reached their hidden mounts safely, leaped to their saddles and were off with scattered blasting of guns, but a few were mowed down in their tracks and left to lie, wounded and dying. There was no mercy shown by the attackers.

The cattlemen split into two groups now, one band of those who were already mounted and who had encircled the sheepmen, taking after the fleeing gunhawks, while the other group corralled the horses and tended to the dead and wounded. Calico's limp and lifeless body was thrown over the saddle of his horse and sent back to the Circle Bar T for burial later. The gunhawk he had killed was left as food for the buzzards already circling overhead.

Even grimmer than when they started, the cowmen gathered their scattered forces and headed for the S Bar 8. But here again, the sheepmen had been forewarned. Pim gathered the ranchmen around him for a council of war. He hadn't expected so much opposition, but he was determined this time to finish off the sheepmen with a crushing blow.

"They're holed up in them barns, men," he grumbled, "and it's goin' to take some heavy gun smoke to hightail 'em out. I figure we might just as well make a day of it here. Croll and the other boys 'll take care of them woolly gunmen we routed out of the cañon. The sheriff's in a safe place where he can't bother us."

"Yuh figure the gal's in the house with the old man?" Pat Zanders asked. "I don't cotton to makin' war on the women folks."

"I reckon she is, Pat," Pim growled back, "and it's just goin' to be too bad for her, unless her old man waves the white flag. Now the thing to do is to sneak up on that barn and set a fire to her. Once we get that burnin' good it may make the old mutton chawer change his tune. Who'll volunteer for the job?"

A tough looking individual whose weathered face and narrowed eyes belied his actual age, spoke up. "Nothin' 'ud give me more pleasure, Pim."

"Then that's settled." Pim wasn't overly anxious to try it himself. He had already had a taste of the sheepmen's expert shooting, a bullet having clipped a neat hole through the crown of his Stetson. "We'll throw slugs at 'em and keep 'em duckin' for cover. Come on let's go."

The cattlemen had left their horses protected in a sandy wash and out of range. Now they slowly began to creep forward from all directions, taking up strategic positions behind any obstacle that would serve as cover. Spike Dummer, the volunteer, under a steady barrage of gunfire continued on, squirming on his belly, making a few inches at a time. The slugs screamed over his head and occasionally kicked up the dust close to him.

Reaching the corral he found protection behind a pile of dead sheep, slaughtered by the cattlemen's bullets, but as he made a dash for the barn, seeking to get beneath the rifle fire and protected by the wooden framework and adobe, one of the gunmen inside caught a glimpse of him. A slug winged its way and caught him in the hip, sending him sprawling. Furious at the interruption of his progress, he threw caution to the wind, and dashed for the barn, his six-gun smoking.

But in that wild dash many another slug found its mark in his body. It was only a miracle that he stayed on his feet long enough to light the mound of hay close to the building. The match flared in his hand for an instant. The dry grass crackled into leaping red tongues of flame, licking upward at the overhanging wooden beams. The cowhand tried to crawl free; did manage to roll his riddled hulk free of the darting fire, then the wooden framework of the building caught. A thick cloud of black smoke billowed out from the barn, effectively screening the man's inert form from further gunfire.

With a loud yell, the sheepmen made a dash for the bunkhouse, scrambling inside in a hail of leaden pellets that stung about them like angry hornets. From here they continued to give the attackers the same kind of medicine.

Pim tried another piece of strategy. Under cover of the burning barn the cowmen moved closer, taking up positions behind the slaughtered sheep. From here he directed the attackers and yelled to the barricaded sheepmen to hang out the white flag or take the consequences.

It was into the midst of this holocaust that the sheriff and Cliff with their ten deputies rode. They came in like charging bulls, six-guns blasting at the cattlemen. The sheriff, sitting his sorrel like a centaur, his bony hands throwing lead slugs right and left, led the sortie. And Cliff was right behind him.

It was too much for the cattlemen. They broke and scurried like frightened coyotes for their horses, cursing Pim for his stupidity in trying to lock the sheriff and the medico up.

"You're all right, Nancy?" Cliff asked anxiously, as he slid from his mount and met the girl at the ranchhouse door.

Her bright hair, partially unloosened and hanging in wisps about her oval face, was streaked with grease and gun-smoke. Her eyes were like twin points of fire. She made him a little curtsy and laughed. "The medico rescues the fair maiden in distress. You're just in time, Doctor. Come right in and go to work." Her voice was bantering.

"Thank God!" The medico couldn't keep the relief he felt from showing.

"And why so anxious about a sheepman's daughter?" she goaded. "Especially Starweather's daughter? That's rather unusual coming from a man who accused my father of the hoof and mouth disease epidemic."

The medico felt his temper flaring again. Must they always meet under such conditions? Was he to spend all his life trying to prove that he was interested only in peace and healing the sick? He choked back the angry retort that leaped to his lips and managed a grin. "I was interested purely from your physician's point of view," he said, coolly. "You and your father have in the past been my patients. Don't you think it would be better if we tended to the wounded first and discussed any differences we might have later?"

She flushed under the sting in his words and turned on her heel. Cliff followed. There were two sheepmen in need of attention inside, but it was nothing serious. Cliff bandaged them up in a hurry and went to the bunkhouse. Here he found a gunhawk of the sheep contingency in a serious way. Cliff fixed him up as best he could temporarily, and gave instructions that the man was to be moved inside the ranchhouse.

The puncher who had fired the barn, lay where he had fallen. It was the sheriff who had discovered him. The medico took one look, noting the gaping wounds. The man's life was ebbing fast. Cliff forced a few drops of liquor between his lips. The cowboy opened his eyes.

"Hello, Doc!" he whispered. "Ain't it funny how yore friends turn agin yuh? I thought them buzzards 'ud know me, but they didn't even stop to take a look. Yo're a square guy, Doc, and I'm danged sorry I can't be one of yore patients. Them buzzards was too quick with their irons. I'm lightin' a shuck soon. Lean closer I want to tell yuh—somethin'." As Cliff leaned closer to hear the whispered words that the puncher was trying to rip from between his clenched teeth, he heard, "It wasn't Starweather that started that hoof—and mouth, it was Carl—"

Spike Dummer's head fell back. A tiny bubble of red-flecked foam appeared at his lips. He was dead.

"Carl!" the medico murmured to himself. "Carl who?" The mystery was getting deeper. Unconsciously the physician began piecing together the few facts that he knew. Could this mysterious Carl be the man from whom Puff Gordon was taking orders? Apparently the dead puncher working on the other side of the fence had been taking orders from the same man.

The medico strode back to the house, ordered hot water in curt tones, and went to work on the sheepman lying so grievously wounded in the spare room. It was a big question whether he could save him. Two bullets had lodged in the man's body, one close to the heart, the other behind the left lung and imbedded in the spine. And this time he had no assistant in the shape of Nancy. She was busy looking after her father and the men, preparing a meal, and cleaning the wounds of the slightly nicked ones.

When the physician had finished and made the man as comfortable as possible, he came out into the living room to find the sheriff and Starweather arguing futilely. The gruff old sheepman looked up.

"How's Ponder, Doc?" he asked.

Cliff shook his head. "Not much chance, Starweather. I don't think he'll live until morning. Dorr, we better get a move on. You want to see Pim and I imagine from the number of wounded here that there's plenty in the other camp."

"If there ain't, it weren't our fault," the sheepman growled. "Lord knows I was aimin' at 'em to kill, the skunks."

Cliff called to Nancy. She came out of the kitchen. "You'll have to watch that patient, Nancy. I'll have to leave him in your hands. There's nothing more I can do."

"Of course, Doctor Monroe, I could hardly expect you to be interested enough to stay and look after him yourself." Her voice was brittle. "No doubt there are lots of mavericks on the Circle Bar T that need your attention."

Cliff's eyes narrowed slightly. "You're right, Nancy. I expect there are and the patient here is too far gone for me to bother any further with." He regarded her steadily, shaking his head. "I can't understand how folks with such apparent intelligence can be so dumb."

"Jist what do yuh mean by that, Doc?" It was Puff who had just come in. Suddenly his voice changed and a new glitter came into his dark eyes. "Well, doggone my hide, if the medico ain't packin' a loaded cutter! Yuh wouldn't like to settle our little affair with the irons now, would yuh, Doc?"

Cliff turned and met the bully's savage glare with a broad grin. "This happened to be an emergency, Gordon." Then he shrugged—"Some other time, perhaps. Right now I am more interested in looking after the wounded, than in making more work for myself."

"Yeah! I thought yuh was yella," the gunman sneered.

But the medico was not to be taunted into any gun play with his adversary. He said, "Come on, Dorr."

The sheriff contained himself until they were once again mounted and on their way, then he exploded. "That ornery side-windin' son of a coyote is sure itchin' to let daylight into you, Cliff. It sure would 'ave done my heart good to see you throw a slug or two into his carcass, if only for the pleasure you got diggin' it out."

The medico grinned. "I'm beginning to feel the same way toward him, Dorr. I'm convinced that he's just a hired killer and I'm beginning to suspect why he hates me so much. I don't roam this country with my eyes and ears closed like the rest of you folks. I've learned plenty and as soon as I can fit the puzzle together I'm going to spring it on you. This range war isn't all the work of Starweather and Pim. There's something else besides that, and some of these days I'm going to find out."

Loping through the Cañon Espectro they discovered the bodies of two more of the sheepmen's gunhawks and also a wounded one. The latter was turned over to two of the men and packed off to the Mullaby ranch hard by after Cliff had patched him up.

But when they finally reached the Circle Bar T, it was easy to see that Pim and his cohorts had made tracks for a healthier climate. Kentucky was the only one left.

"That was a dirty trick to pull on you hombres," he said in a conciliatory tone. "I was hopin' yuh might drop in. There's a couple of the boys needs a mite of attention." He led the two men toward the house. "Pim and the rest of the boys has gone to Beman to celebrate."

"Well, do tell!" the sheriff exclaimed ironically. "Just imagine them boys ridin' thirty miles for a drop of redeye!"

The cowboy reddened. "That's where they said they was goin', Sheriff, and I hankered to go with 'em. My tongue is stuck right smack dab up against the roof of my mouth."

While Cliff dressed the wounds of the two punchers, the three exchanged news of the battle. It was late in the afternoon before Cliff and the sheriff loped back for Painted Springs. The sheriff had given up hope of finding the owner of the Circle Bar T for awhile.

"I tell you, Cliff," he grumbled as they turned their sweat covered mounts into the small corral after giving them a rub-down, "this here range war is gettin' my nanny goat. What can I do against the whole danged countryside? There's a few peaceful ones hereabouts that 'ud like to see peace on the range, but they're in the minority and ridin' hell out of me besides. I ain't no superhuman. All I got is the law and two guns to back it up. That ain't much when every last one of them is a breakin' it hisself."

Cliff laid his hand affectionately on the elder man's shoulder. "You're doing the best you can, Dorr. You can count on me at least, for what little help I can give." His eyes took in the distant range of mountains and he sighed. "It's too bad that such good cow country should be laid waste by a band of hired gunhawks. There ought to be some way to stop them, but I'm frank to admit that right now I don't know how."

And that night as gunfire broke out in sporadic bursts back on the range and in the cañon and washes, the medico sat at his desk, trying to piece together the jigsaw puzzle of the range war. He was definitely sure now that Nancy's father wasn't the real power behind the conflagration. He hadn't been able to believe that Starweather would stoop to such tactics as the planting of the foot and mouth disease, even when all signs pointed to him as the culprit. The words of the wounded puncher beat into his brain. Carl! Who was Carl? There lay the solution to the puzzle. Was he a sheepman or a cattleman?

His mind traveled over the names of the men he knew in the county. Suddenly he remembered. Carl Westover, the owner of the Diamond L spread at the furthest corner of the county's border! But what interest would such a powerful cattleman have in promoting a range war? His spread covered thousands of acres to the south of Brant county. His cattle ranged on prairies that were lush with feed. He was the one man in the state who had no use for more range country.

It was afternoon before the medico arrived to see the wounded man at the Starweather ranch, and the greeting he received from both Starweather and his daughter was about as cold as any greeting he had ever received. Phil Ponder had died in the early morning hours, fighting for breath, and cursing the doctor with the last breath in his body. It was Nancy who told him.

"I think, Doctor Monroe," she said, frostily, "that the sheepmen can do without your services from now on. If you hadn't been so interested in healing the wounded men on the other side of the fence, Phil Ponder would be alive now."

The medico frowned and shook his head. "You're all wrong, Nancy. Ponder didn't have a chance. It was a miracle he lived long enough for me to extract the bullets. Surely you and your father must realize that I am not a miracle man. I can't bring the dead back to life. I did the best I knew how."

Puff Gordon, who had come in and stood draped in the doorway, grinned maliciously. "Yore best ain't none too good, Doc. Yo're a better vet than yuh are a doctor."

Starweather spoke up, his shaggy brows knotted. "Puff is right, Doc. We've had enough of your services. We'd appreciate it if you'd confine your ministrations to the cowmen."

"Yeah, it ain't goin' to be healthy for yuh on this side of the fence," Puff sneered.

"I'm not interested in your threats, Gordon, but I am very much interested in Nancy's. As far as I'm concerned, her word is law. If she wishes me to stay away from all the sheepmen, from the S Bar 8, I'll do just that. But let me refresh your memories. It isn't so many weeks ago that we worked side by side stamping out the smallpox epidemic. It isn't many weeks since I saved your life, Gordon. I don't hesitate in telling you that I think this county and state would be a lot better off without you. In spite of my natural inclinations to let you slide into the great beyond or the great below, where you'll probably end, I used my best efforts to bring you back. I didn't expect any thanks from a hired killer such as you, and I didn't get any. What's the verdict, Nancy?" His gray eyes were studying the blue eyes raised to his.

For an instant he thought he saw compassion, but if it was there, she hid it with a swift dropping of an invisible curtain. He saw her lips compress and hard lines form at her mouth ; saw the muscles at her throat tighten. She glanced away and when her eyes again met his they were as hard and cold as the blued-steel of a six-gun.

"Don't come back, Doctor Monroe," she advised, in a determined voice. "I hate and loath all cattlemen and you are one of them." With that she whirled and fled through the door.

"I guess that's tellin' yuh, Doc," Puff derided. "Now I'm addin' my sayso. There's a slug waitin' for yuh the first time I lay eyes on yuh on this side of the line, whether yuh pack a gun or not."

CHAPTER TEN
THE UNKNOWN STRANGER

It wasn't many days later that the medico gave Puff and his sheepmen a chance to make good their threat. Word was brought to him that another case of smallpox had been uncovered at one of the outlying Mexican huts.

"Yo're just loco, Cliff, to bother with them sheepmen," the sheriff argued. "Let the fools die. Ain't no sense in stickin' yore head into a noose. It Starweather told you to stay away, then you better listen to reason."

Cliff shook his head. "I'm more afraid of another epidemic than I am of Puff's threats. That case has to be looked after. I'm going."

"Yo're as stubborn 'bout some things as them loco ranchers." The sheriff regarded him anxiously. "All right. If you've made up yore mind, I guess arguin' won't do much good. I'll send a couple of the boys along with you."

"You will not. You need every man you can get here."

"Well, you danged mangy fool! Then pack yore six-gun, will you? You want at least a fightin' chance."

The medico's jaw set and his eyes deepened. "Not even a gun, Dorr. The only weapon I'll carry will be my medical kit."

The sheriff looked at him aghast, his mind refusing to believe that a man of Cliff's intelligence would stick his head so thoughtlessly into a noose, but the medico only grinned, gave the sheriff a wave, and mounted his roan.

In a few minutes the dusty main street of Painted Springs was behind him, the grama covered mesa, the foothills, and the desert ahead of him. The sick herder's hut lay to the west close to the arid waste and Cliff's route took him close to the giant Joshua tree and the sandy wash where Puff had met his mysterious friend.

The sun beat down in merciless waves, bringing the sweat to the medico's bronzed skin. His mount's shod hoofs sent up little inverted cones of dry powdery dust with each stride. Crossing the mesa, cutting through the gulches, he reached finally the adobe hovel of the ailing Mexican.

But it took him considerably longer to doctor his patient than he had contemplated, and the sun was a fast disappearing red ball over the distant peaks of the sawtoothed range when he mounted his horse for the trip back. The twilight deepened swiftly, changing the crests of the range into purple and blue, making the hollows lakes of color. Ahead of him, like a lone sentinel guarding the edge of the desert, stood the huge Joshua, its branches sweeping upward in graceful curves, while just beyond lay the gutted wash through which he must pass to reach the higher plateau.

And as he glanced ahead, unconsciously observing the desert growth of fantastic shape, he saw a lone horseman come over the distant rise, poise for a moment, then dip out of sight. The distance was too great for Cliff to distinguish the rider, but a premonition, a sense of impending danger, made the medico alter his course and urge the roan into a more secluded path. Even at that distance Cliff had sensed from the easy grace of the horseman that the lone rider was none other than his enemy Puff. Had the sheepman, he wondered, seen him outward bound and followed him?

There was no time to lose. The medico roweled the roan and guided him as swiftly as possible up the rocky and shale covered sides of the ravine toward an immense boulder near the crest, around which stood clumps of ocotillo, mesquite, and sahuaro. Here he dismounted, tied his horse, and peering from behind the barricade watched the trail below him, his eyes straining in the semi-darkness. In a moment more the rider came leisurely into view and this time there was no mistaking his identity. It was Puff and as he reached the Joshua tree he dropped from the saddle and looked cautiously up and down the watch.

Cliff didn't have much time to cogitate upon the actions of the sheepman for a second rider suddenly appeared and joined the gunman. But it was too dark now to distinguish the features of the newcomer other than to convince the medico that he was a stranger to Brant county. Cliff would have liked to have left his horse in the hiding place and gone forward on foot to investigate, but unarmed he realized the risk and foolhardiness of such a move. Consequently, he remained hidden, his hand clamped to the roan's nostrils, his ears striving to catch at least fragments of the conversation that occasionally floated up to him.

The two men now were distinguishable only by the bright ends of their cigarettes and the medico prayed that the conference would come to a speedy conclusion for the roan was becoming restless under the hand at his nostrils.

Suddenly Cliff heard the creaking of leather and the impact of hoofs against the gravel. Straining his eyes in the blackness of the wash he made out the two men mounted. They hesitated only a moment, wheeled their mounts, and vanished slowly up the wash toward the cut that led to the plateau.

Cliff gave them plenty of time to get out of sight and sound. Finally he too mounted and followed, breathing a bit easier, but wondering who the newcomer had been, that the sheepman met in such an out of the way place. He gave the roan his head as they reached the gulch and started climbing steadily upward. The medico was no longer thinking of possible danger to himself. His mind was busy trying to piece the puzzle together. Consequently when the sing of a rifle bullet rang close to his ears, followed by the report, it startled him so that the half-burned stub of his cigarette dropped from his surprised fingers. Unconsciously his spurs raked the animal's ribs, sending the roan driving ahead at breakneck speed.

Although no more bullets followed his mad flight, he knew that he was being followed, and as he reached the end of the cañon and the wide plain, he heard the thud of more than one rider's mount converging toward him. Realizing that flight was useless, he pulled the roan to a walk and waited for them to overtake him.

"What the hell's yore hurry, stranger," the first rider greeted him. Then he recognized the medico. "Well, doggoned if it ain't the medico!"

Two others came up, followed by Puff. "I reckon yuh don't like to take good advice," the sheepman growled. "What's brought yuh out here in sheep country, Doc?"

Cliff slowly drew the makings from the pocket of his shirt before replying. He resented the bully's words more than he cared to show just then. "That's rather a foolish question, Gordon," he said at last, puffing at his cigarette. "There's only one thing that brings me, and that's sickness. And by the way, are you in the habit of dry-gulching your enemies? Somehow I gained the impression that you were the kind who liked to meet them face to face."

Cliff knew the shot had gone home. Puff snarled, "Dry-gulchin' is too good for cow critters. That was jist a warnin', Doc. Yuh don't seem to understand that yo're not wanted in this country. The next time I'll aim a little lower."

"Umph! I rather thought it was some of your fancy shooting," Cliff replied, coldly. "I never saw a bully yet who had guts enough to stand up and take it. Now if you don't mind, suppose you instruct this hired killer of yours to take his hands off the reins of my horse. I've had a hard day and I'm not particularly anxious to sit out here and chin with you."

Puff bristled, "That's pretty big talk for a medico without an iron. I reckon yore night ain't quite over yet, Doc. Cal! Jest ride along close to the Doc and see that he don't pull no shannanigans. Yuh might as well come along quiet like, Doc. We've decided that it ain't safe for a medico to be ridin' the mesa at this time of night."

There was nothing else for Cliff to do but to comply. It was four against one and they were all well armed. Nor would they have hesitated to drill him if he made a false move. But as they surrounded him and they moved off south at a steady lope, he said:

"This is a pretty serious offense even in Brant county, kidnapping the health officer. You're liable to get a nice stretch in the pen for such tactics, Gordon."

The sheepman made no reply other than a disdainful grunt and the others kept their silence. They pressed steadily on until the twinkling lights of the S Bar 8 ranch came into view. Puff led his captive directly to the door of the ranchhouse, left him sitting out there guarded by the gunmen, while he entered alone. In a few minutes he heard Starweather's gruff voice raised in anger followed by the gunman's snorts of disgust. Finally the owner of the S Bar 8 appeared on the veranda with Nancy close at his heels and Puff bringing up the rear.

Cliff said, "Is this some of your ideas, Starweather, or did your hired gunmen take it into their own hands?"

Starweather grunted, "You should 'ave known better than to cross into sheep country, Doc. I thought we told you the last time you was here that you wasn't wanted."

"If I remember correctly those were your exact words," the medico replied, "and I had no intentions of going against your wishes, but it just happened that one of your herders is sick with smallpox. I could hardly refuse my ministrations under the circumstances. You can see that I am not here on S Bar 8 property of my own free will."

Starweather looked him over coldly. "Appears like you don't realize how well off you are, but I reckon this night's work may make you a mite more careful in the future."

The steady tattoo of thundering hoofs stopped the old man in the midst of his tirade and his warning. A rider came kiting in from the south, stopping his mount precipitously in front of the group.

"The cattlemen is on the prod," he yelled. "They're goin' after Mullaby's spread."

Puff didn't hesitate an instant. He gave a quick command to his men, leaped for his saddle, and was off, the three gunmen at his heels. Cliff looked at the old rancher and at the girl at his side. Age and youth, he thought, fighting side by side, in a senseless battle that would gain them nothing but misery in the end.

He said, "Can I be of any further service?"

The medico's deep voice seemed to arouse the old rancher. His eyes blazed with hatred. "Get out of here, you damned beef eatin' coyote. Get off this spread and stay off."

Nancy put her hand on her father's arm to calm him. "Please, Dad," she protested, in a strained voice, "we might need Doctor Monroe tonight."

"Need him?" the rancher blustered. "Need that ornery polecat? Yo're losin' yore mind, Nancy. We got along all right 'fore he stuck his pryin' nose into this county and I reckon we can again. That there's orders, Doc. If you don't get out and stay out, I'll—" He winced and let out a grunt of pain.

Cliff saw his face gray, quickly dismounted, and came toward the porch. "Better let me help, Starweather. You don't look well."

But the old man waved him away. "Get out, damn you! Get out!"

Cliff looked appealingly at Nancy. "Your father needs attention, Nancy."

The girl squared her trim shoulders and her eyes full of mute appeal met his for an instant. "I can take care of him, Cliff. Please go. You're only making him worse. He hates you."

And as Cliff rode back towards Painted Springs, that look in Nancy's eyes remained in his memory. The fighting spirit that he had seen there before was gone. The incessant struggling against odds was beginning to tell on her. But what could he do to help? How could he, the health officer of Brant county, break up a range war that threatened destruction to the entire countryside? What chance did he have to win the girl with a man of Starweather's implacable hatred on one side, and a man of Pim's vengeance on the other?

He had wanted to ask her if she truthfully shared that hate for him with her father. It was all so senseless. No matter which side he helped, the other immediately became incensed. Now it had reached a point where he was a cattleman in the eyes of the woolly-men. Tomorrow the shoe might be on the other foot. What a fine location he had picked to set up a practice in!

It was late when he unsaddled the roan, gave him a good rub-down, and dropped in at the Mansion House for a tardy meal. Maw Blane was alone. The cowmen's raid into sheep country had taken all the ranchers out of Painted Springs. She hovered over him, administering to his wants, noting the drawn expression about his young eyes.

"It's a downright shame, Doc," she despaired, "that somethin' can't be done to stop this fightin'. Where's it all goin' to end? I'll tell you where. Every sheepman and cattleman in the country 'll be busted higher 'an a kite."

"I know it, Maw, but what can we do about it?" He glanced up at the worried looking woman. "You've been through this sort of thing before. You know what it means. Right now they're out there at each other's throats like a pack of hungry wolves, and—" He wanted to share the knowledge of the meeting he witnessed that night with someone. The decision came suddenly. He told her of it.

"It's just as I suspected," she nodded in understanding. "That there Puff Gordon is at the bottom of it. I always said that no man with as pretty and sweet a daughter as Nancy could be as bad as he was painted."

Cliff then unburdened his heart in full, telling her of the dying puncher's words, of the finding of the cattle tracks before the foot and mouth disease epidemic, even to the girl's enmity toward him.

Maw laid her hand affectionately on his shoulder. "The women folks seem to be about the only ones in this county that has good sense. Maybe the sheriff too," she admitted, grudgingly, "but he can't do nothin'. I reckon I can read right. I'm a goin' over to Beman the day after tomorrow. I'll just drop in and make a friendly call on Katie Westover. If that husband of hers is stirrin' up trouble in this county for his own gains, Katie ought to know about it. You leave it to me to find out, Son. As for Nancy, I wouldn't fret over much. That girl's got a level head on her shoulders. She likes you no matter what she said."

Cliff reddened. The astute woman of the plains had read his secret correctly. And Cliff knew that he had a strong ally in Maw, and the knowledge that she shared the information, while it might not bring matters to a swift and happy ending, lightened his load considerably.

Before the first rays of the sun were visible, news of the night's gruesome warfare had reached Painted Springs. The medico filled his saddle bags with the accoutrements of his trade and again went out to succor the wounded. This time, however, he avoided the sheep country, and rode directly to Pim's ranch, where the wounded had been gathered. It was a calamity indeed. Men had been brought in mortally wounded, and now lay surrounded by their weeping women folk.

Cliff did the best he could, but in spite of his efforts, many of them were hopeless cases, where the most he could offer was a hypodermic of morphine to ease the pain and make their few remaining hours more comfortable. The women took their losses philosophically in most cases, the ways of the frontier were hard, but Cliff couldn't help but feel compassion, for there was many a woman who would go back that night to a lonely ranch to carry on the struggle for existence unaided by the man she had loved and fought side by side with.

Tired almost to the point of exhaustion, the medico returned to Painted Springs and stretched himself out for a much needed rest, but early in the morning that rest was broken by a loud hammering on his door.

He climbed out of bed, glanced at his watch, and wondered sleepily what new calamity had befallen the community. The sight that met his eyes startled him into complete wakefulness. It was Nancy, her blue eyes ringed with deep shadows, her light hair flying about her face, her riding habit covered with dust.

"Good Lord, Nancy!" he exclaimed. "What's happened?"

"It's dad," she sobbed. "He's dying. Come quick, please."

Cliff saw the nervous strain she was under. He guided her to a chair, hastily mixed a bromide to quiet her nerves. "Unless we take care of you first, young lady," he smiled, "you'll never be able to take me back. Now just take it easy for a spell, while I get a few more clothes on. I'll be ready in a jiffy."

It wasn't until later as they rode stirrup to stirrup across the mesa in the early morning hours, that he remembered the warning of the old sheepman and remarked about it.

"I expect I'm putting myself in your hands, Nancy. If any of your father's hired gunmen spot me, there's liable to be a dead medico on the S Bar 8."

"You're afraid, Cliff?" She turned and looked at him steadily.

He saw that the nervous strain had passed and that her old scrapping spirit was coming back. He shook his head. "Hardly that. If a physician ever loses his nerve he might as well quit. No, I'm wondering what the reaction will be. You see I don't carry a gun."

"I'm glad." The words were barely audible.

But as they reached the corral of the S Bar 8 a group of the sheepmen surrounded the medico, hands gripping six-guns, faces grim and relentless. Puff Gordon stood off to one side, a sneer on his dark face, but making no move to interfere with his hirelings. He seemed to welcome the sight of the medico.

And as the medico looked down on the upturned hard faces, he felt a little chill of apprehension sweep over him. What could he do against such a mob? What could Nancy do? This time there would be no warning. Here he was looked upon as a cattleman, an enemy, one to be hated, loathed, and despised. And so he remained in the saddle waiting for either a signal from Nancy or from the grim-jawed men who had surrounded him.

CHAPTER ELEVEN
DOC DEALS A HAND

Nancy had dismounted hurriedly, tied her horse to the corral poles, and now turned to see Cliff surrounded by the hostile sheepmen. In a few quick strides, she broke through the group and reached the medico's side, her hand clutching the pearl handle of her .38 Smith and Wesson.

"What's the meaning of this?" she snapped. "Doctor Monroe is here at my orders. If any one of you lays a finger on him I'll—"

Puff interrupted her. "Jist hold yore horses, Nancy. We got orders not to let this beef vet cross this range. Yore father gave them orders. I'm makin' myself personally responsible for them commands. I was sort of hopin' the doc 'ud come around today. He don't seem to believe nothin' we tell him, so this time we're a goin' to show him. Yuh might jist as well stay on that cayuse, Doc, unless you'd rather walk to the next county."

Cliff said nothing. It was up to Nancy to do the arguing and she did it with a vehemence that drove the men back fuming and spluttering.

"The doctor is neither going to ride nor walk to the next county, Puff," she blazed out, "and the sooner you realize that the better. I'm giving orders now and I'm going to back them up with lead if I have to. Get off that horse, Cliff, and walk ahead of me to the house. I'll see that none of these yellow skunks put a bullet in your back. You'll find dad in the bedroom."

Cliff couldn't quite control the grin that spread over his face as he saw the gunmen's discomfiture. He slid from the roan's back, opened his saddle bags, and procured his medical kit. Without looking backward he marched swiftly towards the ranchhouse and his patient.

Nancy joined him a few minutes later, her temper still at fever heat from her encounter with the sheepmen, but all anxiety over her failing parent who lay gray and lifeless on the bed.

Cliff had already stripped Starweather to the waist, baring his chest, and was administering restorative measures. And for the next two hours, they labored side by side, applying boiling hot towels to the gaunt frame, striving to bring back additional heat into the sheepman's chilling body.

Nancy gave no sign of breaking under the strain until her father was once more breathing regularly, then suddenly she collapsed, sinking into a huddled heap on the floor. Cliff picked her up tenderly and carried her to the sofa in the living room.

"That's better, young lady," he said, as she again opened her eyes and tried to sit up. "Now you just lie there and rest for a spell. I'll look after your father."

"But, Cliff, he won't die will he?"

"Certainly not," the medico denied. "Your father is a long ways from that, young lady. In another twenty-four hours he'll be yelling for the blood of his enemies as loudly as ever."

Her hand stole into his. "Thanks, Cliff. I knew you wouldn't fail me."

He shook his head. "Never, Nancy! Never as long as I live. We can't fail those we love and—" He stopped suddenly and turned away. What was the use of telling this girl he loved her? A bottomless chasm separated them. His face became a mask. He said, with a strictly professional air, "I want you to rest. Now close your eyes and see if you can't get some sleep."

Ten minutes later he peeped into the living room, and for a time stood framed in the doorway watching her. What a glorious girl she was! And yet she looked so frail and helpless. He turned away unable to stand it, went to the kitchen, and ordered breakfast of the cook. And while he ate his mind was busy formulating plans and discarding them for the death of the range war. There must be some way to end the scourge that was ravishing the county. If he could only find it so that peace would again come to the range!

Suddenly his face lit up. He chuckled aloud much to the surprise of the Oriental's unperturbed spirit, finished his breakfast hurriedly and went back to his patients. Several hours later he awakened Nancy, gave her instructions for the care of her father, strode unconcernedly through the group of sheepmen at the corral, forked his horse and headed for town. All the way back he kept grinning and chuckling to himself. It wouldn't end the war permanently, but at least it might put an end to hostilities for a time. He felt sure that the sheriff would fall in with his plans.

Dorr Plum, lean of jaw, tired of eye, from continual efforts to bring peace, heard his plan and laughed. "That's plumb entertainin', Cliff," he commended. "When do you want to start?"

"Today," the medico answered, "but it's up to you to bring 'em into town. I've got enough serum to take care of all the scrappers in these parts and then some. While you're rounding them up from the outlying ranches, I'll start with the men in town. I'll have a notice pasted inside of an hour. Maw 'll help me do the work. I think she'll be right glad of the chance."

The sheriff chuckled. "I know danged well, she'll plumb relish the opportunity of stickin' a needle in some of them cowpokes and gunhawks. Boy, yo're just too doggoned smart to be a medico. I'll have the deputies rounded up and hightailin' for the ranches inside of an hour."

"Don't forget though, Dorr," Cliff advised, "that the deadline is off temporarily and bring in even numbers from both sides. We don't want to play any favorites with the rest of them shooting it out in the meanwhile."

And while the sheriff gathered his deputies, Cliff posted his notice on the board in front of the post office that the county of

Brant and the town of Painted Springs was under quarantine for smallpox and that by orders of the county health officer, every man, woman, and child was to appear at the office of the health officer for immediate vaccination against the disease.

Maw Blane arrayed herself in a white apron, the only one she owned, rolled up her sleeves, and under Cliff's instructions, practiced on the town's inhabitants the art of vaccination.

"This here is more fun than I've had since I was married," she confided to Cliff with a chuckle. "I should have been a nurse."

"You'd have made a good one, Maw. There's no doubt of that, and I hope the stuff is virulent enough to do the work. But remember, go easy on the kids and the women. We'll give them just enough to prove that we're not missing anybody. It's the men folks that I want to wreck temporarily."

That night after the last of the first contingent had been vaccinated, Cliff rode out to the S Bar 8 to take a look at his patients. He found Nancy looking refreshed and her father up on his feet and hobbling about, much the worse for his experience, but rapidly recovering.

"I suppose you've heard about the scare in town," he greeted them. "When you're able you'll both have to come in for vaccination."

Starweather grunted. "That's damned nonsense! They'll not drag me into town for no vaccination."

Cliff grinned. He had every intention of letting both Nancy and her father off with a light dose, but he was not going to make exceptions of them. To be effective, the entire populace had to be taken care of.

"That's just what they will do to you, Starweather, unless you come in of your own free will. Now I'm going to give you a little tip. That attack you had last night was nature's warning to you to be careful. Your heart will stand just so much and no more. Unless you take it easy for a bit, the next time my efforts will be fruitless. I can't bring the dead back to life and you were pretty close to the borderline last night."

Nancy walked out with him to his horse. "You needn't ever fear that you won't be welcomed, Cliff, at the S Bar 8. Dad told Puff today, and there will be no more threats against your life. I don't suppose I can ever thank you enough for what you've done. When do you want me to come into town?"

He had a momentary desire to impart the reasons behind the vaccination order, but fought it down. After all, Nancy was a sheepman's daughter. If the word got out that he was doing it to bring peace in the range war, the whole county would be up in arms.

"Any time, Nancy, within the next day or so. There's no particular hurry about you and your father. I'd like him to have a few days to recover from that heart attack. And thanks for your invitation. I knew that sooner or later you'd realize that I am neither flesh nor fowl, beef nor mutton, but just the county health officer."

Early the next morning, the posse brought in the first of the fighters, three hired gunmen of the sheep contingency, and three of Jim's henchmen. Cliff gave them each a shot of the vaccine large enough to put their gun arms out of commission for at least a couple of weeks. To each he gave the same warning:

"Inside of twenty-four hours the vaccine will begin to have its effect. Your arm will become stiff and you'll notice a pronounced swelling about the wound. Under no circumstances must you use that arm. If you do, I can't be responsible for the results."

Others followed in quick succession. Maw took care of the women and the children, giving them a mere scratch of the needle and a faint trace of the vaccine.

Inside of three days the majority of the county had been treated, but there were still a few recalcitrant ones at large, whom Cliff and the sheriff were exceedingly anxious to reach. Among these were the rancher Pim, Jim Croll, and Puff Gordon, besides several of his hired gunmen. Pim was the first of these to be rounded up by the gaunt sheriff.

He protested vehemently as he was brought into the medico's office. "You ornery bunch of side-winders!" he exploded, "I have had the smallpox. You can't do this to me."

"Have you a doctor's certificate to that effect, Pim?" Cliff asked, trying hard to keep a straight face and winking at the grinning sheriff.

"Course, I ain't. How in hell would I have such a thing. All you got to do is to look at my face. Ain't that proof enough?"

The medico shook his head. "I'm sorry, Pim, but those marks could have been made by chickenpox. No, we can't let anybody off unless they have proof of vaccination." He busied himself filling the vaccine tube and making ready. "Take off your shirt, please. I'll have to give this to you in both arms."

The rancher glowered and stood there with his arms folded across his chest. "I'm doggoned if you'll do it, Doc. There ain't no man goin' to scratch me with that stuff. I've had smallpox, I tell you."

The sheriff made a motion to the two men who had brought in the rancher. "Just toss him on the couch there boys. We ain't got no time to argue. If he gets too uppity, I'll slap him into the calaboose for a spell. I been aimin' to do that anyhow. There ain't no cowman can make a monkey out of the sheriff of this county."

The rancher's face went gray. He knew the sheriff had grounds to do just that thing, and keep him there for a good thirty days. "All right, Doc," he grumbled finally. "I guess yo're dealin' the hand."

"You can sure bet he's dealin' the hand," the sheriff responded laconically, "and the deck's stacked plumb against you."

Jim Croll was the next victim to be dragged in protesting. "How am I goin' to use my iron on them sheepmen, if my arm's all stiff?" he complained, bitterly.

The sheriff guffawed. "You don't need to worry 'bout them woollies, Jim. They're all nursin' sore arms too. I reckon it 'll be a couple of weeks 'fore any of you hombres start pickin' on each other. Just remember this ain't goin' to be no one-sided affair. Yo're all in the same boat like."

Cliff chimed in. "You can take a much needed rest from thumbing the hammer of your six-gun, Jim. I can assure you that there will be a temporary lull in the fighting. We have one more of the sheepmen to handle, then we're through."

Croll followed in the wake of the others. The sheriff knew him as a right-handed shooter only, so he got off with a single vaccination in the right arm, but there was enough vaccine in the dose to insure the complete disability of that arm.

But it took several days for the sheriff and the posse to discover Puff Gordon. The gunman had had word of the deeds that were being perpetrated in the name of medicine and had made hurried tracks for a safer climate. Unfortunately, his curiosity finally got the better of him, and he tried to steal back unobserved, hoping perhaps to stir up additional trouble among the now helpless cattlemen. The opportunity to deal his enemies a crushing blow while they were hors de combat, made him walk almost into the wily sheriff's arms, and that individual disarmed him and dragged him through jeering cowmen to the medico's office.

"This here is against the law," he snarled. "Yuh can't drag a man in without his agreeing to submit. I'll have the marshal on yuh."

"Yo're a fine one to be protestin' about the law," the sheriff answered with a wry laugh. "I suppose it ain't agin the law to go around killin' yore brethren? The ways of the transgressor is hard, Puff. I wouldn't be a mite surprised if this here serum didn't lay you out flat in yore grave. It's powerful stuff, the doc says, and sometimes it acts much like the smallpox."

Puff glared at the medico, hatred blazing from his dark eyes. "I'll get yuh for this, damn yuh, yuh sneakin' polecat."

Cliff regarded him coolly and laughed. "Seems to me I've heard you say that before, Gordon. You must realize that this is done for a purpose. We can't afford to have another epidemic like the last one break out."

"Then why didn't yuh vaccinate me before?" the bully stormed, "when me and Nancy was helpin' yuh with them greasers?"

The medico shrugged. "I didn't have enough of the vaccine unfortunately. Will you please bare your arms to the shoulder?"

The gunman stood spraddle-legged, his lips compressed into a thin line, his black eyes snapping with wrathful yellow lights. "Suppose yuh make me."

"Oh-ho! Would you listen to that ornery mutton eater! What do you suppose he's aimin' to do, Doc? Tear you apart with his bare hands. I reckon he's plumb forgot that last lesson you gave him." The sheriff beckoned to his two deputies. "If the woolly won't listen to reason, boys, take a smart hold on him and put him over there on the couch. How about it, Puff?"

The sheepman wilted, but a crafty look came into his eyes. This might be an opportunity to test his own prowess. Dorr's reference to his past encounter rankled. He peeled off his shirt and extended his arm forward. But as Cliff leaned over to scratch his arm, he brought his fist up with a resounding smack, catching the medico on the side of the head and knocking him backwards. At that instant something hard cracked on his head knocking him into oblivion.

Cliff got to his feet prepared to give the bully something in return, but he was too late. Dorr had seen the coming blow and with the agility of a cougar had brought the butt of his gun down on the sheepman's head. Puff now lay stretched in dreamless sleep on the floor.

"The yellow polecat!" The sheriff holstered his gun. "Are you all right, Cliff? I saw him comin' at you, but I wasn't quick enough. Give him an extra dose for me. The polecat's got it comin' to him."

The medico rubbed his head where the gunman's fist had landed. "That won't be necessary. I'm afraid our friend has already received more than his allowance in that arm. That member is going to be plenty stiff in short order."

"Serves him right. You better take a look at his head too."

Cliff shot the vaccine into the other arm, bound up both wounds, and wiped the blood from the spot where the sheriff's gun butt had connected. A whiff of smelling salts and a glassful of cold water brought the gunman back to life. He felt his head gingerly and winced as he saw the bandages of both arms. Finally he sat up and glared at both the medico and the sheriff.

"You two hombres has got a lot to account for one of these days," he growled. "I ain't forgettin'."

The sheriff grinned. "That's just a sample of what the law and medicine can do to you, Puff. If yo're smart, you'll hightail it out of the county for a spell. Yo're goin' to be right slow on yore trigger finger for a couple of weeks and there's a couple of cowmen that's goin' to recover first."

Cliff nodded in agreement. "That's right! Pim has had smallpox, so he claims, and the chances are that the vaccine won't have much effect on him."

Puff grunted derisively. "Shucks! I could beat that sidewinder usin' my feet."

"Nevertheless, don't forget that deadline goes back tomorrow. If you do decide to stay around these parts you better stick to yore own side." The sheriff led him to the door. "On yore way, woolly. Me and the doc has work to do."

Nancy and her father came in that afternoon and after the vaccination had been performed on both of them, they sat for a time on the veranda of the Mansion House talking to Maw Blane. For the time at least, the old sheepman seemed to have sobered into a mellower state of mind. Both Cliff and the sheriff labored under the hallucination that the sheepman was beginning to see eye to eye with them and was anxious to settle the range war. Even Maw Blane admitted after father and daughter had gone, that it looked like peace had again settled over the county.

"You ought to run for governor, Cliff," the sheriff remarked, his eyes twinkling. "Nancy 'ud look sweet up there in the executive mansion. You'd win this county hands down without a mite of trouble."

The medico reddened to the roots of his hair. "I could do without the governorship if I had her," he grinned a bit wistfully. Then he shook his head—"That would be expecting too much."

"Maybe so," the law officer nodded, "but you might as well hitch yore wagon to a star, Cliff, as to a Gila monster. From the way that young lady looked at you I'm thinkin' that it ain't goin' to be long 'fore the Circuit rider 'll have a splicin' job on his hands." He winked knowingly at the mistress of the Mansion House. "What do you think, Maw? Has our medico got a chance of crawlin' out from under?"

Maw put her hand affectionately on the doctor's arm. "Don't let that old flea-bitten wreck of a misspent life get yore nanny, Doc. He's just so plumb jealous he can't see straight. There never was a woman that 'ud have a thing to do with him. Now, look at that face. How could any petticoat ever get hot flashes over that?"

The sheriff grunted, "That just goes to show you don't know nothin' about it. I had the prettiest gal in the whole of New Mexico followin' me around like a trained hound."

"Then what happened to her?" Maw snorted.

"Oh, she up and married another gent," the law officer responded with a sigh.

"What did you expect her to do?" Maw chuckled and hoisted her heavy weight from the frail rocker. "I got to quit this gassin' and tend to my victuals."

"Great little woman!" the sheriff grinned. "It's too bad she's married. She's sure my type."

"Rubbish!" came a parting shot from the doorway.

CHAPTER TWELVE
CLOUDBURST

Brant county changed overnight from a scene of bloodshed into a tranquil pastoral countryside. True, the dead line that separated the warring factions was again in existence, but there were too many sore arms among the populace to make any of the vengeful ones go hunting for trouble. Puff Gordon had vanished almost immediately and for several days was not to be seen in his accustomed haunts. The Lone Deuce did a thriving business and the Mansion House was full to the point of overflowing at each meal. The mail wagon from Tombstone stopped regularly on schedule, disgorging occasional newcomers and visitors who invariably remarked about the peacefulness of the town, in comparison to its bigger brother, Tombstone, and the hell-roaring cowtown of Beman to the southeast.

But such tranquillity couldn't continue indefinitely where two such bitter factions lived side by side. Puff Gordon appeared on the main street of Painted Springs, his six-guns lying conspicuously handy and began taunting his adversaries on the opposite side. It was quite evident that the bully's arms had healed and were no longer stiff. Within a few days war again broke out in the foothills and range country to the south. They were sporadic outbursts when an occasional sheepman or group met a group from the enemy's camp. Nothing serious resulted from these clashes outside of minor wounds, but it kept the medico on the jump digging out slugs and bandaging the injured.

In the interim, Cliff had made frequent calls at the S Bar 8 not only to inquire after the health of the old sheepman, but to see more of his attractive daughter. Nancy had made many a trip with him across the foothills and to the edge of the desert to visit ailing herders.

It was on one of these trips that Cliff broached the thoughts he had been carrying in his mind for some time. The continual warfare and bloodshed had worried him to the point where he had decided that he was foolish to spend the rest of his days looking after gunshot wounds.

"I'm beginning to think, Nancy," he said as they rode stirrup to stirrup up a narrow cañon, "that I made a mistake when I picked Painted Springs for a home."

Her eyebrows arched in surprise. "I thought you liked Brant county, Cliff. What do you mean? Aren't you busy enough?"

He shook his head. "That's the trouble. I'm too busy treating bullet wounds. I'm heartily sick of all this war, this silly killing. I've been seriously considering pulling up stakes, and starting in fresh in some other community. In spite of all that I've done for both sides, they still look upon me as a sort of hybrid. I am neither beef nor mutton, just a nosey medico who sticks his nose in where it isn't wanted."

"That's ridiculous! What would have become of Pim if you hadn't arrived that day? What would have become of Puff? And where would my father be now, but for your prompt action?"

"You seem to forget, Nancy, that you had very definite convictions about me not many weeks ago. If I remember correctly, I was told to get off the S Bar 8 and stay off."

A tinge of red flashed out at her throat and swiftly mounted to her cheeks. "I hoped you had forgotten that, Cliff. That wasn't very nice reminding me of it."

"Then you're sure you don't feel that way any more?"

"Certainly not!" Twin spots of color burned in her cheeks now.

He sighed and glanced up at the sky where a black cloud was rapidly taking shape and moving toward the foothills. "I'm glad of that, Nancy, but still I think I am playing the fool." He shrugged and wagged his head. "I had hoped that I could make Painted Springs my home. I like the country and I could like the people in it if they would come to their senses."

"Meaning, of course, the sheepmen."

"I didn't say that, Nancy. You know exactly what I mean. We have the salt of the earth in this county and I think just as much of the sheep folks as I do of the cowmen. It's this continual scrapping that is getting my goat. In the end, the entire range will be ruined. There is plenty of room for both."

"And you really are thinking of moving out of the country?" Her eyes were deep pools, unfathomable.

"Exactly," he acknowledged. "I can't see any future in Painted Springs. After all I have to live the same as any other individual. My salary as county health officer is minute, barely enough to keep me in food. The few cases I have had are hardly remunerative. Not that I expected much. Even a doctor has to be cognizant of his patient's finances. Most of the ranchers are on their last legs. The range war and the foot and mouth disease has brought them to the brink of ruin. Now when the cattle market is up and they should be obtaining the excellent prices, they have no cattle."

"Puff will be glad to hear of your decision," she announced, watching him out of the corners of her eyes.

"Yes, I expect he will. He'll have a free rein then to bring the range to its knees. But I can't worry over that. I've done the best I could, spending a good deal of my own money buying medicines, wearing out leather and horses to succor the sick. The warring factions don't seem to realize that Puff has an ax of his own to grind."

"What do you mean by that?" She looked surprised. "Father hired him to protect his sheep."

Cliff shook his head. "I'm just guessing, Nancy, but I'd like to lay a little wager with you that if Puff and his gunhawks together with a few in the opposing camp were removed from the scene, it would spell the immediate death of the range war."

"That's absurd! Pim is at the bottom of all this trouble." Her blue eyes snapped.

Cliff shook his head. "There's more than Percy Pim to this, you mark my words. Pim naturally hates sheep and all that goes with them, but he's a hard-headed old cattleman with a scent for profits. Anyhow, that's beside the point. After all I am only the health officer. It's really none of my business. I've about made up my mind to pull stakes and move to a more peaceful community." He looked up suddenly as a drop of rain hit his face. "We better hurry, Nancy, or we'll get a wetting. That cloud looks like it had plenty of water in it."

For an instant her eyes studied his face. Finally she said, coolly, "I didn't think you would show the white feather, Cliff. I guess I was mistaken."

A clap of thunder followed by a drenching downpour drowned out the rest of her words. "We better get out of this wash," he yelled at her, spurring the roan ahead, "or we're liable to get a good ducking."

The black stallion had leaped ahead and now raced at breakneck speed down the wash. Cliff looked back and his face suddenly went gray. Already a wall of water was sweeping down the wash, threatening to engulf the two riders. He dug his spurs into the roan's belly and yelled at her, "Strike for the high ground. Strike for the high ground."

He saw the stallion turn and clamber up the steep and rocky sides of the wash. Cliff followed close at her heels, but even as he topped the higher rise, he saw that they were still a long ways from being out of danger. The floor of the wash was now knee deep in water and silt, rushing downward at tremendous speed. From all sides of the gulch, smaller rivulets fed down to increase the tons of water already pouring through the narrow defile. Nancy had stopped her horse on the brink, beneath a shelf of overhanging sandstone, where the rain could not penetrate.

"This is no place to stop, Nancy," he cried, as his steaming mount reached her side.

A mocking smile crossed her face. "The white feather again, Doctor? Of course, I have no intentions of stopping here for long. Midnight and I are going across. We don't care to associate with yellow cowmen."

With that she roweled the stallion. The animal hesitated only a moment as the water licked up at his legs and belly, then he sank to his nose, and swimming mightily headed for the far bank. Cliff saw the pale but laughing face of the girl he loved, sink beneath the swirling mass, and bob again to the surface, her hands clinging tightly to the saddle. She looked back once to give him a derisive wave of her hand.

For an instant the animal seemed to be winning forward. Cliff sat as if paralyzed, a prayer on his lips, a lump in his throat. His eyes strained on the figure of the horse and rider, caught the change in Nancy's expression. The stallion was no longer making headway. The swift current had swung him around and was carrying him relentlessly with his burden down the gulch. Neither man nor beast could possibly make any progress against that flood. The angry wall of water was sweeping Nancy and her mount toward the sharp ledge of rocks ahead, around which the torrent lashed and dug at the sandstone.

Cliff saw but one chance to save her. To attempt to breast that current was useless, but on his side of the ravine, and overhanging it, stood a clump of piñons, their branches reaching almost to the water's edge. Roweling the roan, he raced along the bank, coiling the lariat as he rode, the rawhide that had hung useless at his saddle for months. Getting ahead of the struggling stallion and the girl, he draped the loop behind him and swung it with all his might at the scrub pines. The loop settled gracefully over the piñons and the medico with a quick jerk dragged it taut. With a few deft twists he lashed his end to his waist, swung from the saddle and splashed into the water, striking out furiously as the water went over his head. The current and his own strong arms carried him directly into the path of the horse and rider.

Somehow he managed to get his hand clamped into the stallion's bridle as it flashed by. The shock of the added weight, lashed as he was to the clump of piñons, almost pulled his arm from its socket and his legs from his hips. The rope tightened, pulling the horse and the girl into the center of the torrent and safe for the moment from the jagged rocks.

Cliff held on grimly, but it was his strength that was greater than the tenacity of the piñon's roots for their gravel bed. With a ripping crash, the roots of the scrub pines gave way and splashed into the water. Almost instantly, the rushing stream picked up stallion, girl, and medico, and hurled them forward.

Keeping one hand securely locked in the horse's bridle, Cliff's other arm encircled the waist of the girl. Her eyes met his for an instant and he gave her a smile of encouragement. Her light hair, unloosened by the torrent, clung to her oval face in a cloudy mass. Her lips were blue from the chill of the icy water.

The lariat with its burden of piñons dragged at his waist with terrific force, the rawhide biting into his flesh. Yet the mass served as a rudder that seemed to keep them in midstream.

Then the unexpected happened. The bundle of piñons caught on some sharp projection on the cañon's side, jerked once at the medico's waist, making him wince with pain. The stallion swung around as the bridle pulled at him.

Again the piñons caught, dragged, and finally with a tremendous wrench became locked behind some obstruction. Cliff had to release his hold on the bridle. No single human being could have withstood the punishment of that lariat at his hips. His hand slipped back and caught at the girl's arms, dragging her bodily from the saddle. The horse, free of its burden, was whirled off downstream.

Clinging tightly to Nancy, Cliff soon found that the rope was swinging them ashore, and at last his feet felt the hard gravel beneath. He staggered, dripping and half-drowned, to the bank to sink exhausted.

A jerk at his waist reminded him of the rope still encircling his hips. He cut it loose with his pocket knife. He was none too soon. Even as the rawhide parted, it flew from his grasp and slid out of sight into the silt and mud, dragged on by the heavy weight of the now released piñons.

Holding the half-unconscious form of the girl in his arms, he sat fighting for breath, a great relief sweeping over him. They were safe. The rain had ceased and the sun was fighting to break through the blackness above. Even now the angry torrent was beginning to subside. The sound of Nancy's voice brought him back to realities and his eyes met hers. They were a deep blue now, with a new light in them which he had never seen there before.

A grin creased his eyes into myriad tiny lines. His lips brushed hers and he strained her close. "Lord, honey," he whispered, huskily. "I thought I'd lost you. Don't ever do that again."

"I really didn't think you were yellow, Cliff," she murmured. "I was so frightened until I saw you there at my side. Then—I guess I didn't care much any more—as long as you were with me." Her arms went up and about his neck, her fingers ruffling his wet hair. "You're not going to move away, are you?"

He shook his head and smiled. "Not if you want me to stay, Nancy. You know that. It will take more than a range war and a dozen Puffs to get rid of me now. Do you want me to make Painted Springs my home?"

"Yes——" The word was barely audible, but still it was loud enough for him to hear, and his lips again met hers.

For a moment they remained in close communion, two kindred spirits suddenly awakened to an age-old fact. It was the whinny of Cliff's roan from the opposite bank that aroused them. Nancy scrambled to her feet, her face suffused with color, but it took Cliff longer to get up than he expected. His legs were numb from the torture of the rawhide.

They both heard the ring of shod hoofs on gravel. An instant later a lone rider topped the rise and dipped down into the gulley. It was Puff Gordon. He saw the roan first and a grin of evident satisfaction crossed his lean face. Then he saw Nancy and the medico on the opposite side and a look of chagrin followed.

"Hey, Nancy!" he called. "Where's yore stallion?"

"He went down in the cloudburst, Puff. Will you follow down and see if you can find him? Take Cliff's horse with you and we'll meet you further down where the water's shallower."

"We've got to get you home in a hurry, young lady," the medico announced as he took her arm and they started down the wash. "You're wet through. First thing I know I'll have a pneumonia case on my hands."

She laughed up at him happily. "I think I'd rather like that, Cliff. Then I'd be sure that you weren't traipsing around with a lot of cowmen."

"Don't breathe it to a soul, darling," he answered, his gray eyes twinkling, "but I'm now a confirmed sheepman."

Puff hove into view, bringing the roan and the black stallion. Nancy broke away from Cliff and ran to her horse. "Oh, he's hurt," she exclaimed. The stallion was limping badly.

"Ain't serious, Nancy," the sheepman protested. "Jist a scratched tendon." His eyes met Cliff's and hardened instantly. "Here's yore roan, Doc. Don't look to me like he got a duckin'. Where was you when Nancy and the stallion was havin' their bath?"

The doctor's answer was tart. "Crawling on my hands and knees through a desert cactus. What do you think?"

Nancy suppressed a laugh. Puff's discomfiture was obvious. "You'll have to lead Midnight back to the ranch, Puff. I wouldn't dare ride him in that condition. Cliff can take me on his horse." She gave the doctor a mischievous wink, that made his heart beat violently and brought a flush to his face.

Puff's eyes narrowed to slits and the muscles at his neck became as taut as bow strings. With a snarl and meaningless mutter he sullenly rode off.

Cliff helped the girl to the saddle and with a quick leap landed on behind. He put his arms around her slim waist and leaning closer kissed the back of her blonde head. "I've been wanting to do that since the first day I met you, honey," he whispered. "Do you mind?"

She shook her head, glancing sideways to look at him. But there was no happiness in her eyes, only a troubled smile. "I'm afraid, Cliff."

"Afraid of me? Nonsense! There's nothing to be frightened of. In spite of everything we have each other. Now let me see a real smile."

His happiness was contagious. "Don't forget I've got you where I want you," she laughed back at him.

"Where ever that is, honey, that's where I want to be."

And so laughing and talking, they went slowly back towards the Starweather ranch, left the roan at the corral and side by side walked to the veranda of the ranchhouse.

But the sight of the glowering old sheepman waiting for them, threw a cold blanket on the pair. The rancher's eyes were cold and forbidding. He greeted Cliff with:

"I seem to be eternally goin' into yore debt, Doc. Puff tells me that you saved Nancy's life today. I appreciate that, but——" He hesitated and glared at the medico—"don't think that entitles you to any liberties with my daughter. I reckon I've made myself clear. Yo're always welcome at the S Bar 8, except in one way. I ain't hankerin' after a son-in-law, particularly one of yore breed.

When Nancy makes up her mind she wants to get married, she'll pick a good sheepman, not a beef eatin' medico."

Cliff struggled mightily to hold his temper. Puff must have witnessed the rescue and had wasted no time in telling the owner of the S Bar 8. Then if he had witnessed the rescue, he had no doubt seen him kiss Nancy. Well, the fat was in the fire. There was no use trying to argue with the sheepman in his present frame of mind. He stared coolly back at Starweather, his gray eyes inscrutable.

"We'll settle that later, Starweather. The most important thing now is to see that Nancy has a hot bath and a change of clothes." There was a hidden threat in the words that boded ill for anyone who tried to cross him, and the old sheepman caught it.

But Cliff gave Nancy a wave of his hand, saluted the sheepman, and without waiting for any more words, strode to the corral, mounted, and headed for Painted Springs. The events of the day fled across his mind like a panorama. At least his case was not hopeless as far as Nancy was concerned. There were only three men who stood between him and happiness. Pim, Puff, and Starweather. Some day, he knew, he was going to be forced to a show-down with all three. Pim because of his connection with the range war, Puff for several reasons, and Nancy's father for the consent he must have to marry his daughter.

The medico smiled grimly as the roan beat a steady tattoo on the hard baked mesa, damp now from the heavy rain, but still too hard to have a sudden cloudburst make any great impression on it. Some premonition told them that the first conflict would come with Puff. The time wasn't far off when that tough-jawed killer was going to have his hands full.

CHAPTER THIRTEEN FEATHERS FOR THE DOC

For several days Cliff had no opportunity to stop at the S Bar 8. Maw Blane had gone to Beman for a visit, assuring the medico that she would bring back proof that the big cattleman, Carl Westover, was either implicated or innocent of backing the range war. The conflict between the two warring factions had simmered out and both sides were marking time. The medico's duties as county health officer had kept him chained to his office, filling out reports, and tending to the few patients who came into town to see him.

"Yo're gettin' plumb unsociable, Cliff," the sheriff complained, when the medico declined to take time off for a jaunt to one of the neighboring ranches.

"Can't help it, Dorr. These reports for the state examiner are a long time overdue. One more day and I'll be caught up. It's the first chance I've had."

"Ain't no sense in workin' as hard as you do over this ornery herd of shorthorns. There's none of them that appreciate it. Look at that polecat Pim! You saved his hide for him once and he ain't got no love for you. He's as mad at you as that sidewinder Puff."

Cliff shrugged. "What's a few enemies more or less? When a man's loved by everyone, Dorr, it's a sure sign that there's something wrong with him. Either that or he's going to sprout wings. I can assure you that I haven't felt any of the latter growing between my shoulder blades."

The sheriff had to go on about his business still grumbling. He liked to ride with the medico for several reasons. In the first place he was beginning to realize that Cliff knew more about this range war than he cared to admit. In the second place, Cliff was excellent company and the county's inhabitants refrained from unpacking their artillery when he was close at hand. The sheriff, twenty years the medico's senior, was unconsciously leaning on Cliff's broad shoulders and depending on him to pull rabbits out of the hat in some magical way and stop the sanguinary fighting that had been stalking the range.

Cliff had finished at last with his final report, had lunched heartily at the Mansion House, although the cooking was not up to par due to Maw's absence, and had settled himself for a siesta on the hotel's veranda. The town was tranquil. The main dusty street with its rows of paintless frame buildings was deserted. The sun, beating down mercilessly had reduced the mud holes to hard packed adobe. Only the medico's roan stood at the hitching rail in the shade, his broom tail flipping at the flies.

Into the midst of the peaceful scene, a Mexican herder came. He dropped the reins of his pinto over the rail of the Lone Deuce, dropped lightly to the ground, and called to the doctor. Cliff got up and walked unhurriedly across the street, his high-heel boots sending up little puffy clouds of powdery alkali, for even the Mexican dared not cross the dead line.

The herder broke into a jargon of Spanish and English. He was excited and voluble. Cliff heard him out, wondering a little why the man's eyes were so shifty, but putting it down to fear more than anything else.

"I'll go with you at once, Juan," the medico said. With that he turned on his heel, crossed the street, and climbed the rickety stairs to his office.

While he packed his necessary instruments and medicines, he cogitated briefly upon the news the herder had imparted. Cliff had thought that he knew every herder in the county, but the news that there was another sick one, in an out of the way corner of the desert came as a surprise. Nor had he ever heard of the Mexican, Alberto Valdez. He decided it must be a new man sent in to replace one of those who had died from the recent smallpox epidemic. He glanced up and his eyes caught the glint of the gun hanging in its holster on a nail in the wall. Some premonition prompted him to reach for it.

Then he laughed and replaced it. "I must be getting soft," he grunted aloud.

A moment later he was astride the roan and riding side by side with the Mexican. They rode north, crossed the plateau, dipped into washes and gullies, and finally entered a deep cañon. On all sides were the signs of the recent cloudburst. Scrub pines, mesquite, and huge boulders lay on the floor of the arroyo, washed there by the terrific downpour.

The Mexican was not taciturn. He answered Cliff's questions mostly with, "Quien sabe?"

Coming out of the deep gulch at last, the saffron-hued desert stretched for miles in front of them, the sun sending up shimmering waves of heat from its shale and lava surface. Mounds of jagged rock, sahuaros, waving desiccated plumes of ocotillo broke up the flat plain, hiding the death that lurked within its confines.

His guide turned and followed the bed of a sandy wash, and as the two riders rounded a pinnacle of sandstone, Cliff saw ahead of him, the crude hut of a herder with its corral of sahuaro poles. There were no signs of life about the adobe shack, although Cliff thought he heard the whinny of a horse from close by.

They dismounted at the door and the Mexican motioned Cliff to go inside. Leaving the roan in the care of his guide, he pushed open the door and stepped inside. For a moment, his eyes blinded by the bright sun failed to discern the occupants of the room. The single window of the dwelling had been covered with a garment to shut out the light. The prod of a gun muzzle in his back and Puff's guttural voice startled him.

"Well now, ain't this lucky! We been waitin' for yuh."

The medico's eyes accustomed now to the light, saw that the gunman was not alone. Two more of his gunhawks were with him and all three had their six-guns in their palms. Cliff knew that he was trapped and instantly regretted that he had left his own .45 hanging on his office wall.

"What's the meaning of this, Gordon?" He stood stiffly facing the sheepman.

Puff's laugh was mocking. "Jist a little friendly palaver. What did yuh think?"

"Where's the patient that Juan asked me to see?"

The sheepman broke into a loud guffaw. "I was afraid yuh might not come peaceable unless I run a sandy on yuh. Jist set right down and make yoreself comfortable. There ain't no sick greaser. I thought yuh might like to spill a little of what yuh know 'fore the rest of the boys get here. Open that door, Stiff. The doc ain't goin' to run away. We're givin' a little jamboree in yore honor, Doc. It's goin' to be a right pleasant sight. The boys is heatin' the tar up now over close to the Diamond 4." He chuckled and nodded with satisfaction. "Hank's raisin' a lot of chickens over there and has a bagful of feathers."

The medico saw that escape was impossible. He felt sure that none of the men would hesitate to use their irons, if he made one false move. There was no fear in the doctor's make-up, but right now he was full of apprehension as to the outcome. This adobe hut was miles off the beaten track and in sheepman territory. Even the Diamond 4, Hank Finley's sheep spread, was little frequented. As was his usual custom, Cliff had left word for the sheriff as to his whereabouts in case some sudden sickness demanded his presence, but Dorr Plum had ridden off early that morning to be gone the entire day. There wasn't a chance that the sheriff would suspect the sheepmen of such a play and come to his aid.

"You're probably the lowest example of human intelligence it has been my pleasure to know, Gordon. You're afraid to dry-gulch me for fear you might get strung up from the nearest tree, so you take this form of gang attack to show your animosity. Did Carl suggest this, or was this your own idea?" It was just a shot in the dark on Cliff's part.

The gunman's eyes blazed open in sudden astonishment, then narrowed. "I kind a thought yuh was noseyin' around and lettin' yore ears stand up too straight," Puff snarled. "That sure cooks yore goose. Yo're goin' out of this county with more speed than yuh come in. Stiff, take a look. Do yuh see them other buzzards yet?"

The hired killer stepped to the door and shaded his eyes with his palm. "Yep," he announced at last. "They're comin' up the wash now."

Puff got to his feet, holstered his six-gun, and motioned to Cliff to go out. The other gunhawk walked directly behind him, his iron ready, in case the medico made a wrong move. He was forced to mount, his legs were securely tied beneath the roan's belly, and his hands were lashed to the saddle horn. Three more men of the sheep contingency, all of them squint-eyed, lean-visaged men, came loping up the wash and joined them. In a moment the cavalcade got under way with the bully Puff in the lead.

Cliff held his tongue as did the gunhawks. The medico was trying to conceive some means of escape, while his captors were looking forward to the coming tar and feather party with keen enjoyment. There was only one man, a youngster in his teens, who showed any sympathy. Cliff had doctored him for a minor gunshot wound some weeks earlier, but Puff noticed the interest and snarled a curse at him, forcing the kid to mask his face into hatred for the medico.

It was almost sundown when the party reached the Diamond 4. A huge fire had been built and a large kettle of tar was simmering and boiling above it. Here more men had gathered to witness the jamboree. The medico was untied, hauled by rough hands from the roan, and pushed forward to a stake driven into the ground, where he was again securely fastened. Cliff felt grimly that now he knew how those old witches in bygone days suffered as they were burned at the stake. His was to be no torture to his body as bad as that, but rather torture to his inner feelings, something that he would remember as long as he lived. He knew that once the news spread, he would be laughed out of the county. The cattlemen as a whole wouldn't mourn his passing. Most of them considered him as a busybody anyhow.

But still the crowd of men, milling about, joking, tending the fire, and keeping a sharp eye on him, failed to start the procedure. Finley, the owner of the sheep ranch, apparently had other ideas. Food was brought from the ranchhouse and the men squatted about the fire. After what seemed interminable hours to the medico, whose legs were cramped, Puff pushed aside his tin plate, rolled the makings, and stood up.

"Well, gents," he laughed coarsely, "I reckon it's about time we sent the medico of Painted Springs on his last ride out of the county. Unsling that bucket of tar and bring out them feathers. I'm itchin' to see what this hombre looks like when he's all dressed up." He strolled nonchalantly over to Cliff. "I ain't never seen yuh in the flesh, Doc, but I'm goin' to get a right good look at yuh now. Come here, Stiff, and you, Hank. Untie the medico and get them clothes off of him."

The medico had an insane desire to lash out at the bully's grinning face, as his arms were released, and the two men started to rip the clothes from his back. His fist caught the man called Stiff a resounding blow that knocked the gunman sprawling. The other ducked just in time to avoid his left as it swung upwards and outwards.

Puff guffawed. "I told yuh to be careful. The doc packs a mean wallop." His six-gun flashed into his hand. "Come here, Kid. Try yore hand at it. If he tries any more monkey business, I'll nick his ears."

"Aw, let someone else do it," the Kid objected. "I ain't got nothin' agin the doc. If yuh ask me, Puff, yo're jist goin' plain loco."

"Nobody's askin' yuh," the sheepman barked. "Jist do as yo're told, 'fore I smack yuh down."

"Yeah? You and who else, yuh big overgrown polecat!" the Kid shot back venomously. "Do yore own dirty work."

There came mingled shouts of, "Yo're right, Kid," and, "Teach him his manners, Puff."

The sun had long since vanished over the distant range. The men's faces were lit up only by the licking red flames of the fire, throwing their features into sharp outline. Cliff waited tensely. His hands were untied. This fact seemed to have been overlooked in the sudden rigidity of his enemies. The Kid stood facing Puff, his eyes twin flecks of fire in his strained face.

Cliff saw the sheepman slowly holster his gun and stare at his henchman who had deliberately questioned his commands. Suddenly, unexpectedly, his fist lashed out. "I'll show yuh who's givin' orders here," he gritted.

But the Kid was just as quick, he ducked the swiftly winging blow, dodged and struck back, catching the sheepman on the side of the head. Then all bedlam broke loose. It appeared to be the signal for a division of the enemy. The crowd broke up into a milling, cursing, fighting mob. A man crashing against the medico, throwing him back against the stake, brought Cliff to a realization that his chance for escape had come. Swiftly, he leaned down and with his pocket knife cut the rawhide that bound his ankles to the post. And just as swiftly, he faded from the ring of the firelight toward a clump of sheltering cottonwoods.

From the trees he made swift flight toward the barn and the corrals where his roan had been tied. But before he had reached the barn, he knew that his escape had been discovered. He heard Puff's voice raised in anger, followed by the shouts of the other gunmen. Then came the pound of many feet on the hard ground, racing toward his hide-out.

Cliff changed his mind about his mount. It was a long ways to Painted Springs on foot, but that was better than to risk a bullet in his back. He cut down through a gulley and doubled on his tracks, heading for the ranchhouse. A light flashing out from that dwelling suddenly uncovered him. He heard the sing of slugs winging close to him and the blast of six-guns. He ducked, reached the veranda, kicked open the door, and slammed it shut behind him. A shotgun hung suspended from the wall. The medico grabbed it, saw that it was loaded, and swiftly hid himself in a strategic position behind the door.

But even as he got under cover, there came from the direction of the corrals and barns, the sound of more gunfire and the yells and yips of fighting men. On top of this came the thud of many hoofs. To Cliff, holed up behind his barricade, it sounded like a full-fledged battle was in progress.

The medico wasn't far wrong as he discovered later. The cattlemen had picked this particular night to raid the Diamond 4. They had surprised the sheepmen and those individuals were now forking their horses with all the speed they could muster and heading for unknown parts, leaving the owner of the Diamond 4 to fight it out alone.

Finally the gunfire stopped, there came the tap of many high-heeled boots on the veranda, and Kentucky Landers rocked into the sitting room, his gun still smoking.

Cliff saw him first. "Put up that iron, Kentucky," he growled in a fierce voice, "before I let daylight into you." The puncher didn't even turn around to see who his assailant was. He promptly reached for the sky. Then Cliff laughed. "That's all right, Kentucky. I just wanted to see if I couldn't surprise you."

"Well, God Awmighty!" the cowboy exploded, recognizing the voice. "What you doin' in a sheep pen?" Then his eyes bulged as he saw that the medico was nude to the waist.

Cliff laid the shotgun across the chair. "I just came in to get dressed, Kentucky. You boys arrived in time. The sheepmen were about to decorate me with a pretty coat of tar and feathers." The puncher listened wide-eyed as Cliff told him of the day's events.

"The lousy, mangy, coyotes!" he exclaimed, as the medico completed his robing. "But doggoned if it don't serve yuh right. You'd ought to know better than to have dealin's with them mutton eaters." He grinned. "Anyhow yo're Johnny-on-the-spot. There's a couple of woolly nurses out here yellin' from pain and I think a couple of my boys is nursin' slugs. Better have a look at 'em as long as yo're here."

Cliff followed the puncher out to the barn, made swift work of the injured, for none of them had serious wounds, and was soon in the cavalcade of cowhands that cut back through the foothills for cow country. They stopped at the Circle Bar T, ate a hearty dinner, and were soon spread out on their way to their respective spreads.

Kentucky rode into Painted Springs as an escort for the medico and for another reason which he divulged later. "Yo're jest plumb loco, Cliff," he contended, "to go ridin' this county without an iron."

"Maybe so, Kentucky," the medico responded, "but so far I've been able to take care of myself without one. Tonight was really the first time that I've felt the need of a shooting iron. Perhaps it's just as well. There would no doubt be a dead medico for this county to mourn over."

"Hell's fire!" the puncher snorted. "Yuh used to be faster 'n chained lightnin' back there in Texas. I ain't forgettin' the time yuh throwed down on that bad hombre at the Shootin' Star, kicked his gun clear out of his hand with one slug, and then mauled him plenty."

"Well, that's best forgotten," Cliff shrugged. "I'm a physician now."

They reached the livery stable, the doctor unsaddled, gave the roan a good rub-down, and turned him loose to graze. Kentucky followed him up to his rooms, something apparently bothering him. Finally he said:

"Yuh wouldn't change yore mind, now would yuh, Cliff."

But Cliff had sensed what was coming. He grinned. "For an old hand like you, I think I will. Take a look in that medicine case. You'll find a bottle of your favorite snake poison. I'll donate it to the cause, but you make tracks for the Circle Bar T before you uncork it."

The cowboy's gratitude knew no bounds. He held the liquor up to the light, shook it, watching the bead form, and chortled, "Bottled sunshine! Cliff, you've earned my undyin' gratitude. I'm a goin' to arrive at the Circle Bar T all lit up like Aunt Mandy's barn on a Saturday night. They ain't goin' to be a drop left. Me and the spirits is goin' to commune tonight."

The cowhand had no sooner forked his horse and left town, when the sheriff called to Cliff, and climbed the rickety stairs to his office.

"Hear anythin' about that fracas at the Diamond 4 tonight?" he asked. "Finley jest rode into town on the prod threatenin' to get my scalp if I didn't do somethin' about these killin' cowmen."

Cliff did and proceeded to explain his part in the night's events. The sheriff got angrily to his feet when he had finished. "Ain't no mutton eatin' ornery son of a prairie wolf goin' to get away with them kind of things in this county. I'm goin' to round up a posse and chase that polecat clear out of the state."

"Hold your horses, Dorr!" The medico put a restraining hand on the sheriff's arm. "Leave that little matter for Puff and me to settle. I learned a little more news tonight and something tells me that Puff Gordon is close to the end of his rope. I've a hunch that this range war is going to be settled very shortly."

The sheriff subsided. "I reckon if that's the way you feel about it my hands is tied. Go to it, Cliff, but I'd sure like to get on the inside track. If this keeps up much longer I'm goin' to throw away my tin badge and hightail it for a more peaceable climate."

And on the road to the Circle Bar T, a singing cowhand loped across the mesa, the reins of his mount looped over his saddle horn, while his hands made frequent passes towards his mouth. Kentucky Landers was making up for lost time and doing a thorough job of it.

CHAPTER FOURTEEN
PUFF RUNS WILD

Out at the S Bar 8, Nancy was beginning to wonder why Cliff hadn't dropped in to see her. Having no means of communication other than horse flesh and shank's mare, she was not cognizant of the events that were transpiring in the town of Painted Springs. Her father, since the day he had heard of the medico's heroic feat in saving his daughter's life, and had bluntly told Cliff that it was useless for him to consider himself as a possible son-in-law, had withdrawn into his shell. Nancy heard no news from him.

But from bits of conversation overheard in the region of the bunkhouse, and other suspicious actions, she finally pieced enough together to get a bird's eye view of the tar and feather party at the Diamond 4. Her blood boiled and she went straight to Starweather, accusing him of having a part in it.

"I never imagined," she blazed, "that you of all people would lend your hand to such a low-down, despicable, and filthy trick. Just like a pack of wolves after a defenseless sheep. I'm ashamed to admit that you're my father."

Now if there was one person in the world that the grizzled old sheepman loved, it was his daughter. He idolized her and well he might. She was more like a son than a daughter, filling the gap created by the death of both her brother and her mother, helping in the business of the ranch, the raising and marketing of sheep, and running the ranchhouse with rare acumen. She was the one person that could make the stubborn sheepman eat dirt.

"Now, Nancy," he argued sheepishly. "You wouldn't accuse yore old dad of such nefarious schemes, would you? The medico was jest gettin' too nosey and the boys only wanted to give him a scare. I didn't know a thing about it until the next mornin'."

"But still you think it was all right. How you can stand there and defend such actions on the part of your men is more than I can understand! Cliff is a fine man and trying hard to do his work in spite of all the opposition. I certainly admire him for sticking to it. I'm beginning to think he and the sheriff are the only ones in this county left with a grain of sense."

"Now, don't you get all riled up over that medico." Her father's eyes became flinty in their hardness. "I reckon the doc's all right, but just the same I ain't hankerin' after him for a son-in-law."

"Then you might as well quit your squealing," she burst out, "because that's just what he's going to be. Cliff and I are engaged to be married."

"Is that so?" He rapped his cane down sharply on the arm of his chair, and his beetled brows seemed to assume even larger proportions as his forehead creased into deep furrows. "I've spoiled you, that's what I've done. Spoiled you! My own daughter stands there and tells me she's goin' to marry the worst busybody in the whole county. Well—you ain't. Damnit! You ain't goin' to marry that beef eatin' medico. That's final."

Nancy's large blue eyes changed from azure to violet, and from violet to indigo. The pupils dilated to twice their normal size. Her lips compressed into a tight straight line, and her chin jutted out with determination.

"I've never crossed you in a single thing, Dad," she countered. "I've tried my best to take Jim's place. Now—" Her voice broke for an instant, but she recovered herself—"you tell me I can't have the only thing in the world that I really want."

"Yes, and I mean it too, doggone it," he snorted back. "I ain't goin' to have that medico for a son-in-law, come hell and high water. What's the matter with Puff? He was aces high 'til this ornery doc came a buttin' in. Now there's my idea of a two-fisted, fightin' sheepman. There ain't a better man in the whole state of Arizona."

"Two fisted!" she scorned. "Of course he's two fisted, but what good are they? I know. He eats with them. Cliff knocked the feathers out of him the first time Puff tried to pull a gun on him. Even the Kid stood up and told him what kind of a skunk he was last night."

The sheepman sighed and shook his head. "I ain't goin' to argue with you, Nancy. I've said my piece. If you want to get spliced there's only one man in the county I'll give my consent to, and it ain't the medico. I was sort of hopin' that maybe you wouldn't want to do that for awhile. Yore old dad's gettin' along and that flip-flop my heart did awhile back kind of scared me."

She was instantly contrite. "Don't you worry, Dad. I'm not going to run off and leave you."

"Then you'll promise me you won't marry the medico?"

"No, I won't promise that, but I'll agree not to marry him without your consent. I'm going to take a run out to Geosta's place to see his boy."

There was unshed tears in her eyes, as she mounted and loped off on the black stallion, toward the adobe hut of the herder, and a great weight dragging at her heart. Cliff was right. The range would never be conducive to happiness until the war had been settled. She was beginning to see eye to eye with her sweetheart now. It was a senseless feud. Bloodshed, death, and ruin faced both cattlemen and sheepmen unless peace should reign again.

Back at the S Bar 8, Puff Gordon had found his boss and had listened hard-eyed to the old man's recital of her love for the medico.

"When I was yore age, Puff," Starweather harangued, "I didn't let no grass grow under my feet when I was courtin'. Maybe times is changed, but a rival's a rival in any age. It's up to you to beat him out in some way if you want Nancy bad enough."

Not many hours later, Puff was seen to top the rise to the west and vanish into the many gullies and washes that crossed the plateau. He rode steadily until the edge of the desert had been reached, stopped, stared about with moody eyes, and rolled the makings. For several minutes he sat there, puffing at the butt dangling from his thin lips. Finally he wheeled the horse, and headed north at an easy lope.

Nancy, unaware of the news her father had imparted to the gunman, reached the hut of Manuel Geosta, dismounted, and called to the herder. The little boy, the flesh once more covering his bony frame, came running to meet her. The girl caught him in her strong young arms and swung him upward to the back of the black stallion.

"I know what little boys like," she laughed. "Especially little boys who are good and who eat the right kind of food. I'm taking him for a spin on the desert, Maria," she called to the fat Mexican woman who had appeared sleepy-eyed from the adobe hovel. "We'll be back in a jiffy."

With the grace of a cougar, she swung herself into the saddle, holding the child tight in her arms. The stallion seemed to sense the fragility of his extra burden, and at the touch of his mistress's spurs broke into an easy lope.

And as the girl rode with an easy grace, cradling the small child, the stallion's stride covering the cactus spotted plain, she told stories of the distant range ; stories of the hidden wealth and the beauties of nature that filled the young man's undeveloped brain with air castles.

Mile after mile, the stallion moved with effortless ease, his nose pointed at the Dragoon mountains many miles to the west. So absorbed did Nancy become in her efforts that the sun was but a half-ball of red fire in the west before she realized that she had gone much further than she intended. The child in her arms, lulled to sleep by the girl's soft voice and the rocking motion of the horse, was totally unconscious of the impending danger.

Twilight comes swiftly in the west. The stars began to twinkle overhead before they were half way to their destination. The stallion made good time under the touch of the girl's spurs, but it was not good enough. Soon they were enveloped in a blanket of impenetrable blackness with only the stars to guide them.

The stallion's steady tattoo on the sun-baked shale, the occasional throaty howl of some distant coyote, and the child's steady breathing were the only sounds that Nancy could hear.

Then far ahead, she thought she heard another sound, the clip-clop of other riders. The stallion neighed suddenly. Three riders came out of the blackness and intercepted her. And as they surrounded her mount, she realized suddenly that this was no rescue party looking for her. Her hand flew to the .38 in its holster, but a hand quicker than her own, wrenched the gun from her hand, and tossed it with a sneering laugh into the mesquite.

"Who are you?" she demanded, "and what do you want?" There was no fear in her voice, only a slight apprehension over the safety of the youngster in her charge.

The child stirred and opened his large black eyes. "Qué hay?" he questioned.

"What 'll we do with the kid?" a gruff voice came from the blackness.

"Drop the brat. We can't be bothered with no kids where we're goin'," another voice answered.

The third rider who had been hanging back behind his fellows, urged his horse closer. He tried to disguise his voice, but Nancy recognized it instantly. He grunted, "Drop the little greaser, ma'am. Somebody 'll find him in the morning."

"I'll do nothing of the kind, Puff," Nancy blazed out. "What do you mean by this? Give me back my gun at once and escort me to Manuel's hut."

The other two gunmen chuckled. "I told yuh she'd recognize yuh, Puff," one of them burst out. "Now what yuh aimin' to do?"

Puff moved his horse closer to the girl. "We're takin' yuh across the border, Nancy. You and me is goin' to get spliced."

Nancy couldn't believe her ears. "Are you crazy, Puff Gordon? Have you completely lost your mind? Stop this nonsense and take me back."

The gunman chuckled mirthlessly. "I ain't crazy and I ain't lost my mind. This here is yore paw's idea. Give me the kid. I'll take him back and drop him at the hut."

The girl argued in vain, but she did manage to whisper to the child to tell his father to notify the sheriff of her abduction. Puff took the bundle and vanished into the blackness. The other two ranged their mounts on each side of her, one of them keeping a tight hold on the stallion's reins. Finally Puff reappeared, and with Nancy between them, they struck off across the desert, heading for the border and veering away from the range to the west.

By midnight they had made camp in a small box cañon out of sight of any prying eyes. The gunman was so sure of cooperation on the part of his employer that he wasn't in the least hurried. After a tasteless dinner of beans and stale bread, she was furnished with a blanket, and told to lie down and rest.

She tried arguing with the gunman at breakfast, but he merely laughed at her. And while the other two men foraged for feed for their horses, and made ready for the day's progress to the south, Puff lay watching her out of smoldering eyes, making love to her.

"I always did have a hankerin' after yuh, Nancy, and I reckon my chances was pretty good until that medico come along." He chuckled. "There's one hombre that 'll sure be surprised when he finds his gal has flown."

Nancy kept her silence, her eyes watching the gunman's cruel face. She wondered how she could have seen anything romantic in the leering thin lips and the pitchy-colored eyes of the sheepman. Thank God, she knew him now for what he was!

Puff continued, unconscious of the hatred that blazed from her eyes. "I've loved yuh ever since I've knowed yuh, Nancy. Yore dad give the idea. Jest as soon as we get across the border, we'll find a padre and get hooked nice and tight. But there ain't no hurry. Yore old man 'll guess what's happened when yuh turn up missin'."

Nancy couldn't quite believe that her father would countenance such a thing and yet the gunman seemed so sure of himself, that there seemed no other answer. She said at last in icy tones, "Did you ever stop to consider that I might not agree to marrying you?"

"Sure. I figured yuh might object, but I reckon I can make yuh see straight. Yo're a right pretty female, Nancy, and bein' married to me is a lot better than bein' tied to some greaser. There's plenty of 'em below the border that 'ud pay a right good price for a gal with corn-colored hair. Most of them greasers is kind of brunette. The light ones is at a premium. Yeah, I reckon you'll be only too glad to tie yoreself to an American."

"That's the first time I ever heard of a jailbird calling himself an American," she derided. "Why you're nothing but a hired killer."

The gunman reddened under her gaze, took a quick glance up the cañon and saw that his partners in crime were out of sight, reached out and picked the struggling girl up into his arms. Holding her tight, he pressed his face close to hers.

"Maybe you'll change yore tune, Nancy, 'fore we get to the border." His lips crushed hers.

There was a sting in the kiss that was decidedly unpleasant to the girl and with all consuming fury, she bared her teeth and bit viciously at his lip. The gunman let out a curse and dropped her to the ground, clamping his hand to his injured mouth.

"Yuh ornery bitin' fool!" he gritted. "Don't never try that agin." Then he laughed—"Quite a spitfire, ain't yuh? I'll tame yuh though. They don't come too tough for Puff Gordon. Hey, you buzzards! Get a move on them horses. We're headin' south pronto."

Nancy lay back on the turf where she had fallen and bit her own lip in fury and chagrin. The future looked decidedly unpleasant at that moment, with her father backing up his gunman. Then Cliff's sun-burned face and twinkling gray eyes flashed before her. Had Juan given the alarm? Or had the small boy been unable to fathom the instructions imparted to him? She mustn't give up hope.

The clip-clop of the approaching mounts aroused her. There might be a chance to escape. She would fight to the last ditch. Anything would be better than being married to Puff Gordon.

She mounted the stallion as it was brought up to her, and without even a protest followed the gunman up the cañon and on to the higher plateau. Close to the top she surreptitiously dropped her quirt. It was a new day, and the distant hills and peaks were crested with coral, the hollows reservoirs of purple, but to Nancy it was a drab, unfriendly scene.

She soon found that Puff was totally unhurried. They rode leisurely towards the south, stopping in the heat of the day for lunch and a short siesta, plodding on again as the sun's slanting rays no longer baked the mesa. His actions only served to convince her of her father's approval of the plan and to make the weight at her heart even heavier.

Manuel, if apprised of her danger by his small son, would naturally go straight to her father. He in turn would grin and tell the Mexican that there was nothing to fear. By night her tortured thoughts had driven all hope of rescue from her mind. Her only hope now lay in her own ability to elude her captors.

But if Puff was sure of his own position, he still wasn't taking any chances of letting his prisoner escape. He took a short length of rope, bound it securely to her ankles and tied the other end to his wrist. Then he calmly stretched himself out in his blanket and went peacefully to sleep.

For some little time the girl lay there on her back watching the constellations above. Finally, stealthily and quietly, she got her fingers to work on the knots that bound her ankles. It was a tedious job for the gunman had done his job thoroughly and several times awoke to test the tautness of the rawhide.

But at last she had her ankles free, and slipping silently from her blanket, she crawled on her hands and knees towards the hobbled animals. She managed to get the saddle on and the cinch tightened, before the gunman stirred and discovered that his prisoner had vanished.

Nancy made a flying leap to the stallion's back, dug in her spurs and headed down the cañon. She heard the blast of a six-gun from behind her. Her mount shuddered, stumbled, suddenly went to his knees and pitched her headlong. She was dimly conscious as she sailed through the air that this was her last chance; that marriage to the sheepman was now inevitable. Then her head hit something hard and unyielding, knocking her into oblivion.

But even as she lay stunned and helpless, the sound of more gunfire reverberated in the cañon, mixed with the excited yells of men.

CHAPTER FIFTEEN
THE MEDICO LETS LOOSE

Both Cliff and the sheriff in their respective offices heard the thunder of hoofs, as Starweather and three of his sheepmen galloped into Painted Springs, ignored the dead line and dragged their mounts to a stop. The sheriff came barging out, a six-gun in either hand, expecting trouble. Cliff came down his shaky stairway on the bound.

He landed on the board walk in time to take in the tense figures of cowmen and sheepmen facing each other, with the sheriff covering the entire group, and threatening to let daylight into the first man who made a move for his iron.

It was Starweather who broke the tension. He sat like a centaur on the big gelding, his shaggy brows drawn together in a knot, his wrinkled face gray with fury and apprehension. “My daughter’s been kidnapped by Puff,” he flung out in a rasping voice. “I want a posse.”

“God Awmighty!” the sheriff rasped. “When?”

The old sheepman was almost beside himself but he managed to give the details as far as known. It was Jim Croll who first pulled his hand away from the walnut butt of his six-gun and in two quick strides reached the sheepman’s side, his hand outstretched.

“By God, you’ll get a posse, Burke!” he raged, “and we’ll bring that yella coyote back by his heels. Get goin’ there, Runt,” he turned and flashed the order to one of the punchers. “Ride like hell and round-up the boys.”

The cowboy didn't wait for further orders. There wasn't a cowhand in the county who didn't believe that the sun rose and set in Nancy Starweather. They would have cut off their hands to be of service to her. Runt was gone in a whirl of dust.

Starweather had gripped the hand of the cattleman. "Thanks, Jim!" he mumbled. "I reckon we should 'ave buried the hatchet—" His hand clutched suddenly at his throat. His huge frame swayed in the saddle.

Cliff and the rancher caught him before he fell. With the aid of the two sheep hands, they carried him into the Mansion House and stretched him out. The medico with the aid of Maw Blane went immediately to work restoring him. And finally as the men began to gather in front of the sheriff's office, they managed to get the old man comfortable and breathing easier. Fighting and stubborn as a mule, he insisted on going with the posse.

"If you want to see your daughter again, Starweather," Cliff snapped back at him, "you'll remain right here. That's the second warning you've had from that pumper of yours and I can't do much for you if you have another one. Maw will take good care of you and we'll bring Nancy back. You don't need to worry about that."

The medico gave swift instructions to Maw on the care of the patient, ran to his office, grabbed his holster and six-gun from the wall, and joined the men and the sheriff.

They were a grim-lipped crowd that spurred their mounts toward the southwest and the border. Cliff rode close to the sheriff and that individual chawed incessantly at the quid of tobacco in his mouth, urging his mount steadily onward and keeping silent.

As they cut down through the Cañon Espectro and slowed their horses to a steady trot, the sheriff glanced out of the corner of his eye at the medico, let fly a wad of brown juice at a passing clump of mesquite and grunted.

"You ain't aimin' to fire that cannon now, are you, Cliff?"

"You know darned well I am," Cliff answered with a wry grin. "And I'm not expecting to miss my target either. When these hired killers start kidnapping women, it's time for even a physician to buckle on his armament. I only hope I get the opportunity of meeting that bully alone. It will be more than just a fist fight, I can assure you."

The sheriff chuckled grimly. "I kind a thought you might change your mind. Well, you ain't goin' to get no chance if I can help it. That gunhawk's comin' back to Painted Springs alive to answer to the law."

There came derisive hoots from the men behind. "There ain't goin' to be enough left of him, Sheriff." And—"It's about twenty to one. Yo're sure goin' to have yore hands full, Dorr."

"Jest the same that hombre's comin' back whole and not in pieces," the law officer growled.

Reaching the edge of the desert, the posse stopped at Manuel Geosta's hut only long enough to hear his story and to get some inkling of which way the gunman had gone. They broke up into smaller parties, spread out fan-wise, and headed across the arid waste, one party for the Dragoon range. The sheriff and the medico with five others went directly south towards the border.

Occasionally some cowhand would let out a yell as he discovered what appeared to be signs. With the sun at its zenith they topped the rise, dipped into the box cañon and discovered the dead ashes of a recent fire. Nancy's quirt was picked up and examined as they again reached the plateau. There was no question now in their minds but that they were on the right trail, and they urged their mounts to a swifter gait.

Cylinders of six-guns were twirled to see that they were in good working order. Sharps' rifles were unloosened from their scabbards, loaded and replaced, in readiness for prompt action when the need arose.

There was no time taken out for lunch. The men who were hungry munched at hard biscuits or bread, and drank from their canteens as they rode. Mile after mile, hour after hour, the posse swept on relentlessly until the sun dipped behind the jagged crests.

It was a puncher of mixed Indian breed who discovered the tell-tale signs of smoke in a deep ravine far ahead of them. The sheriff gave quick commands. The posse spread out and began circling, cutting through the gullies and washes, working ever closer to the tiny flicker of a campfire that winked off and on like a prearranged signal.

Cliff left his roan in a deep gully and finally went forward on foot. He knew that the other men were doing the same. Crawling to a rocky ledge he saw three figures stretched prone on the ground, and even as he watched, saw one of the mounds of flesh and blanket stir; saw a figure slip into the shadows and an instant later caught a glimpse of a horse and rider come flying up the cañon.

The medico's eyes straining to get a better view of the running animal and its burden failed to see another one of the prone figures leap to its feet, but he saw the flash of the gun and heard the detonation of the man's gun. Then he saw horse and rider, waver for a moment, and crumple.

It was too much for the medico to stand. He let loose with his six-gun even though the range was too great to do any damage, scrambled to his feet, and went leaping, tumbling, and cursing down the ravine's side. And from every direction he heard the rest of the posse following suit; heard the sheriff's deep voice booming out orders.

Cliff sped straight for the prone figures of horse and rider, reached them and lifted the girl into his arms.

"Nancy," he whispered. "Nancy, darling!"

There came a faint stirring of her body and a sigh escaped from her lips. Finally she opened her eyes and stared at the medico in disbelief. "Is it really you, Cliff?"

"There's the proof," he answered, pressing his lips to hers. "Did that skunk shoot you?"

"No," she winced, "but Midnight. Is he dead?"

The medico set her on her feet, keeping his arm about her waist, for she was still groggy from the blow on her head. Together they reached the inert figure of the stallion, already stiffening in death.

"Nancy!" the sheriff's voice boomed down the cañon, as he came hurrying towards them. "Are you all right."

Explanations quickly followed. Puff, still convinced that the sheepman would back him up, had given up without a struggle. Only one of his gunhawks had showed fight, but a well-aimed slug from one of the posse's guns had finished him in short order.

Puff and his crony had been lashed to their mounts and the posse gathered for the trek back. Nancy rode the dead gunman's mount, Cliff keeping close by her side, still worried over the bad knock on her skull. There was no thought of food or rest. The sheriff was anxious to get his prisoners under lock and key, and both Nancy and the medico were worried over Starweather's condition. The sun was just appearing over the mesa when tired and dust-covered the cavalcade reached the main street of Painted Springs.

The sheriff made haste to get his prisoners behind the bars. Nancy and the medico went straight to the old sheepman. For the first time, that individual softened enough to give the doctor his hand. Maw Blane whipped up a breakfast that any hotel chef would have been proud of.

But as soon as breakfast was over, Starweather insisted on seeing his gunman alone and the sheriff escorted him there and left them together.

Almost immediately a crowd began to gather in front of the sheriff's office and the twin cells that were located directly behind it. Each hour brought new riders to town, both sheepmen and cattlemen. By noon the street was thronged with weather-beaten, lean-faced punchers, herders, and ranchers.

Pim was among the group that rode in from the Circle Bar T. "It's too bad you didn't string them coyotes up 'fore you brought 'em in," he booed at Cliff. "It 'ud save the county a lot of expense."

The medico shrugged. "There's still law and order in this community, even if most of you men don't seem to realize it. The sheriff will handle the case in the proper way, you can be sure of that."

"There's only one way to treat them kind of polecats," Pim retorted, "and that's to string 'em up to the nearest tree."

There came a chorus of assent from those close enough to hear the cattleman's words. "That's right, Pim," a puncher yelled. "Let's drag the skunk out by his heels."

It didn't take a clairvoyant to sense the temper of the men gathered in a knot in front of Cliff. All they needed was a leader.

At this moment the sheriff followed by the grizzled sheepman appeared at the door. Dorr Plum took one look at the sneering faces, hitched his guns around to a handier position and looked the crowd over with cold eyes.

"Don't you hombres get any smart ideas," he growled. "Starweather here, ain't goin' to press the charges agin the prisoners. He's got reasons of his own."

The sheepman stood up gaunt and straight beside the sheriff. "That's correct, men," his voice boomed out. "I reckon it was a few smart words I let drop to Puff that gave him the idea. I ain't goin' to press no kidnapping charges. They're both goin' free."

Cliff was just as surprised as the rest of the crowd, but he figured that the sheepman no doubt had excellent reasons for letting the prisoners go and said nothing, contenting himself with ranging his six feet of bone and muscle alongside of the sheriff and the sheepman.

But this was too much for Pim. He had come to town for the express purpose of witnessing the demise of his worst enemy. To find that he had come on a wild goose chase was more than he could bear. Then to see the medico apparently siding with the sheepman and the sheriff was like adding insult to injury. Cliff was the closest and on him he vented his spleen.

"Why you damned meddlin' medico!" he ranted. "Yo're just another one of them mutton eatin' polecats from the other side. It's just too bad them sheepmen didn't finish that tar and feather party. I'd have sure enjoyed watchin' you running around sproutin' wings."

Cliff had taken a lot of insults from the cowman since his arrival in Painted Springs. For the past twenty four hours he had been worried to death over his sweetheart, and ridden miles without sleep to aid in her rescue. The range war had gnawed at him until he had almost considered giving up his practice and moving to a more healthful and peaceful clime. This unexpected tirade from the man whose life he had saved was the climax. His face turned from a light bronze to the color of a beet. His eyes darkened to the chilly shade of mined slate. For the first time he was conscious of the six-gun strapped at his hip and longed to use it. If ever a man had it coming to him, Pim had.

"I think that's about all the insults I'm going to take from you, Pim," he grated, unable to hold his temper in check, but keeping his voice down to a menacing tone. "From now on this Colt and I are inseparable. The next time you call me a meddling medico or a mutton-eating sheepman, reach for your iron and reach fast, because I'm going to let you have it."

"Well, now ain't that somethin'!" Pim drawled. "The medico's turnin' gunhawk as well as sheepman. Any time you're hankerin' after a quick and painless end, Doc, I'll be glad to accommodate you. I ain't never liked yore guts and I reckon I never will. This county 'ud be a heap of a sight better off without you. I'll be plumb delighted to salivate you."

The physician's face twitched, but otherwise he gave no sign of the anger that was boiling within him. He wondered if he was still as handy with his Colt as he had been in the past on his father's ranch. He decided suddenly that it wouldn't hurt to give the fire-eating Pim something to think about. He didn't want Pim to think that he was crossing guns with a novice. He glanced at the faces confronting him, at the roof of the Lone Deuce, and his eyes came back to rest on the mirthless ones of his enemy.

"See that weathercock over there on the roof of Tim's place?" he questioned.

Pim turned his head and looked, then nodded. "Sure! I suppose you think I can't hit it." With the swiftness of a striking cougar his hand flowed to his hip. Almost simultaneously with that swift movement came the sharp report of his .45. A neat hole appeared in the body of the cock. The rancher turned and glanced triumphantly at the medico. "Not bad shootin' for a cowhand!" The six-gun slid back into its holster.

The medico shrugged. "I'm afraid it isn't good enough, Pim. I never shoot to wound a man, and that's especially true of your case. I have no desire to extract any more slugs from your filthy carcass. When I throw down I always aim for the eyes."

No one saw the medico's hand or could follow it in its swift flight, as it descended to his hip, came up with the iron, and pointed it at the weathercock. But they all heard the detonation and saw daylight where the cock's eye should have been. A gasp of astonishment came from the crowd. Pim had shot true, but there wasn't a man now who didn't realize that the owner of the Circle Bar T had a tough assignment on his hands.

Cliff holstered his weapon and regarded the rancher with a cold glitter in his gray eyes. "That's about where I'll aim my slug, Pim," he taunted. "I never did approve of hanging for murderers and you're about the worst example of one I've seen since I arrived in this county. You won't have quite as easy a time killing me off as you did Jim Starweather."

The shot went home. Pim's face blanched for an instant, followed by a brick red that suffused his leathery face. He snarled a curse at the medico, at Starweather, and at the sheriff, forked his horse, and with his punchers at his heels galloped out of town.

The owner of the S Bar 8 laid a hand on his shoulder. "I reckon I'm pretty much in your debt already, Doc," he mumbled, "but I ain't askin' you to avenge the murder of my son. You better leave that to me."

The sheriff took hold of his other arm. "Gosh awmighty!" he exclaimed. "I didn't know you was that fast and true with an iron. Why, I ain't seen such shootin' since the days when I was in Abilene and Wild Bill Hickock was marshal."

With the spitfire Pim out of the way, the news that the sheepman was not going to prosecute his hired gunman, and that Puff would be freed, soon emptied the town. There was plenty of work to be done on the ranches and cattlemen and sheepmen alike drove their hirelings back to their labors.

Puff had declined to accept his freedom until he could leave safely, but was finally released just as Cliff, Starweather, and his daughter mounted their horses and started for the S Bar 8. Knowing that there would be no possible chance of his meeting the cattleman Pim while in sheep territory, Cliff had parked his gun in its accustomed place on his office wall.

Puff, standing in the doorway of the sheriff's office, had seen the medico go up to his rooms, and had seen him come down minus the weapon. He had also overheard the altercation between Pim and the medico, had heard the shots and been told of the results of the doctor's marksmanship. The daylight showing through the weathercock on the Lone Deuce gave mute testimony to the truth of his informer's tale.

When at last the street was again tranquil and Starweather and his party had long since vanished over the distant rise, the gunman accepted his shooting irons from the sheriff, and in company with the lone survivor of his original triumvirate, strolled across the street and entered the swinging portals of the Lone Deuce.

The gunman was no coward, but he was a cautious man. An idea had been sizzling in his head for some time now, and as the fiery liquid coursed through his veins, it began to take shape. Fast as he knew himself to be with a six-gun, he realized that the medico was a better shot and considerably swifter in getting his gun into action. Puff therefor had no more desire to test his skill against the medico. So far, in every encounter, he had come off second best.

Now he had a plan, that if carried to consummation, would eliminate his two worst enemies from the scene of his courtship, and leave the field uncontested. If successful, there would be no nosey medico to interfere with his work and that of his mysterious boss.

However, he needed help and the only one he could turn to was the gunhawk at his elbow. Coming to a sudden decision, he motioned the man out of earshot of the bartender and gave him whispered instructions.

"The medico 'll be ridin' back this way along 'bout night. You tell him that Jim Croll's been throwed from his horse and got a broken leg and internal injuries. Tell him he's got to hurry, that the word was brought in to the sheriff and he asked yuh to come out and meet him. Make it plain that he hasn't time to go back to his office. He always carries that kit of his wherever he goes. As soon as yuh tell him, yuh hightail it for the meetin' place."

The gunhawk was accustomed to taking orders from Puff without question. At dusk he forked his horse and vanished at a leisurely trot over the distant rise.

Cliff had an enjoyable evening with Nancy and her father, and after dinner when the sheepman had been ordered to bed by the medico, he had his first opportunity to tell the girl exactly what he thought of her. It was well past midnight when he saddled the roan, gave his sweetheart a fond farewell, and headed toward Painted Springs. Half way there he saw a horseman top the rise in front of him and come loping to meet him.

The gunman carried out his orders to the letter. Cliff immediately wheeled his horse and urged the tired roan at a swift pace toward the spread of Jim Croll's.

He passed the Circle Bar T, giving the ranchhouse a wide berth, for he had no desire to encounter Pim, now that his gun hung in his office. By midnight he had reached the Lazy Arrow and was surprised to find the place dark.

Dropping from his mount he halloed and rapped loudly on the door. Jim Croll, very much on his feet, opened the door for him. Cliff took one look at the man and knew that he had been sent on a wild goose chase.

Croll grinned when Cliff had explained the reasons for his late call. "Just some more of them sheepmen's shananigans, Doc. Ain't no horse ever throwed me yet. You might as well spend the night here, long as yore this far from town. Me and the missus is startin' out early in the mornin' with the kids for New Mexico. We're goin' down there to visit some of her relations. I expect we'll be gone for 'bout three months. I'm hopin' to drive back a herd of shorthorns to fill up the gaps left by that hoof and mouth epidemic."

Cliff accepted the invitation more on account of his horse than for his own bodily comfort. Early the next morning he saw Croll and his family leave, and soon was on his way back to Painted Springs. This time he gave the Circle Bar T an even wider berth, arriving in town unobserved, and in plenty of time to shave and clean up for one of Maw's plentiful breakfasts.

CHAPTER SIXTEEN MURDER AT THE CIRCLE BAR T

After seeing his henchman safely on his errand, Puff returned to the bar of the Lone Deuce. He was now the only customer and as Tim Roney set a bottle and glass in front of him, the gunman said:

"I reckon I'm leavin' this county, Tim. I'm about fed up with these mutton eaters. Gun wages ain't enough when the whole pack is too yella to string with yuh."

The bartender smiled knowingly. It wasn't the first time that Puff had made such an announcement. "Kind of overplayed your hand a mite, Puff, when you kidnapped the crinolina. If you ask me, yo're lucky to be out of the calaboose and not danglin' from the short end of a rope. For awhile there this mornin' I thought I was goin' to have to go into mournin' for a customer. You can thank that medico for savin' your ornery hide. If he and Pim hadn't got to arguin' it might have been a different story. That medico surprised me no end. He's a friendly cuss and tends to his business, but he's a bad man to rile."

Puff reddened a little under the jibe and his dark eyes narrowed slightly. "That's jist the trouble with that hombre. He's got his nose into everybody's business. He's ridin' for a fall, I'm thinkin'. Pim's liable to let daylight into him the first time they meet up."

"Are you goin' away for good, Puff, or just temporary?"

"I don' know. Maybe for good. I figured I'd take a run over to the next county and see if I couldn't get myself a steady job. The sheepmen in these parts is gettin' soft. If it hadn't been for that meddlin' medico we'd have had them cattlemen licked to a frazzle." Puff tossed off the three fingers of corn liquor, choking a little as the fiery fluid flowed down his throat. "Cripes!" he exploded. "That stuff is sure pizen."

Tim grunted, "There ain't any better corn in the whole county. Yo're gettin' soft yourself."

The gunman wiped his mouth with the back of his hand. "Maybe so, Tim. Maybe so." He regarded the bartender through narrowed lids. "If anybody comes askin' for me, yuh can tell 'em that I've lit a shuck."

Tim grinned wickedly. "Leavin' the gal flat, eh? Maybe she'd like to know where at you can be found."

The gunman hitched up his gun belt ignoring the jibe. "Well, so long, Tim. I'm hightailin' for Bonita. Give my regards to the boys."

At a swinging gait, he turned and headed for the swinging doors. As he reached them he turned and said, "Don't forget, Tim. Bonita's the place."

Tim watched him thoughtfully as he swung on to his horse and vanished toward the north at an easy lope. "Umph!" he grunted aloud. "Good riddance if you ask me, but too good to be true. That side-winder's too tough and too sweet on Nancy to pull a run-out. I wonder what in tarnation he's up to. Sufferin' cripes, but I wish this cussed range war 'ud simmer out. Business is certainly all shot plumb to hell."

There being no more customers and no prospects of any, the bartender and owner of the Lone Deuce closed his doors and locked them. Still trying to fathom the reasons for the gunman's sudden plan to go to Bonita, he blew out the oil lamps, and made ready for bed. Several times as he sat on the edge of the bed he shook his head and muttered.

One by one, the lights of Painted Springs winked out, leaving only the lamp over the entrance of the Mansion House to cast lurid shadows on the deserted street, an invitation to any late traveler to enter and partake of the hostelry's hospitality.

The sheriff, fagged out from his twenty four hour trek across the desert, had stretched himself for a short nap on his cot, but the nap had lengthened into the sleep of utter exhaustion.

Into the silent sleeping outskirts of the town, a horse and rider came, the animal's footfalls muffled by the heavy pads of sheepskin wound over his shod hoofs. At some little distance from the main habitations, the rider reined in, dropped silently to the ground, hitched up his gun belt, and leaving the horse behind an old tumble-down adobe hut, started warily up the alley that ran parallel with the main street.

Reaching the rear of the jail and the medico's office, he skirted between two buildings, and stole stealthily towards the main street. For an instant he hesitated, his sharp eyes making a swift inventory of his surroundings, his ears straining to catch any signs of life. Faintly there came to him the noise of the law officer's heavy breathing. A grin split the face of the horseman.

Without the faintest sound, he eased himself past the sheriff's office and noiselessly mounted the stairs that led to Cliff's rooms above. The door was unlocked for the medico kept his reception room open at all times for patients. The man stepped inside. A match flared momentarily revealing the doctor's gun belt hanging from a peg on the wall. A hand reach up and dragged the six-gun from its moorings. A moment later the door closed softly and the thief retraced his steps, passed the sheriff's office, and back to his waiting mount.

Safely out of sight of the town again, the man took his own gun from its holster and dropped it into a saddle pocket. The medico's .45 he slipped into its place after testing the weight of the weapon and hefting it to get the feel of the butt.

Then he roweled the horse and skirting the town, loped directly south, heading deeper into cattle country. After several miles he guided his mount into a deep wash which effectively screened him from the eyes of any late traveler.

For some time he followed the winding, boulder-strewn floor of the gully until he reached the destination he had been seeking. Dropping soundlessly from the saddle, he threw his reins over the mount's head, palmed the six-gun, and scrambled up the rocky side of the wash.

Not over a hundred yards directly ahead of him stood the ranchhouse and the out-buildings of the Circle Bar T, and seeing no signs of life and hearing nothing, he began to move relentlessly but noiselessly forward, until the plank floor of the veranda was beneath his feet.

Luck favored him. The door was unlocked and he entered the living room leaving the entranceway unobstructed for a hasty retreat.

But his entrance, stealthy as it had been, had awakened the rancher. Pim came barging into the room, gun in hand, a lamp held high. At that instant there came the deafening detonation of the intruder's .45, three shots in rapid succession. The owner of the Circle Bar T stiffened and fell forward jerkily.

The murderer, with a quick twist, threw the medico's gun toward the lifeless figure, turned, and fled through the door and across the intervening space to the gulley. Lights flashed on almost immediately in the bunkhouse, and men in all stages of dress and undress came barging out, but the mysterious rider didn't hesitate for an instant. He spurred his mount and went thundering down the gulley, the tattoo of the horse's padded feet finally fading into the distance.

Once he stopped and listened. No sounds of pursuit came to his ears and he laughed mirthlessly. Unperturbed by his recent killing, he rolled the makings, lit the fag, and drew the smoke deep into his lungs. Remembering the pads on his horse's hoofs, he dismounted, removed them and tossed them into the chaparral. From the saddle pocket he drew his own six-gun, twirled the cylinder from force of habit, and pressed it into its holster. A moment later horse and rider vanished at a swift pace into the cañons and water-gutted arroyos that criss-crossed the mesa.

On the desert's rim, the gunman who had notified the medico of the hurt Jim Croll, sat cold and angry on his mount close to the giant Joshua tree. A cigarette dangled from his lips. Off and on, he mumbled a curse, glancing again and again up the deserted wash. Finally he heard the sound of shod feet on gravel. Puff rode slowly up.

"Where in all tarnation yuh been?" the gunman grumbled. "I been here most two hours."

Puff shrugged. He was not in the habit of telling his hired gunhawks of his plans. "Had a bit of unfinished business to attend to. I'm headin' for Bonita. Tell the boss I won't be back for a couple of weeks." With that he wheeled his horse, roweled his mount, and went loping off up the wash to the north.

But the man he had left behind cursed him roundly. "It's a wonder the tight-lipped skunk couldn't a told me that earlier in the evenin'. To hell with this loco country! I'm gettin' sick of bein' played for a goat. I've got most of my pay. Let old Starweather keep the rest. I'm movin' to a more friendly range, where maybe the wages is less, but the men ain't so proddy."

Far to the north, Puff was making good time toward the distant town of Bonita, but it was late the next afternoon before he jogged up to the livery stable, saw that his horse was properly cared for, and swaggered over to the town's rambling structure of a hotel. He procured a room and for three hours slept soundly and dreamlessly.

Awake again, he shaved, changed to a fresh shirt, and went down for his dinner. From the now empty dining room, he strolled over to the gambling palace, had a drink or two and sat in at a game of stud poker. Aside from the keen looks which he gave every newcomer to the bar, he didn't appear in the least worried.

Finally he saw a tall, bushy-eyed individual make a place for himself at the bar. Puff caught the man's glance, nodded, cut short his game, and joined him. Together they repaired to a room in the rear.

"What the hell are you doing here?" the man questioned.

The gunman shrugged. "It was gettin' a mite unhealthy around Brant county, Carl. That damned medico has outdrawn me on every hand. Even old Starweather is gettin' soft. We ain't gettin' nowhere down there."

"No?" The man's brows drooped lower as his forehead creased into deep furrows. "You're not telling me any news. Looks to me like we need a new man down there to liven things up. You're gettin' too sweet on that gal and too proddy over that doc. Now you listen to me, Puff. I don't usually threaten the men who are working for me, but don't forget that I know enough about you to send you up for a nice long stretch in the pen. Ralph and I have sunk a cart-full of money into this deal and we're not quitting. What we want is action and plenty of it. I know that damned medico ruined our scheme to kill off the cattle with that epidemic, but there are plenty of other ways to skin a cat."

"Yeah?" the gunman jeered. "Well suppose yuh tell me, and don't go makin' no threats, neither." His lips set grimly. "I ain't takin' nothin' from you two grasshoppers. Don't yuh forget for a minute that I'm holdin' the ace card in the hole. The marshal 'ud be right interested in knowin' where yuh picked up them diseased cattle and jist how yuh run 'em across the border."

The man laughed. "Don't get your dander up, gunhawk. I guess we're all in the same boat, but the last time I saw you, you were figuring on marrying Starweather's daughter and taking up sheep raising in a big way. What's the matter? Has that medico beaten your time with the girl?"

"Yuh can jest bet yore bottom dollar he ain't," Puff snarled. "That hombre's ridin' for a fall that 'll be heard all over the state."

The man looked curious, and Puff told him of the kidnapping and the altercation between Pim and the medico.

"Serves you right for trying such a fool trick, Puff," he preached. "You're lucky that bunch of cowhands didn't string you up. But I still fail to see the connection between that affair and this medico. It looks to me as if the doc was on an even better footing than he was before. If he can use an iron as well as you say, Pim is most likely to be the one that will travel the road to Boothill. However, that's jake with us. He's been a fly in the ointment from the beginning. You might have a much easier task if that cowman was removed from the range."

"That's jist what I figured," Puff replied, with irony. "I worked out a plan that 'll remove both the medico and that side-winder Pim." However he had no intentions of divulging that plan to his employer and frankly told him so. "I ain't spillin' nothin' until the right time comes, but unless I drawed to a bobtail flush, that hombre's got his horns sawed off so close he won't be botherin' us any more."

His employer grinned. "Tight lipped, eh? Well, that's all right, Puff. That's one reason I hired you. You're one of the few gun-fighters that has sense enough to keep his trap shut. I think I'm beginning to see the reason for your arrival in our metropolis. There's nothing like a good alibi. Your name on the register of the hotel, the word of these men, all counts with a jury."

The gunman knew that his secret had been guessed, but his face was an inscrutable mask. He was an excellent poker player.

"I'm spendin' the night here, Carl," he announced, after quickly rolling himself a cigarette. "Yuh better arrange to meet me about day after tomorrow in the same place. I might have some good news for yuh."

A few minutes later he joined the players at the poker table, later passed the time of day with the bartender, and started through the swinging doors for the street and the hotel.

As he reached the boardwalk, a man stepped out of the shadows and confronted him. "I told yuh we'd meet up sometime, Puff," the newcomer spat. "Yuh better notch yore sights for I'm aimin' to salivate yuh right pronto. This country's too clean to have its face marred with boils."

For just an instant the gunman studied the face of his opponent, trying to remember where he had seen him. Then suddenly it all came back. The small ranch on the Lobo, the bearded, hollow-eyed man that he had left for dead. He saw his opponent's muscles tighten; read the flicker of leaping killer-lights in his eyes, read other indubitable signs and knew that he was as close to death as he ever would be again in his adventurous life.

At that moment Puff had no desire to indulge in gunplay. There were a number of things back in Painted Springs that required his attention, but he had no alternative. The gunman moved swiftly. Faster perhaps than he had ever moved before. His right hand snaked in the gun-snatch as he flung aside and down, and a smile creased his lips as he felt the butt in his palm.

But his opponent was equally as swift. The detonation of two six-guns reverberated in the semi-darkness of Bonita's main street. Puff felt a sledge hammer blow connect with his middle and with a grunt of surprise he rolled over backward from his crouching position. His opponent pitched forward on his face and lay still.

There came an excited and milling crowd pushing from the saloon. The sheepman was dimly conscious of being picked up and carried for some distance and deposited on a table. Strange voices were jumbled in his ears. His belly ached and burned, making him grunt with pain. A shot of red-eye forced between his clenched teeth brought him back to consciousness.

A strange medico had removed his trousers and was industriously digging away at his ribs. Puff winced and forced a grin. "Where did that polecat nick me?" he gritted.

The doctor completed his work before replying. "You're a lucky stiff, man," he said, straightening up. "That slug caught you full on the navel, but your belt buckle deflected it off to one side. Your friend wasn't so fortunate."

At this point the town's marshal arrived. A witness had overheard the warning given the gunman and had tarried long enough to see the fight. Puff was in the clear, but leaving for Painted Springs in the morning was out of the question.

And as they carried him back to his hotel room, the sheepman thought with an inward smile of satisfaction, that he couldn't have picked a better night for a gun fight. Here was an alibi that was hand picked. Even the town marshal had a record of him and could swear to his whereabouts.

CHAPTER SEVENTEEN MAW HANDLES THE SHARPS

Cliff had finished his breakfast and a long talk with Maw Blane. Carl Westover, the big cattleman from Beman, had proved his innocence of any hand in the range war to Maw's entire satisfaction. That left the medico just where he had started. Puff's mysterious boss was still an unknown quantity. Cliff's puzzle was still shy of several pieces.

He glanced into Plum's office, but that worthy individual was not in. Finally he sat himself down on the cool veranda of the Mansion House, rolled himself a smoke and stared thoughtfully at the mauve peaks of the Dragoons. There were several things troubling him. His anger at the sheepman who had sent him on the ride to Croll's ranch had simmered out, leaving only curiosity as to the reasons behind the man's behavior. He intended to question the sheriff when that individual appeared.

He heard Maw Blane industriously wielding her broom inside the hotel. "Better come out and sit for a bit, Maw," he called to her. "It's a beautiful morning."

"Can't take the time now, Doc," she responded. "That lazy good-for-nothing husband of mine has another one of his spells."

Cliff grinned. Paw Blane's lazy spells were nothing new to the medico. "Give him a dose of castor oil, Maw, or some calomel. Maybe his liver needs turning over."

"Ain't nothin' wrong with his liver," the woman complained. "He's just naturally sluggish. Why I ever married such a no-account is more than I can fathom."

The sound of a party of horsemen approaching the town from the south interrupted further conversation. Cliff recognized them as punchers from the Circle Bar T, as they reined in their mounts in front of the Mansion House. It was unusual for the cowhands of Pim's ranch to be in town that early and he wondered.

The swart men dropped silently to the ground and grim of eye, clumped in their high-heeled boots up on to the veranda and to the medico. Jed Townes, a fire-eating old puncher and a life-long friend of Pim, was in the lead. Cliff saw Kentucky Landers hanging in the background. Something unusual was up. That much the medico sensed from the dogged looks of the men.

Jed pushed forward and thrust a gun toward Cliff, butt foremost. "Is that yore shootin' iron, Doc?" he asked, stiffly.

Cliff took the six-gun and turned it over in his hand revealing his initials cut in the walnut stock. He nodded, "Yes, that's mine. How did you get hold of it?"

"We found it alongside of Pim's corpse," the puncher ground out, glancing with triumphant eyes at the cowhands around him. "Where did yuh think we'd find it?"

If a bomb had been placed in the doctor's lap it wouldn't have surprised him more. "Pim's corpse! Good heavens, Jed! What's happened to Pim?"

The cowboy nodded. "That's what I said. Somebody dry-gulched him long about midnight. Findin' yore loaded cutter lyin' close to him, we figured yuh might be able to tell us somethin' about it." There was menace in the words.

Cliff suddenly had the answer to one of his riddles. That sheepman who had sent him on his wild goose chase! Had the man stolen his gun, killed the rancher, and left the iron there to point the finger of suspicion at him? It certainly looked like it. It was a good thing he had spent the night at Jim Croll's. Jim would corroborate his testimony.

"Naturally Pim's death is a shock," he answered, "but I'm afraid I can't help you much." Then briefly he told of his meeting with the sheepman, and of his spending the night at the Lazy Arrow. "I haven't any idea how my Colt got there. Some one must have stolen it from my office. I left it there when I went to the S Bar 8."

"That's rani-cum-bugerie," the puncher refuted. "It jist don't make sense. Yuh threatened to shoot Pim on sight. We all heard yuh. It ain't likely that you'd ride into cattle country without yore six-gun."

"I had no intention of riding into cow country," the medico responded somewhat hotly, "but when a man's life is at stake you don't stop to worry over threats made in the heat of anger. There are several people who saw me leave here yesterday with the Starweathers, and I think they can all assure you that I was unarmed."

Maw had been listening from the doorway. "That's right, Jed. The doctor didn't have his gun belt on when he left."

"It don't mean nothin'," the fuming cowhand retorted. "He could 'ave come back here and gotten it. Yuh had to ride past the Circle Bar T to reach the Lazy Arrow. Yuh could 'ave done it easy."

The medico had a tough time keeping his anger in check. Suddenly he remembered that Jim Croll had left early that morning and by now would be many miles on his way. There was one witness that couldn't be reached.

"From your conversation, Jed," he said, hotly, "I gather that you are accusing me of the murder of your boss. That's ridiculous! It's true that Pim and I had a little altercation yesterday and that I did threaten to shoot him on sight, but I would hardly resort to the tactics you have suggested. I can assure you that I gave the Circle Bar T a wide berth last night. I'm not crazy enough to sail past there at night without a gun after the argument Pim and I had. Nor would I resort to ambushing a man. Even though I am a physician, I think I demonstrated to all of you that I know how to use an iron and can shoot as fast as the next man."

"Yeah! That's jist the point," the puncher hurled back. "Pim was gosh awmighty quick with his cutter, and when we found him he had his gun in his hand, yet there wasn't a cartridge exploded. There's only two other men that could out-draw him. You and Puff Gordon."

"Then why not find Puff? His enmity was surely as great as mine."

"I reckon Puff's in the clear this time. Yuh can't hang it on him. Tim Roney told us early this mornin' that Puff had left right after dinner for Bonita, sayin' he wasn't comin' back. One of the gunhawks told us the same thing."

"It looks like you men had me in a corner," Cliff said thoughtfully. "About the only thing I can prove is that I had dinner with Nancy and her father. Jim and his family left early this morning for New Mexico. He expects to be gone for at least a month. Suppose we go find the sheriff."

Jed looked meaningly at the circle of faces about him. His eyes came back to meet the medico's. "I reckon we don't need the law hornin' in. I'll have the boys get yore horse and we'll move on to the Circle Bar T. I've always been able to smell a skunk when I get close enough to one, and this ain't no exception."

Cliff stood up and faced his accusers, his eyes narrowing. The charge was absurd, but he realized it was no laughing matter. These men were swift to deal out justice, as they mis-named it, and if they happened to string up the wrong man, well—it was just an unfortunate occurrence.

"You want to find the real murderer of Pim," he challenged. "So do I, yet I'm sure you men are not bloodthirsty enough to want to take the life of an innocent man. You men are still laboring under the impression that I am an ally of the sheepmen, and you're losing sight of the real facts. I'm innocent and I know if given time that I can prove it. In the eyes of the law a man is considered innocent until he is proved guilty. The right thing to do is to find the sheriff, have me indicted by the grand jury if the evidence is sufficient and bring me to trial in a court of justice."

"There ain't no use of yore tryin' to argue yore way out of it, Doc," the puncher snarled back. "We got the proof and the motive for the crime. That's about all we need. We'll hold court out at the Circle Bar T and give yuh a chance to say yore piece before a hand picked jury of yore peers." His hand dropped menacingly to the butt of his gun. "Yuh might as well come along peaceful, unless yo're hankerin' to go horizontal."

Kentucky put a word for the medico, but it was like trying to stem a flood with a single sandbag. He was told to mind his own business. The doctor's roan was saddled and brought from the stable. Cliff was forced to mount and to submit docilely while his hands were lashed behind him and his feet tied securely beneath the animal's belly. Surrounded on all sides by his wardens, the cavalcade went swiftly out of town in the direction of Pim's spread.

But Cliff had one ally in the person of Maw Blane. She had heard the accusations and knowing that it was useless to argue, had routed her lazy husband out of bed with instructions to find the sheriff pronto. While the leather-faced punchers were getting the medico's horse, she had saddled her own mount from the stable in the rear of the hotel, had found her husband's Sharps and a six-gun, and had gotten a lead on the lynching party, determined to do battle for the young doctor at all costs.

The big gelding was swift and she reached the outbuildings of the Circle Bar T considerably ahead of the cowboys. Apparently unobserved, Maw rode her horse directly in to the barn, climbed laboriously to the hay loft, and took up a strategic position commanding the house and corrals. She had guessed that if any lynching was done, the rope and pulley used for lifting hay into the loft would be the instrument of death.

Lying flat and peering out through the door, she saw the horsemen approach the ranch at a steady gait, the medico in the center. They dismounted at the corrals, pushed Cliff ahead of them, and entered the ranchhouse.

Maw sent up a mute prayer for the safety of the doctor, edged closer to the doorway, and took a firm grip on her rifle, placing the .38 handily beside her. After what seemed hours, she saw one of the punchers come out of the back door and approach the barn.

She watched him as he fashioned a noose of the heavy rope, and she smiled grimly, muttering, "Don't you worry, Doc. There's goin' to be a parcel of dead cowhands if they don't listen to reason. Old Judge Sharps is goin' to try this case and not no salty jiggers from the short grass."

Soon the rest of the party filed out of the house, their prisoner in the lead. Cliff was a bit paler than usual, but he held his head high, and stared straight ahead, walking with an unfaltering step, which brought a chuckle of appreciation to the woman's set lips.

Maw waited stiffly until she saw one of the punchers start for the corral. Fearing they might change their minds and use some other means than the rope at hand, she barked out:

"Hoist yore claws, you ornery parcel of coyotes."

The unexpected female voice coming from above them, focused all eyes on the glinting barrel of the Sharps and the gray head and snapping eyes behind it. Jed Townes was the first to recover from his astonishment. His hand dropped swiftly to his holster. The Sharps cracked once and the puncher let out a howl of pain, clutching at his shoulder.

"Let that be a lesson to the rest of you side-winders," Maw shrilled down at them. The rest of the men were now reaching for the sky. They had had the skill of the hotel's mistress demonstrated.

But she was at loss what to do next. She couldn't hold such a group of men indefinitely with their hands upraised. Suddenly she saw Kentucky Landers, noticed that he quite apparently approved of the interruption, and knew that he was a friend of Cliff's. She called to him.

"Kentucky, just move around there and deprive them other waddies of their artillery."

The puncher's face split into a wide grin. He didn't hesitate an instant. It took him but a moment to remove guns from holsters and pile them neatly in the place designated by the woman.

This completed to her satisfaction, she directed him to untie the medico, who now stood chuckling at the discomfiture of his captors.

"Help yoreself to a couple of them shootin' irons, Doc, and keep an eye on them hombres while I get down to earth."

"Thanks, Maw." Cliff reacted quickly to the suggestion.

A moment later, her hair awry, and her clothes covered with hay, she descended and faced the growling punchers. "Yo're a fine parcel of yella polecats," she berated them. "A person 'ud think you'd have more sense than to try and lynch an innocent man. What's this country comin' to anyhow? We got law and order in this community. Can't you use yore heads for anythin' except to hang yore hats on? Do you think for a minute that if the doc had a done that he'd a throwed his gun now for everybody to see? It's plumb ridiculous. And you, Kentucky, I'm surprised at you."

The puncher looked crestfallen and ashamed. "I couldn't do nothin', Maw."

"Maybe you couldn't, but you could 'ave made a stab at it. Cliff, get yore horse and mine and we'll hightail it back to Painted Springs. Yo're in my custody and I'm turnin' you over to the sheriff and the grand jury. Kentucky, rastle them shootin' irons and put 'em in the medico's saddle bags. You boys can pick 'em up at the Mansion House, anytime you feel up to it. Maybe you better go along with us, Jed. It looks to me like that shoulder of yores might need some medical attention and I reckon you'd like to see that the Doc is put in a safe place."

Not many minutes later, Maw, Jed, and the medico, left the spread of the Circle Bar T behind them and vanished over the rise, leaving a bunch of humbled and flabbergasted punchers in their wake.

Half way to town, the horsemen met the sheriff and his posse. Cliff was turned over to Plum, while Maw went back to her duties with a final word of encouragement to the medico.

Cliff told the sheriff as much as he knew about Pim's death and of his own actions on the night of the murder.

"Daggoned funny!" Dorr mused. "I know you ain't guilty, Cliff, but the evidence sure points your way. I don't like to do it, but the safest place for you is in the calaboose until these mavericks sort of calm down. I'll see that Maw brings you the right sort of victuals. In the meanwhile, I'll sashay out to the Circle Bar T and to the S Bar 8. I'm right anxious to check up on Puff and Nancy'll probably like to hear the news."

Cliff took his misfortune with stoical calmness. He knew that the sheriff was right. He had just had one experience with the temper of the cattlemen. But for Maw's timely intervention he knew that right now he would have been dangling from the wrong end of a rope. He had no fears but that he could prove his innocence when the proper time came.

He thanked Maw again when she brought him his lunch and learned from her that the sheriff was acting swiftly. The grand jury had been impaneled and would go into session that afternoon in the main dining room of the Mansion House, which constituted eating place as well as court room.

Late that afternoon the sheriff brought him further news. The grand jury had indicted him for murder in the first degree and he was to be held without bail.

"This county has gone plumb loco," that worthy fumed. "The only evidence they got is that your gun was found at the scene of the crime and that you was out all night. They're lettin' their petty grievances get the better of their judgment. I don't mind tellin' you, Cliff, yo're in a tight spot." He shook his head disconsolately. "Puff ain't been seen in the sheep country, and neither has that gunhawk that told you to go see Jim Croll. I've sent a man after Jim, but there's no tellin' where he is by now."

The medico nodded. "I know it looks bad, Dorr, and I haven't much chance of proving my innocence while I'm locked up here, but I can't believe that a jury would convict me on such flimsy evidence."

The sheriff frowned. "Yo're forgettin' that the jury 'll be cattlemen. Pim was their leader and well liked in spite of his hot temper. Your argument that mornin', 'll go a long ways towards swingin' the jury to a conviction. It's too bad you had to show them mavericks what a good shot you was."

Cliff grinned in remembrance. "I couldn't resist the temptation, Dorr. Pim was so sure of himself and actually I wanted to prove to myself that I was as good as in the old days. Putting a bullet through that cock's eye right above Pim's slug did my heart good."

"Well, keep your shirt tucked in." The law officer grinned back. "All the water ain't over the dam yet, by a jugful."

"I hope there's more than a jugful left."

The door clanged shut and the sheriff's hulk moved out of sight. Late in the afternoon, Cliff busy reading some of his medical books, had an unexpected caller. He heard Nancy's voice in the sheriff's office, followed by the heavy tread of the deputy's boots. A moment later she was locked in his cell.

"Cliff, darling!" she cried, melting into his outstretched arms, and clinging to him.

The medico held her tight, his lips brushing the crown of her light hair. "There's nothing to worry about, honey. It will just take a little time. You don't believe that I killed Pim, do you?"

"Certainly not. The whole charge is preposterous. But how can you prove it?"

"That's just what is bothering me, honey. If I could get out of here, there might be a chance. Puff Gordon had a hand in this somehow and if I could get to Bonita, I believe I could prove it as well as discover a few facts that might end this range war once and for all. But what's the use? I'm in and there's some very stout bars to keep me in, besides some Colts in the hands of several capable deputies. Dorr isn't taking any chances on losing his prisoner."

The girl shuddered. "To think you were almost killed by those cowhands! It frightens me. They might try it again." If she could only help him to escape. With a jury of cattlemen he wouldn't have a chance. "I'd feel a lot better for your safety if you were in Bonita."

Cliff suddenly had an idea. "If you can smuggle me in a pair of six-guns and get Maw to loan me a horse, there might be a chance, Nancy. Could you do it?"

In whispers then, he outlined a plan of escape. "If I do get out safely I want you to tell Dorr that I'll be back for the trial without fail. If I know that man, and I think I do, he'll cover my tracks by telling the ranchers that he's moved me to the next county for safe keeping."

Nancy's eyes were shining. This was her chance to save the man she loved; to repay him in some small measure for what he had done for her. The thought that he would take his life in his hands to make good his escape brought a twitch of fear to her lips, but her voice was steady when she answered.

"I'll bring your dinner instead of Maw, Cliff."

Once again he held her close, and she could feel the steady throb of his heart against hers ; feel the confidence that radiated from him, nerving her for the coming ordeal.

The deputy came at her call and unlocked the cell door. He glanced a bit suspiciously at Cliff, bringing a smile of amusement to that young man's face.

"There's nothing to worry about, Tom. The young lady didn't deliver any firearms." He threw back his coat to reveal that his pockets were empty.

The deputy grinned back. "That's all right, Doc. I reckon yuh got more horse sense than most of these critters around here, but I'll say this much. It ain't healthy to be loose. Dorr heard they was goin' to try a raid on the jail tonight. Them hombres are a goin' to get a taste of lead if they try any of them shananigans."

The medico shrugged. "I'm not worried, Tom."

When the deputy had gone, Cliff started to make a more careful examination of his quarters. The walls were a mixture of heavy beams and adobe too thick to get through, even if he had the tools to do it with. The iron bars, at the single window, which looked out on the back alley of the main street, were deeply imbedded and solid as rock. There was no escape possible that way. His only hope lay through the cell door, catching the unsuspecting Tom off guard at the possible risk of wounding the man or being wounded or killed himself.

CHAPTER EIGHTEEN
ESCAPE

Puff Gordon had made unusual time considering the flesh wound that irked his sides. He reached Painted Springs just at dusk, dismounted as usual in front of the Lone Deuce, hitched his gun belt a bit higher, and gave a cursory glance up and down the main street. There were no outward signs of the turmoil that seethed below the surface. Several horses stood idly swishing flies from their flanks, as they stood at the Mansion House hitching rail.

The gunman pushed open the swinging doors and strode in. He was almost instantly greeted by several of the sheepmen who were either lounging at the bar or playing cards. The news of the medico's arrest and of the events that had recently transpired were given him after which the gunman merely vouchsafed that he had been to Bonita on urgent personal business in reply to their inquiries.

"Yuh better let the sheriff know where yuh been, Puff," one of them suggested. "He's lookin' for yuh."

Puff laughed. "Well, I'm right here. That sure is good news about Pim. That saves me a heap of trouble. With him and that nosey medico both out of the way, we ought to finish off this argument right pronto."

After further conversation wherein the gunman gave little information about his own doings outside of to admit that he had been in a gun fight, he finished his drink and unbuckling his gun belt, handed it across to Tim Roney. Then leisurely he sauntered across the street and into the sheriff's office.

"So you've come back!" Dorr looked up from his desk to meet the gunman's eyes. "You must 'ave crossed trails with that deputy I sent over to Bonita."

"I understood yuh was lookin' for me, sheriff," Puff jeered, "so I came right over."

"Humph! Sit down there and let's hear your alibi. And don't leave out none of the details."

It was while Puff was explaining his absence to the sheriff and telling that individual that he had plenty of witnesses in Bonita to corroborate him, that Nancy came in with a tray of food for the prisoner.

She paled a bit as she saw the gunman, recovered herself, and swept on by him with only a nod, her eyes only showing the distaste she felt.

"Right pretty waitress yuh got, Sheriff," the gunman remarked, loud enough for her to hear, and grinned as he saw the red creep up the back of her neck. "I wouldn't mind languishin' in one of them cells myself."

"Yeah!" the law officer snorted, "and I'd be tickled to have you. Don't count yore horses too soon. You may be in there yet."

"There is always that chance," the gunman answered with an easy laugh.

Nancy returned now empty handed, and passed by him without even a glance, only the twin spots of color in her rounded cheeks revealing the feeling of revulsion that she felt in having to come that close to him. As she reached the door, she spoke directly to the sheriff.

"Maw's having dinner a little earlier tonight, Dorr. You better come in early. There is quite a big table to feed."

"Thanks, Nancy. I reckon this gunhawk can come back later. If you know what's good for you, Puff, you'll stick around town for a spell until I get a chance to check on them witnesses."

Nancy continued on her way into the Mansion House with a fervent prayer that the sheriff would follow her immediately.

He did. If there was one thing the law officer enjoyed, it was the Mansion House victuals, so sending Puff back to the Lone Deuce and leaving word with his deputy, he was soon working industriously at a heaping plate of hot food.

Back in his cell unobserved, Cliff had twirled the cylinders of the twin six-guns that Nancy had delivered to him surreptitiously, took up a position close to the iron grating, and called to the deputy. That individual came tapping back unsuspecting. Cliff pushed the empty tray beneath the door and as the man stooped to pick it up, a hand shot out and gripped his throat in a vise-like grip, preventing any outcry.

At the same instant, the muzzle of a .45 was shoved into his middle. The hand that had clawed at the holster remained dangling at his side.

"Unlock that door, Tom. Quick!" Cliff ordered grimly.

The jutting jaw, the cold eyes, and the tense lines about the medico's face did as much to convince the deputy as did the hard barrel of the gun poking at his ribs. He knew that his life hung by a thread and life was more precious at that instant than the incarceration of a damned medico who could hit the eye of a weathercock at fifty paces.

Gasping and fumbling, he inserted the key in the lock. The door swung outward and Cliff followed it, still hanging tenaciously to his victim. Releasing his hold on the man's throat, he swiftly deprived him of his gun and pushed him inside the cell.

"Just lay down there on the cot, Tom, and keep quiet. I don't intend to harm you, but there's a few things that will have to be attended to before I leave."

The deputy was young and valued his life, so he submitted docilely while Cliff bound him securely and shoved a gag in his mouth improvised from the strips of the blanket. He heard the cell door clang shut and knew that his prisoner had flown. He immediately struggled mightily to release himself and make an outcry, but the medico had done a thorough job.

Gun in hand, Cliff peered into the office, saw that it was empty, and with catlike steps reached the door. For only a moment he hesitated on the threshold, then slipped into the shadows, cut down between the two buildings and reached the stable of the Mansion House in the rear.

Maw had done a thorough job. The big gelding was saddled and ready, the saddle pockets filled with food. He made a swift examination of the alley, mounted, and keeping the horse in the darkest part, rode slowly out of town. As he passed the last building, he dug in his spurs, letting the gelding break into a swift gallop that soon took him over the rise to the north.

Nancy, sitting along side of the sheriff at the dinner table, kept that gentleman busy answering questions. There had been no outcry from the jail, but she thought she had detected the sound of receding hoofs in the alley. She had seen the law officer's ears perk up as if he too heard it and she had immediately started talking a little louder so as to drown the noise out if possible by her own voice.

But much as the sheriff enjoyed his victuals, he was not the kind to loiter after the meal was finished. He ate with a swiftness that appalled the girl. With a prayer that her lover had made good his escape, she watched the sheriff vanish through the door on his way back to his office.

But something else happened at that moment to heighten her fears for Cliff's safety, and to make the sheriff scurry for his office with all possible speed, dragging out his guns as he ran. A large party of horsemen came whirling down the main street and stopped suddenly in front of the jail. There were at least twenty men in the group and all of them were heavily armed, rifles resting across their knees.

The men inside the Mansion House came pouring out to face them. Not that they intended to interfere with such a well-armed group, but because they wanted to see what would transpire.

Pat Zanders, the owner of the Squared X, was the spokesman for the group. He dropped heavily to the ground and approached the gaunt figure of the frock coated sheriff who stood framed in his door, a gun in each hand.

"I reckon yuh know what we came for, Dorr," the rancher announced, gruffly. "We don't want to hurt nobody and we figured yuh might listen to reason. Will yuh give up the prisoner or have we got to come and get him?"

Nancy, standing by the door of the Mansion House among the interested spectators, saw the grin of amusement that flashed across the sheriff's face, followed by the determined set to his jaw. She wondered a little about that grin. What made him so sure of himself? Then she heard Plum's hard voice in reply.

"It kind of looks like you'd have to come and get him, doesn't it, Pat? It takes more 'n a parcel of cowmen to scare me off. Cliff's my prisoner and I'm responsible for his safety until he's tried and either acquitted or convicted. You elected me sheriff of this county and I'm aimin' to uphold my oath of office."

"Don't be a danged old fool, Dorr," the rancher argued. "Yuh ain't got a chance. The boys 'ave got their gunsights notched on yuh right now."

The girl studied the grim faces of the men on their mounts. She was torn between the fear that Cliff hadn't escaped and the anxiety that the sheriff might be killed needlessly. There was no doubt in her mind but what these men would go to any lengths to accomplish their purpose, even to the murdering of the sheriff.

In a few quick strides she ranged her slender figure alongside of the law officer, her eyes blazing with fury. "I thought that even cattlemen had a code of honor," she snapped, "but I see they haven't. If you want the doctor you'll have to kill us both."

This seemed to shame some of the cowhands, but not all of them. Pat Zanders looked a bit nonplussed and uncertain, until the cries of his men urged him on.

"Yuh better stand aside, Miss Nancy," he advised. "We don't want to hurt yuh, nor the sheriff neither."

The sheriff leaned closer to her and winked his eye. "Ain't nothin' to worry over, Nancy. I can handle these mavericks," he whispered. "I don't think there's anythin' but a hogtied deputy back there."

"I hope you're right."

Nancy backed off, aware now that the sheriff was not as big a fool as she imagined him to have been. He must know that Cliff had made good his escape. This was just a stall for time, to give her lover a better chance to put additional distance between himself and a posse.

With the girl out of the way, the rancher became more insistent. "Get out of the way, Dorr, before some of the boys get itchy fingers. We want that medico and we're a goin' to have him."

"Looks like they ain't no law left in this danged county," the sheriff sighed at last, sheathing his guns. "I reckon there's nothin' more I can do about it. There ain't no sense in two of us dyin'. But yo're makin' a big mistake, Pat. The medico's innocent."

Puff, along with several other sheepmen, had been watching from the opposite side of the street. The gunman was grinning in anticipation. They would make short work of the medico once they got him outside of the jail, and Nancy would be on hand to witness it.

Pat Zanders and three of the men rushed past the sheriff and thumped on through the office and to the cells. The sheriff was the only one who heard their first astonished cries. In a moment they came barging back.

"Yo're a hell of a sheriff, Dorr," the rancher exploded in fury. "That ain't the medico. That's one of yore damned deputies. Yore prisoner's gone."

The sheriff looked startled. "That so? That's funny. He was there jest 'fore I went in for dinner. Come to think of it, now——" His eyes twinkled and a slow grin spread over his face—"that you bring it to my attention, I sent the medico over to the jail at Beman. I figured some of you hot-headed hombres might come a lookin' for him."

The owner of the Squared X had all he could do to control his temper, while Puff from the other side of the street gave vent to curses of chagrin.

Later when the street was again empty, the sheriff went in, released his deputy and upbraided him for his stupidity. "Yo're a fine example of the law, Tom Baggot, lettin' a doctor truss you up like that. You had ought to be ashamed of yourself. I covered yore tracks for you, so's the people of this county 'll just think it was a trick. If anybody asks you, tell 'em that the prisoner has been taken to Beman for safe keepin' and that I was the one that tied you up. Unless I miss my guess, Cliff 'll be back here to stand trial."

"Ain't yuh goin' to put a posse on his trail?"

"Course not, you simple minded jigger. If I did that the whole town 'ud know that the prisoner had escaped. Cliff's innocent and I'm givin' him a chance to prove it. I was afraid you'd notice the outline of that .45 barrel under the napkin when Nancy brought his tray in, but neither you nor Puff saw it. You got to pay more attention to details, Tom, if you ever want to be a good law officer. Be more observin'."

The deputy left to get his dinner and the sheriff met Nancy on the veranda. "Yo're a better sheriff, Nancy, than I am," the law officer extolled. "That was a right smart move on your part."

The girl reddened and smiled. "You knew it all the time, Dorr Plum, and I thought I was pulling wool over your eyes. Thanks. I always thought you were the salt of the earth and now I'm positive of it. Cliff told me to tell you that he'd be back for the trial and not to worry."

"Shucks! I knew that, Nancy. They're ain't a finer man in the whole state of Arizona. Cliff's the only man in this county outside of myself that's got a head on his shoulders. He's a goin' to make some gal a right fine husband."

"You just bet he is, Dorr." Her eyes shone with hidden fires. "He's never failed me yet. He won't now, but you and I have got to help. Will you?"

"You know daggoned well I will, Nancy."

Her hand rested in his for just a moment, then she mounted her horse, and vanished into the darkness toward the S Bar 8. A moment later, Puff stole out of the Lone Deuce, forked his horse, and followed. The gunman wanted information. He had been sadly disappointed when the lynching party failed to appear with the medico, and he had a hunch from the little conversation that had carried across the street to his keen ears that Nancy knew more about the medico's whereabouts than she had divulged to the sheriff.

But Nancy's big bay was fast and she was in a hurry to get home to her father whom she had neglected the entire day, and was unsaddling and turning her mount loose to graze when the gunman caught up with her.

"That bay's a mighty fast horse, Nancy," he remarked, as he reined in his mount close to the corral. "Yuh sure went a foggin' after yuh left town."

"Yes, he's rather fast," she replied coldly, "but not as fast as Midnight, the horse you killed."

"Now, don't talk thataway, Nancy. I'm sorry I did that to yuh. I was hopin' yuh might forget and let bygones be bygones."

"I've learned to forget you, I can assure you, Mister Gordon," she snapped back. "We've seen too much of your kind already in this county. The range would be better off without you."

The gunman's eyes flickered dangerously. "Yuh may be singin' another tune when that damned medico is swingin' from a noose."

It was too dark for Puff to see the expression that crossed Nancy's face at that moment. If he had seen it, he wouldn't have felt so sure of himself.

"I don't think it will be Cliff who does the swinging, Mister Gordon," her reply came back. "There's another man in this county that's going to pay for that crime."

"Well now that 'ud be jest too bad, Nancy," he mocked. "I'd hate to see another man swing for the medico's crime. That wouldn't be justice." He slid from his horse and faced her. His voice took on an angrier tone. "You better not plan on ever marryin' that hombre. Yore dad's given me first chance and I ain't lettin' no beef-eatin' medico beat my time."

"How interesting! I don't suppose that you considered my wishes for a moment. You wouldn't. Men of your type seem to think that they can take whatever they wish. Will you please get out of my way. I am anxious to go in the house."

Puff reached for her, determined to have at least a kiss for his hard ride even if it was forced, but Nancy was too quick for him. Her quirt made a swishing sound in the air and landed with a smack across his dark face, biting into his tough skin and raising a livid welt. Before he could recover himself, she had fled to the safety of the ranchhouse.

Puff cursed and wiped the blood from his face, forked his horse, and roweling the animal cruelly, thundered away in the darkness toward his rendezvous with the mysterious Carl.

Following the ridges, loping through the cañons far to the north, Cliff traveled the unbeaten trail to Bonita. And as he rode he wondered if after all this was to be a wild goose chase. What evidence could he possibly unearth in the next county? But somehow or other he must pick up the signs that would lead to the solution of the range war which now was definitely linked with the murder of Pim. The unknown Carl and the gunman who had sent the medico on his useless trip to the Lazy Arrow must both be found and made to talk. Cliff knew that he had all the pieces of the puzzle if he could but fit them together properly.

Looking at the slouched deeply tanned figure of the medico astride the big gelding, no one would have suspected him of being a physician. The habiliments of his trade had been left behind. He was now a wandering cowpoke on the loose. His legs were encased in worn and scratched leather chaps. The butt of a long barreled .45 protruded from its black holster lashed to his thigh.

At the S Bar 8 many miles to the south, Nancy had been trying to get her parent to assist her in proving the medico's innocence, but she was getting nowhere with that stubborn, grizzled sheepman. Much as he was pleased over the death of his enemy, he was still inclined to think that Cliff had had a hand in it. He had seen hatred blaze in the medico's eyes that day when he had threatened Pim, and he was inclined to believe that Cliff was only getting his just desserts. The medico had been a thorn in the sheepman's side now for months with his meddling into matters that didn't concern him. But what galled him the most was that no matter which way he turned, he was continually getting himself into the physician's debt. He had seen his daughter's rising interest in that young man and looked upon the coming trial and certain conviction of Cliff as a way out of his dilemma.

Not such a great distance from the S Bar 8 on the edge of the desert, Puff was in subdued conversation with his employer from the neighboring county.

"Jist as soon as the trial's over and they've buried that meddlin' doc, we'll run them mavericks clear out of the state. They're goin' to get a real taste of gun smoke."

"It's about time," came the grumbling reply. "But how are you going to handle Starweather? It may not be so easy now that you and the gal have had a falling out."

"Leave that to me," the gunman snarled. "I'll meet yuh down here the day after the trial."

But the bully of Painted Springs was never destined to meet his employer under the candelabra arms of the Joshua tree. If he had but known it, the circumstances of their next rendezvous would be far from pleasant both from the gunman's viewpoint and from that of his employer.

CHAPTER NINETEEN
THE FINGER OF SUSPICION

Painted Springs was awake at an early hour on the morning of the trial. The Dragoon range to the west was a mass of mauve peaks, banked with shadows of purple and the mesa was a vast ocean of color. The sun coming up over the chaparral studded uplands tinted the horizon with golden radiance. Here and there dust motes proclaimed the near arrival of some new cowhand or sheepman. Inverted cones of dry, powdery soil announced the coming to town of buckboards with their loads of human freight.

Horses of every description, age, and color, swished their broom-like tails at the hitching rails. Wagons, buggies, vehicles of every kind were drawn up in side streets.

Children played in the dusty street, supremely indifferent to the grim and voiceless menace that stalked Painted Springs. Men stood singly and in groups, conversing in low tones, greeting the newcomers, and commenting upon the dryness of the season.

Even at this early hour the Lone Deuce was doing a thriving business. The dead line had been thrown aside for the occasion upon mutual consent of both sides. Cowhands stood shoulder to shoulder with sheepmen at Tim's long bar even though there was no fraternization. There was hardly a man who didn't carry a six-gun strapped down to his thigh, but there were none who were anxious to use them.

There was much speculation as to the outcome of the trial.

"The doc's guilty," a short, stocky, puncher contended, "and I reckon that's all there is to it. That jury 'll settle his hash pronto."

"I don' know," his companion argued. "It don't seem good sense to shoot a man and leave yore loaded cutter. Course, he may have gotten scared and dropped it."

"They'd ought to give him a medal instead of a noose," a sheepman proclaimed to his cronies at the opposite end of the bar and out of earshot of the punchers. "That Percy Pim was a no-account son of a mangy coyote."

Locked in his cell, Cliff was talking with his attorney, Henry Montgomery, an old classmate from college. "That's about all there is, Hank. I know who's behind the range war and the reasons for it, but I haven't a clue as to the murderer of Pim. Did you locate Jim Croll?"

"Yes. That will be one point in your favor, Cliff. Croll ought to be here shortly. Thank goodness we managed to get Judge Frame from Beman. That other judge may be all right, but he's too good a cattleman to have on the bench."

The sheriff came to the door and pushed the key into the lock. "We're all set, Cliff. Court is about to go in session." His hand rested heavily on the medico's shoulder as Cliff filed out through the door, a heavily armed deputy on each side of him. "Keep your shirt on, Son. They ain't got a noose around yore neck yet."

Cliff thanked him with a reassuring nod, and head erect and looking straight in front of him, marched through the crowd of men and women lounging on the sidewalk into the hotel.

Painted Springs was not yet large enough to boast of a courthouse even though it was the county seat, and the Mansion House dining room, being the largest single room in town, had been requisitioned for that purpose. Flanked by the two deputies and followed by the frock-coated sheriff and his attorney, the doctor passed through the crowd inside the hotel and into the dining room.

Gilbert Frame, the presiding judge from the nearby town of Beman, sat on a platform improvised from empty packing cases and planks. In front of him was a plain table. To the judge's left the twelve men who had been drawn for jury service were arranged in two rows. They all eagerly trained their eyes on the prisoner as he took his place at a table in front of them.

Cliff met their gaze with eyes that were steadfast and unwavering. One or two of them were strangers, but the rest he knew. They were all ranchers of the county, men of tenacious purpose, men whom he thought would dispense justice according to their beliefs, but there wasn't a friendly eye among them. They watched the prisoner stoically, their feelings disguised by expressionless poker faces.

The medico's gray eyes traveled leisurely about the room, giving no sign of recognition to anyone. Every available chair, box, and bench, had been crowded into the room, filling it to overflowing. Even the windows were filled with strained and curious faces.

Cliff had hoped he would catch a glimpse of the one person that he wanted to see more than any other, but if Nancy was present, she was effectually hidden from his sight. But he did catch sight of his enemy Puff. That individual, surrounded by a half dozen of his gunhawks, was lounging with his back to the wall, an arrogant, self-satisfied expression on his swart face, his eyes black and intensely bright like a bird's.

One of the deputies, pressed into service to act as bailiff, stood up, cleared his throat, and in a hoarse, quavering voice, read the indictment. A hush fell on the room as he finished and all eyes were concentrated on the prisoner.

The judge looked toward the prisoner. "What is the prisoner's plea?"

Hank Montgomery answered for Cliff. He stood up and said in a clear voice, "Not guilty."

A bedlam of voices broke out from the assembled crowd. The judge looked them over sternly and rapped with his fist for quiet. The trial was on. Cliff took the witness chair and in a clear voice detailed his actions on the night of the murder.

The jury listened attentively. The medico's Colt was produced by the prosecuting attorney, a pock-marked bearded man from an adjoining county. Slowly and relentlessly, he built up the circumstantial evidence against the doctor, bringing witnesses to corroborate his statements; telling of the medico's threats, of his swift and unerring ability to use a gun. The jury was impressed.

His attorney rose swiftly in rebuttal. "I am willing to concede to the court that the evidence produced points strongly to my client as the murderer of Percy Pim, yet I contend that there is other evidence which must be introduced which is indirectly responsible for the death of the owner of the Circle Bar T and directly responsible for the range war which has been ravaging this county. You men are all aware of the services rendered by the prisoner in his position as county health officer and as medical advisor, but let us review them. Doctor Monroe's first duty, his first patient on his arrival in Painted Springs, was the deceased. By expert medical skill he brought Pim back from the divide and restored him to good health. Would such a man deliberately take the life of his erstwhile patient? I doubt it."

There were murmurs of both approval and disapproval. The attorney went on.

"Not many months ago, a holocaust in the shape of a smallpox epidemic descended upon the herders of this community. In spite of obvious danger to himself, the accused labored mightily, having as assistants Miss Nancy Starweather and one Puff Gordon, a hired gunhawk of the sheep contingency. After weeks of unceasing, heart-breaking work, the accused brought the epidemic under control, thereby saving the lives of innumerable citizens of this community. Would such a man murder another in cold blood, leaving his instrument of death for all to see? I think not."

An objection by the prosecuting attorney was overruled by the judge.

"On the heels of the smallpox epidemic came a calamity to the cattlemen of this county, the foot and mouth disease. The accused, with the assistance of John Ferris, government inspector, stamped out the disease with a ruthless and ferocious tenacity. But even after the disease had been checked, Doctor Monroe went further. He discovered where the disease had originated and today knows the perpetrators of that dastardly trick."

This brought startled exclamations from the crowd. The judge again had to rap for order and admonish them sternly that they would all be ejected and the doors closed.

Cliff had been watching Puff out of the corner of his eye and saw the gunman start, when Hank had made that announcement. He also saw one of the gunhawks slip unobtrusively through the crowd, evidently at the sheepman's command.

But as the trial progressed and witness after witness was brought to the stand to testify, the medico knew by the expressions on the faces of the jury that they were all convinced of his guilt. Jim Croll's corroboration of his testimony that he had spent the night at the Lazy Arrow seemed to make some impression on them, but the prosecutor had expected that. Very cleverly he showed that Cliff could very easily have killed the rancher and still arrived at Croll's ranch at the time specified.

The evidence against the prisoner became more damning as the day wore on. He was neither beef nor mutton. He was pictured as a quarrelsome meddler, a man of hot temper, a rarity among country physicians who could shoot to kill with lightning swiftness.

The medico glancing about the stuffy and hazy room, could discern no look of pity or sympathy on the faces of the crowd. He realized that his case was well nigh hopeless. He had been damned and condemned to die even before the trial had started. Hank had again called him to the stand, asking him to detail to the crowd the information he had gathered. The medico took his seat and began.

"Since the day of my arrival, I have tried earnestly to do my duties as county health officer, to administer to the sick, and to be a respected citizen of this county. From the first I have been accused of being first a sheepman, then a cattleman. Also from the first I have known that this range war was not the result of a local feud. I mention this because the murder of Percy Pim is directly linked to it. In the town of Bonita there are two unscrupulous men, Carl Mansic and Ralph Brenden, who are greedy for additional range." The medico looked directly at Puff Gordon, his gray eyes accusing. "Those two men have hired the gunhawks that have been ravaging the range. They are not sheepmen. They are cattlemen who hope by making the free range unsuited for animals of any kind, to purchase it for a song when you cattlemen and sheepmen have been driven from your homes and moved to more peaceful communities."

The prosecutor entered an objection at this point, which stopped the medico. Cliff had only to glance at the jury to realize that he had made no impression. They were interested, but not to the extent of forgetting that the medico was all they believed him to be, a meddler and a murderer.

They stood up as the judge gave them instructions. There was no question in the minds of anyone in that room as to the outcome. There wasn't a shred of sympathy for the doctor, except from one or two helpless sources. The verdict had been signed, sealed, and delivered on the range, not in the court room.

A sudden commotion from the rear of the room, stopped the judge in the midst of his instructions. He rapped for order. Breathless, her faced flushed, her eyes bright with determination, came Nancy. She reached the judge's desk, gave him a nod, and asked to take the stand. The prosecutor objected but was overruled. Gilbert Frame was not the kind of a man who would refuse the slight demands of an exceptionally pretty girl. He bowed gallantly and held the witness chair for her. With set lips and snapping eyes, she gave her testimony. It was more of an accusation against the ranchers of the county than any plea for the prisoner.

"On the night of the murder," she began in a cool voice, "Doctor Monroe had dinner with my father and me at the S Bar 8. He was entirely unarmed and I cautioned him of his foolhardiness. He left about ten that night to return to town. Before he reached there he was stopped by Gila Flint, a gunman, and told to go at once to the Lazy Arrow. That order was given to Gila by Puff Gordon." She turned and faced that individual, her eyes like pools of fire. "It was you, Puff Gordon, who killed Pim. You thought your alibi would protect you. You planned this out, knowing that it would remove two of your opponents. You left the Lone Deuce at dusk, but you didn't go directly to Bonita. You were seen in Doctor Monroe's office that night ; seen to steal the doctor's gun from its holster. I have a witness to that effect."

It was like the explosion of a bombshell. All eyes were trained on the gunman and his hired gunhawks. But miraculously Puff kept his temper. Only the cold glitter in his black eyes gave evidence of the turmoil that was seething within him.

"Prove it," he called loudly, arrogantly, folding his arms across his chest. "I wasn't anywheres near the doc's office. I was half way to Bonita when the crime was committed. Where's yore witness?"

The sheriff came pushing and pulling Manuel Geosta toward the judge.

Puff took one look at the witness. His face blanched slightly, then the muscles about his jaw and lips tightened. "You dirty sneakin' greaser," he gritted. There came the sudden and unexpected blast of a .45 reverberating in the crowded room. Acrid smoke drifted across the faces of the jury, the judge, and the prisoner at the bar. A woman screamed.

The gunman's voice cut through the haze. "Claw the sky, you polecats! Every last one of yuh or I'll let daylight into yuh."

There wasn't a dissenting voice. Every man in the room had been deprived of his irons before being admitted to the court. Where the gunman had contrived to conceal his weapon no one knew. The sheriff had been the only one outside of his deputies who had carried a six-gun and he now lay flat on his face, beside the inert form of the Mexican.

Puff and his henchmen, all armed, covered the crowd, menacing them. Over the barrel of his .45 Puff was glaring at the medico, his shoulders slouched, his eyes black as midnight and flickering dangerously. "I ought to kill yuh, yuh mangy meddlin' medico, but I reckon you'd like to have an even break." He laughed hoarsely. "This town's getting too warm for comfort, so I'm pullin' my freight pronto, but 'fore I go, I'd like to meet yuh alone and settle our difficulties. You've blocked me at every turn and I'm just about fed up with it. When this court adjourns and when the sun sets over the Dragoons I'm coming a gunnin' for yuh. If yuh ain't armed I'm goin' to gunwhip yuh to death. The sheepmen are backin' me up from the other side of the street, and if any man other than the Doc sticks his head out a door, he'll get his face blasted."

The medico got slowly to his feet. He smiled, but his lips were a straight line. This time the gunman had overplayed his hand. There would be no quarter asked and none given. Puff had killed his best friend, Dorr Plum, and had thereby committed murder and desecrated a court of justice. He, as the county health officer, would have to uphold the law of the community and avenge the sheriff's death.

He knew from the expressions of the faces about him that this was the acid test. But a moment before he had been a murderer, a rat to be hanged without the least compunction, an outcast of society. Now if he could rid the county of this murderous, thieving gunman, he could once and for all settle the range feud, bring peace to the community, and place himself in an enviable position. If he failed to accept the gunhawk's challenge, he would be again an outcast shunned by the entire county.

For just an instant his eyes met those of Nancy's beseeching him not to accept. Her face was blanched to the color of chalk, her eyes were pleading. Resolutely he tore his gaze from hers and faced the swart gunman.

"That isn't such a big order, Puff," he mocked, with a tinge of humor that twisted his lips grotesquely. "You've tried about every shady way your warped brain could devise to get me out of the county. It just happens that nothing would give me greater pleasure than to send a stinking rat like you where you belong. Now if you'll take your gunmen and get out, I'll get busy with these two men you've shot."

Puff merely sneered in reply. The failure of his plans had made him desperate. He had thrown caution to the winds. He had lost Nancy. The medico had outwitted him at every turn. He was filled with a consuming hatred that had driven all thought of self-preservation from his mind. He had but one thought left, to salivate the medico, to put him once and for all out of his way.

With his gunhawks at his heels menacing the crowd, he backed through the door and into the street. Cliff hardly waited for him to vanish before he had his medical kit brought to him, and had carried the two men to more comfortable quarters. The Mexican was beyond hope, but with Dorr there was a chance. The slug had gone clean through Manuel, struck Dorr in the chest, and deflecting from a rib had traveled downward to lodge in the abdomen.

Cliff worked with cunning and skill, a silent prayer on his lips that his efforts would be crowned with success. It was still several hours to the appointed time. He forgot the gunman's challenge in his anxiety over his patient. Making the Mexican as comfortable as possible, he spent all of his time on the sheriff. It was a delicate operation that required nerveless fingers and steady hands. There were intricate parts of the man's anatomy that had to be avoided for fear of instant death. The slug was deeply imbedded in the tissues, the soft lead having mushroomed to make a jagged hole.

Nancy stood by his side, handing him the carefully sterilized instruments as he called for them. Several times she bit her lips and swayed uncertainly as a spurt of blood from some unseen vein or artery threatened life. Maw sat in the background, her face a pasty gray, her hands busy with steaming water and hot cloths.

The room was pregnant with death. The occupants felt it and fought on grimly. Geosta in one corner was still alive, but his breathing was becoming shorter and more difficult. Dorr was unconscious. He was not aware of the capable and gentle fingers probing over his abdomen.

The bright sun, dropping relentlessly behind the Dragoon range of jig-saw peaks, shot out golden lances, throwing the brush fringed bases into deep shadows of purple. Broad bands of color appeared over the horizon while over the town of Painted Springs a brooding hush descended, and made itself felt to the crowded mass of humanity packed into the lobby of the Mansion House. A life hung in the balance; a life suspended by a gossamer thread.

CHAPTER TWENTY
MORPHINE INSTEAD OF BULLETS

Time seemed interminable to the tight-lipped girl who stood tense by the medico's side. It wasn't the first time that Nancy had seen Cliff operate and probe for a leaden slug, but here the life of a dear friend hung by a slender thread. Perhaps no other man was as near and dear to her outside of her father as this grizzled veteran of the plains.

Fearing the shock might kill his patient, Cliff had used an anaesthetic and the sheriff's gaunt frame lay stretched in almost lifeless immobility beneath her eyes. The man's spasmodic breathing gave the only sign of life.

But at last Cliff straightened. In his slender fingers lay a pair of bright forceps. "I've got it," he muttered. His voice held a combination of relief and grim determination.

"Thank God!" came from Nancy's lips. It was all she could manage to say. It had taken every ounce of her courage to stand there practically helpless while the life's blood slowly oozed from the man she loved. She swayed uncertainly. The basin in her hand tipped, spilling some of its contents.

The medico looked at her sharply. "Hold yourself, Nancy. We're not through yet. Don't fail me now."

With a supreme effort of will she recovered herself. Her hand traveled across her forehead. "I won't faint, Cliff. I won't fail you."

He dared not take additional time to caution her further. There was still a great deal of intricate surgery to perform before the sheriff would be safe. There were minute veins and arteries to be cauterized and tied. Each tissue had to be replaced in its proper setting. Each delicate part of the sheriff's anatomy had to be handled with infinite care.

But at last the task was completed. It was nature's turn to begin her slow healing processes. The medico took the basin from Nancy's outstretched hands and helped her to a chair. There was nothing more he could do for his friend. The arm of surgery had reached as far as it could. Time and watchful care was needed now.

From his medicine kit he produced a bottle of pills. One of these he dropped into a glass of water and handed it to the girl. "Drink that, honey," he ordered with a smile of encouragement. "You look pretty well tuckered out."

Maw Blane, gray of face, hiding the state of her own nerves, had risen from her chair. "Will he live, Doc? Is there any chance?"

Cliff put his hand on her shoulder. "If he doesn't it won't be the fault of my two helpers. All we can do now is hope for the best."

Maw nodded, made some lame excuse that she was needed elsewhere, and hurried out. She was wise enough to sense that these two wanted to be alone. A hush fell on the room as the door was closed. Nancy sat staring straight ahead of her in a sort of dumb unhappiness.

Her blue eyes drifted toward the window. For the first time she noticed that the sun had sunk to a brilliant ball of crimson over the purple shadows of the Dragoon peaks. Twilight was near. A cold hand clutched at her heart, bringing her hands to her throat in a gesture of fear. Within an hour the man she loved more than life itself was going out to face almost certain death. Her lips twitched convulsively and a wave of nausea and apprehension engulfed her. Her mouth formed words of entreaty, but no sound came from them. She was struggling mightily to control herself.

Suddenly the pent up flood could be stemmed no longer. Cliff had moved to the window and was looking absently into the now barren street. Beasts and humans had been removed to safer places. Nancy rose from her chair and reached the medico's side. Her hands clutched his in a convulsive gesture.

"Don't meet him, Cliff," she whispered. "Please don't." In her mind's eye she had seen a horrible picture. Cliff was facing the gunman Puff. Each man stood tense, hands gripping their instruments of death. She saw the spurts of blue flame, saw her lover sway, his body jerk spasmodically. Then she saw him fall writhing to the dust, his face contorted with pain ; saw Puff with a sneer on his handsome face turn on his heel and with a grunt of unconcealed triumph vanish from view.

Cliff's voice broke the hallucination. It cut into her dream, gentle, modulated, and soothing. "There's nothing to worry about, honey. We still have an hour. You're upset and nervous."

"I'm afraid. Terribly afraid." The premonition of disaster overwhelmed her. Her eyes met his imploringly. "Why should you risk your life to kill that murderer? It isn't fair. You're not the sheriff."

His hands were soothing. He drew her close into his arms, his gray eyes somber now. "You forget, Nancy. Dorr is close to death. Brant county has no sheriff at this moment. It is up to me to rid this county of a vile killer."

"No! You are the health officer. You are here to save lives, not to take them. Let the ranchers hunt him down. It isn't up to you to avenge the death of Pim. Please, darling! For my sake give up the idea." A sudden cunning crossed her face, adding new brilliance to the blueness of her eyes. Her voice dropped to a whisper. "My horse is in the stable. Take him and fly to the ranch."

He shook his head slowly, and his lips set in a straight line. "That isn't like you, Nancy. Surely you wouldn't want me to do that. You're losing your senses. Not even a medico would dare pull a trick like that and hope to face his friends again. They would say I was yellow and I couldn't blame them much. No, you don't really mean that."

"But I do, Cliff. I do. Puff will kill you just as he killed Pim. He's heartless and cruel. He hates you." The words flowed out in angry appeal, hysterically.

"Hush, honey! It won't be as simple as that. Have you no faith in me? I know what Puff Gordon is; know the kind of a criminal I have to face. He'll never meet me face to face. Deep in his heart he's afraid." A mocking glint came into his eyes, twisting his lips into a sardonic grin. "You don't need to worry. There 'll be a corpse delivered to the cemetery, but it won't be me. I know how to handle that rat."

Nancy sensed the change that had come over her lover. This was a new side, a side which she had never seen before. He was no longer the gentle-handed physician anxious over the life and health of his patients. His eyes flickered with dancing killer lights that chilled her. His lips had contracted to a grim line of determination.

For a moment the sight unnerved her. She drew back afraid, but her voice when she answered was cold. "You are determined to meet him. You will go in spite of my entreaty; in spite of my wishes. The death of your enemy then is more important than my love, our happiness?"

His face softened momentarily. "Nancy, you know that I would do anything in the world for you. There is no need for me to tell you that I've loved you since the first day I met you, but what you're asking now is impossible. I must meet Puff as I promised. I could never face a person in this county again unless I do. Would you have me scuttle for cover like a frightened coyote, after the threats he's made, leaving him to go free, perhaps to continue his crimes? I'm sure you wouldn't. Deep in your heart you couldn't feel otherwise."

The expression of her face changed. Twin spots of crimson burned in her cheeks. A grimness came to her generous mouth. "You say you love me! You don't know the meaning of the word. In spite of my entreaties you will do what I've begged you not to do. Isn't my happiness to be considered?"

"It is your happiness and mine that I am considering. How could we possibly find happiness with that murderer dogging our footsteps? I have done all that is humanly possible to avoid this encounter. I have been laughed at by cattlemen and sheepmen alike ; called a meddling medico, a nosey, blundering fool. The time has come. Once and for all this range war is to be settled. Either Puff Gordon or the health officer will get out."

His stubbornness made her furious. Her eyes were no longer entreating. She blazed at him, "Go to your death, you fool! Die for Brant county if that's what you wish. They won't make a martyr of you. They'll think as I do. The medico got what was coming to him for his meddling. He should have stuck to his little bright instruments and his pill bottles. But if you live, don't come whining back to me. You told me once that Brant county was full of lunatics. Maybe we are, but at least we're not fools. If you meet Puff Gordon, I never want to see you again."

A dull red suffused his face, accentuating the chill of his gray eyes. "Surely you don't mean that, Nancy?" A doubt had risen in his mind. Was she anxious over his safety or over the safety of the gunhawk?

She thought he was weakening and woman-like pressed her point. "I do mean it, Cliff. Every word of it. If you meet and harm Puff Gordon, I never want to see you again."

His sudden suspicion had been confirmed by her words. It was not his safety, but Puff's that worried her. Then the gunman after all was the man she really loved. Well, he'd save the scoundrel for her. He had said he would do anything in the world for her, but this would be the last thing he would do. It would not be a fight to the death as he had planned, but merely a vindication, a proof of his own superiority. Puff would feel his heavy hand as he had never felt it before. He would knock all the beauty from his face. Oh, it would be a thorough job! With that accomplished he would leave. Painted Springs was no place for a medico. What they needed was a mortician!

His answer when it came at last, coldly and distinctly, drew a pallor to her face. "I'll save your killer for you, Nancy. He may be a pretty mess to look at when I get through with him, but he'll still be alive. That much I'll promise. And I'll not come back begging for your favors. I'll leave Painted Springs for good. The gunman will be my wedding present to you." A mocking grin creased his lips. "I wish you lots of luck with your murdering bridegroom."

The hot words made her clutch at the window frame for support. Incredulously, unable to believe what she had heard, she stood mutely staring at him. The man she loved had insulted her, accused her of being in love with a killer. Her teeth sank into her taut lips in anger and dismay.

Cliff gave her no more attention. Leaving her standing there by the window, he called Maw, and gave her swift instructions for the care of the patients in his absence. He made a hurried examination of the two men. Suddenly his eyes lit on the gun belt and the stag-handled .45s of the law officer's. Without a moment's hesitation he buckled them to his waist and thighs.

Seemingly unaware of Nancy's burning gaze, he opened his medical kit and poured into his hand a number of grayish pills from a bottle. He dropped these into his pocket, opened the door, and strode out into the crowded hotel lobby.

Maw looked first at Nancy and then at the medico's back. "Well, I declare!" she exclaimed. "What's eatin' the doc? He stalked out like he'd seen a ghost. Never did I see the likes of it."

Nancy, pale and trembling, managed a shrug. "I guess that's what he did see, Maw. The fool believes that I'm in love with Puff. He refused to listen to me. I begged him not to go."

"Here now, child!" The older woman put her arm around the girl's slim waist. "You two been fightin'. That ain't no way to send yore man out to meet the devil."

Nancy's nerves had reached the breaking point. Tears fringed her lower lids, but she fought them back and squared her shoulders. "I was the fool, Maw. I know it now. I just couldn't bear the thought of Cliff facing that fiend." She made a rush for the door, determined to make amends, but Maw's grim fingers stopped her.

"It's too late, Nancy." The older woman pointed towards the west. "It's sunset."

Bleakly, Nancy followed with her eyes the direction of Maw's outstretched hand. Only a faint rosy glow remained to outline the distant range, making the Dragoon mountains like a strip of jagged cardboard. Tiny flickering spots of yellow were appearing in the deep blue of the sky overhead.

The older woman kept a firm grip on her arm. "Our place is here, Nancy. That's where the doc 'ud want us. That's man's work out there and Cliff Monroe is a real man, don't mistake that. Unless I miss my guess there 'll be one dead sheepman 'fore the sun rises tomorrow mornin'."

Cliff was in the lobby surrounded by a group of now friendly ranchers. They were all giving him advice, but most of it was unintelligible to the medico. His thoughts were back in the sick room with the girl he loved. The curious attributed his chilly composure to the coming encounter.

It was Kentucky Landers who broke the spell and brought a hush to the crowded room. A delegation of sheepmen and cattlemen had met to clear the street, to see that the gun fight was fair. The puncher came shuffling through the door, the tap of his high-heeled boots, sounding like a dirge. He stopped directly in front of Cliff and held out his hand.

"I always knew you was a white man, Cliff. I'm wishin' you luck. No matter what happens I reckon we cowmen 'll have a lot to thank you for. Tonight ends the range war."

Cliff gripped his hand with fingers that were as cold as the steel barrels of the .45s in his gun belt. "Thanks, Kentucky! That's the best news I've heard since I arrived."

There followed whispered advice on the puncher's part, and the silent handshakes of his friends. The medico hitched up his gun belt, took each iron from its holster, and made a swift examination to see that they were fully loaded and in good condition. Turning on his heel, he strode through the crowd, into the dining room, and out to the kitchen door. With a wink at Maw's helper, who was standing there gawking at him, he vanished into the blackness of the night.

In the sick man's room, Nancy and Maw sat side by side at the bedside of the sheriff. Nancy clung grimly to the wrinkled and work-worn hand of the hotel's mistress. They were both too full of apprehension to talk. As they stared silently at the patient, his eyelids flickered and slowly opened.

"Hello, Nancy!" he mumbled. "Hello, Maw! Where's the medico?"

Maw answered. Nancy was too choked to speak. "He'll be back pretty soon, Dorr. He just stepped out for a minute."

The sheriff's eyes rested on the older woman's. He seemed to sense that something was amiss. Painted Springs was too ominously quiet. "Where'd he go? What's goin' on now in this inferno? Tell me, doggone yore blasted hides or I'll romp out of this here bed and find out for myself."

They both realized the futility of trying to keep the encounter a secret. Dorr was that kind of a man. The doctor had ordered absolute quiet. Unless they told him, the sheriff would get out of bed and find out for himself even if it killed him. So Maw told him.

When she had finished, Dorr grunted and a twinkle came into his pain-wracked eyes. "I reckon this is one time when that malo hombre has bitten off a bigger piece than he can chaw properly. That gunman's goin' to look like a piece of Swiss cheese when Cliff gets done with him."

"Yo're right, Dorr," Maw replied, "but Nancy here is a heap worried just the same."

The sheriff put his hand over the girl's and his lips twisted into a smile of encouragement. "Keep yore shirt on, Nancy," he murmured. "There ain't a man in this county can lick that medico. Puff's goin' to get just what's comin' to him."

The law officer's eyes closed. Maw aroused him long enough to give him a drink of some concoction ordered by the doctor. A moment later he was breathing regularly, deep in drugged slumber.

The two women remained motionless. Nancy still clung to the gnarled hand of the sheriff, deriving comfort from it. Maw's chair rocking back and forth, squeaked, and made the girl jump nervously. Restlessly she dropped Dorr's hand and stood up.

"I can't stand it, Maw," she cried. "I can't stand it, I tell you. I must go to him. I can't let him die thinking that I love Puff Gordon."

Before the older woman could interfere, Nancy had crossed the intervening space, and had scurried through the door.

The lobby was a mass of subdued humanity. Tables had been barricaded behind the windows to prevent any stray bullets from reaching the onlookers. Children had been placed in places of safety. One or two of the more foolhardy were peeking through the cracks, watching the dimly-lit street.

Without even a word to anyone, the girl followed in the path of the medico, through the dining room and into the big kitchen.

"Hey, don't you go out there, Miss Nancy," Maw's helper cried out in alarm, as she reached the kitchen door.

The advice was useless. Almost before the words were out of his mouth, she was swallowed up in the blackness. At that instant, there came the detonation of a six-gun, followed by four more shots in rapid succession. The girl stopped dead in her tracks. She was too late. Cliff——

It was Maw who found her lying in the alley and dragged her back to the safety of the hotel's walls, soothing her as best she could, whispering words of encouragement. The detonation of another single shot reverberated outside, followed by ominous silence, then a man's curses.

Nancy groaned. Maw slipped an arm about her shoulder. "He'll come back, child. Don't you fret. It 'll take more 'an a murderin' gunhawk to catch that boy nappin'. Just wait and see."

CHAPTER TWENTY-ONE DOC KEEPS HIS PROMISE

Once again the medico of Painted Springs had left behind the habiliments of his trade. No one encountering the tall, broad shouldered, and gun-belted man who made his way stealthily up the alley would have suspected him of being a physician. There was no sympathy now in his slate-colored eyes, only a grimness about the straight line of his mouth, a relentlessness of purpose to the set of his jaws.

Reaching the end of the line of frame buildings that fronted the main street, he turned and moving cautiously along the adobe wall of the last dwelling, he reached the street. For a time he stood there, his body in the shadows, his eyes peering keenly up the darkened street. Shades and windows had been barricaded. Only here and there a faint ray of light escaped in a pencil-like slit, making the shadows even more pronounced.

Somewhere concealed in one of those black patches Puff Gordon was slouched. Of that much the medico was convinced. But how many more of his henchmen were concealed in other strategic places, he could only guess. Yet he knew they were there. The gunman was not brave enough to meet him according to the rules. He had planned to meet the medico with the odds in his favor. Fearing some such treachery on the part of his opponent, Cliff had used the back door of the Mansion House.

Fortunately there was no moon. The flat mesa and the foothills were meaningless mounds of blackness. A horse from some hitching post in the rear of the Lone Deuce neighed, the sound cutting through the silence with the sharpness of a keen blade. The medico shifted his position slightly, stooped low and picked up a pebble the size of his thumb.

For a moment he stood watching a spot further down the street where he thought he had detected a slight movement. Suddenly his hand shot back and he hurled the pebble. The stone caromed off a wooden upright and rattled to rest on the plank sidewalk.

A spurt of blue flame followed by the detonation of a heavy caliber gun, came instantly on the heels of the pebble's rattle. Simultaneously came the report of three more shots in rapid succession. A grin split the medico's face. His ruse had worked. He now knew the location of Puff and his three henchmen.

The first shot had undoubtedly come from the nervous fingers of the gunman. The three following had been the death volley from his gunhawks. They had guessed that their leader had seen the medico. They were taking no chances. It was to have been four against one.

Nancy's parting words were still rankling in Cliff's mind. He had left the Mansion House with a determination to spare the gunman's life, to bring him to trial as he himself had been brought before the bar of justice. Nancy should have her killer-lover, but he would not be a pleasant sight to gaze upon. Cliff had every intention of changing the shape and contour of the bully's face beyond recognition. Shooting was too good for the gunman. His best friend lay at death's door, pushed there by a slug from Puff's six-gun. The medico knew the sheriff's code. Dorr would have gone to any extreme to bring the killer to trial. That was what Cliff intended to do. Puff Gordon must be made to answer for his crimes at the regularly constituted bar of justice.

As the last shot reverberated from the wooden walls of the buildings, Cliff darted from his place of concealment, reached the opposite side of the street and faded into the shadows. The four gunhawks he had surmised would be too intent on the spot they had aimed at to notice him cross at that end of town.

With cat-like tread, he slipped silently from one shadow to the next towards the spot where he had seen the nearest gunman's spurt of flame. That individual, intent, cautious, and waiting for what he thought was the medico to make another move, was unaware of the danger that lurked in his rear. His first intimation was the muzzle of a Colt shoved cruelly into his back, and the medico's hissing words.

"Drop that iron back into your holster."

Even as his hand obeyed the command, his neck was encircled by sinews of steel, choking off all outcry. He was dragged bodily backward, off the board walk and between two buildings. Cliff backed him up against the wall and with his free hand produced two grayish colored pills from his pocket. Holding the now thoroughly frightened gun fighter in place with the muzzle of his gun, he forced him to swallow the pellets.

The man sputtered and choked, mouthing a curse, but Cliff's steel fingers at his throat and the barrel of the gun in his abdomen convinced him that there was no way out of it.

The pills had no sooner vanished when the physician's fist came like a battering ram from the darkness and connected with the side of his head. The man's knees collapsed and his body went limp.

"That will give you a little temporary rest," Cliff grinned, "and the morphine will do the rest."

Removing the gunman's holster and gun belt, he placed it in a dark corner out of reach. It was now only three against one. The odds were improving. Again he reached the sidewalk. But now he was in a dilemma. Was the nearest gunman Puff or one of his henchmen?

There was only one way to find out. He began slipping stealthily toward the spot where the first gun flash had appeared. A voice hissed at him from the shadows.

"Is that you, Spike?"

It wasn't Puff's voice. It was one of his gunhawks. Cliff answered hoarsely in a low voice, "Did we drill that damned medico?" In a few noiseless strides he reached the gunhawk's side.

Too late, the man recognized him. The butt of the medico's six-gun crashed against the side of his head, cutting the outcry off, crumpling him to his knees. Cliff followed the same procedure with him. He dragged the inert body of the gunman further back between the buildings, forced two more of the morphine tablets between his clenched teeth, deprived him of his armament, and left him to sleep. Although the man was unconscious and unable to swallow, he knew that the two pellets would gradually dissolve and work into his system.

But Puff, on edge from the oppressive silence, had grown suspicious. He was beginning to have qualms that all was not well with his two cronies. Anyhow he wasn't taking any chances with friend or foe. A life meant nothing to him. If he should kill one of his own men by mistake, well—it was too bad. He had heard the man's partial outcry and the gurgling sound that a man makes when something heavy and relentless hits him. He thought he had detected the scraping of boots dragged over planking.

Now he stood tense, listening intently. A board creaked faintly. The gunman's nervous fingers thumbed back the hammer of his six-gun. Cliff saw the spurt of blue flame, then a shower of adobe mud blinded him as the slug imbedded itself in the wall close to his head. Puff's face had been outlined for just a second.

Drawing back behind the barrier of the wall, Cliff wiped the smarting dust from his eyes, and simulating the gunman's jargon, called out in a furious voice, "Yuh loco polecat! I ain't the medico."

A harsh laugh came from the gunman concealed further up the street, followed by another ominous silence. Now Cliff had a real problem to face. Puff faced him hidden between two buildings. Beyond the bully another gunhawk lay in hiding hoping to catch him between two fires. There was only one solution. He must retrace his steps to the nearest alleyway, circle behind the gambling palace and saloon, and reach that furthest man from behind.

But there was grave danger in that. Puff was already on the alert. The slightest sound might bring down the gunman's fire on his head, might end his plans swiftly.

Glancing up at the roofs above him, he noticed a projection. His eyes glinted with renewed hope. Drawing his body further back into the niche, Cliff swiftly drew off his riding boots. With a cougar-like spring he locked his fingers in the projection and slowly pulled himself bodily to the roof. His feet encased in heavy socks made no sound as he crossed the wooden slats.

He reached a skylight and peered down. It revealed the interior of the Lone Deuce. Tim Roney was busy polishing his glassware with a soiled rag. A dozen men stood at the bar, their eyes belying their cool attitude. One man was sprawled in a chair, his head lolling on his chest grotesquely, his eyes closed, his mouth open. Too much red-eye had driven all anxiety or interest in the proceedings from his body.

Cliff's eyes swept the occupants of the room. He had wanted to assure himself that the man who shot at him was Puff. Now he was sure. He left the skylight and moved silently to the far edge of the roof. Dropping his long legs over the side, he descended to the ground, passed the rear of the general store, and finally reached the passageway where the third gunhawk had concealed himself.

That worthy never knew what hit him. Something hard and unyielding descended on his head, bursting like a skyrocket, knocking him completely and efficiently into oblivion. Cliff followed the same procedure with this one. The morphine tablets were forced into his mouth and he was deprived of his armament.

The odds were now even. Cliff retraced his steps, climbed back to the roof of the Lone Deuce and reached a spot directly over his enemy's head. He crouched to leap.

The thunder of an approaching rider, startled both the medico and his opponent. They both saw him and recognized him almost simultaneously. It was Burke Starweather. Nancy had escaped from him that day determined to save Cliff's life. In spite of his gout, in spite of his heart attacks, he had managed to get on his horse at last and come in pursuit. He knew nothing of the menace that hovered over Painted Springs.

Cliff's warning shout died on his lips. He saw the gunman's arm come up, saw the spurt of bluish-yellow flame, heard the detonation of the .45. Too late to save Nancy's father, he catapulted over the edge and landed on the gunman's back.

The gun went spinning from Puff's hand. The medico's fist caught him in the face, bringing a grunting curse to his lips. He was picked up bodily and hurled to the center of the street.

But Puff was fighting for his life now. There was no doubt in his mind as to who his assailant was. Recovering his equilibrium quickly, he crouched and met the medico's next onslaught with a driving right to his midriff.

"I might 'ave known you'd try some of yore sneakin' tricks," he snarled, baring his teeth. "This is one time when yo're goin' to wish you'd used an iron."

Cliff didn't answer. He was consumed with a hatred that was foreign to his habitual nature. But still he didn't lose his cunning. He knew that his enemy was a worthy opponent with any sort of weapon. He partially avoided the gunman's right, struck out with his left, striving to reach a vital spot.

Back and forth, the two men fought like mountain lions at bay, while in front of the Mansion House lay the helpless form of Nancy's father, a silent witness to the struggle. He was still alive, but his leg was doubled under him, broken by the fall of his heavy poundage from the saddle.

Puff's bullet had penetrated his lung. His breathing was gasping and difficult, but in spite of the pain that wracked him, his old eyes were glued to the two struggling figures half-way across the street.

Inside the Mansion House men stood tense, waiting. No one dared to open the doors or to peer out. Nancy had come stumbling back into the room with Maw and sat hunched in a chair, her face chalk-white. Only the sheriff's measured breathing broke the silence of that room. The girl did not know that in the dust of the street, her father was the only witness to the battle as his life slowly ebbed.

In the Lone Deuce Tim Roney continued to wipe his glassware. If he had known how to pray, the Irishman would have done so for the health of the medico. His customers still waited at the bar, waiting for either Puff to announce his victory or to hear the shouts of success from the opposite side of the street.

It was the drunk but lately sprawled in his chair who broke the tension. He came to, looked vacantly around, stumbled to his feet and went ambling for the door. Some one yelled at him, but the man was totally unconscious of any danger to himself. He had forgotten all about the encounter.

Reaching the barricaded door and before anyone could stop him, he pushed the tables aside, pulled open the shutters, and fell out. The noise of the fight now penetrated to the ears of the sheepmen. For a moment they hesitated. Then in a body they made a concerted rush for the door. If there was one thing both a sheepman and a cowman loved it was a fist fight, and here was one that promised to be a knockout.

Knowing of Puff's plans for ambushing the medico, they wondered how he had avoided death, but avoided it he had, for shoulder to shoulder, giving blow for blow, the bully and the medico swayed back and forth in the center of the street, their shuffling steps sending up little puffs of powdery dust.

Hearing the shouts of the sheep contingency brought another flood of humanity from the Mansion House. Windows were swiftly unbarricaded. A flood of light poured out on the main street from unshuttered windows, silhouetting the two fighters. The sidewalks became packed with jostling men, urging on the two combatants. This was a fight the like of which had never been seen in Painted Springs.

Nancy came scurrying out, pushed her way through the crowd and saw her father huddled in the dust. With a cry of horror, she reached his side, calling for help. But the grizzled sheepman knew that his time was short. He stopped her.

"Puff shot me," he grunted, "and it ain't no use to try and save me. Just sit here beside me, Nancy, and hold my hand. I'm goin' out with my boots on, but God Awmighty what a scrap I'm seein'. What started this fracas anyhow?"

The girl knew that argument was useless. There was no man in Brant county as stubborn as Burke Starweather. Quickly she told him of the day's events, of the sheriff's wounds, of Puff's threats, and holding tight to his knotty hands watched the battle.

Cliff, tall, straight, and broad of shoulder seemed to her the personification of righteousness. Puff was satan, from the crown of his coal black hair to the tips of his high-heeled boots. The gunman, noting that his opponent was shoeless had several times stamped cruelly on his stocking feet. After that the medico had managed to dance out of reach of those sharp heels.

As Puff drove in a vicious right, Nancy cried out, "Kill him, Cliff! Kill him!"

Cliff heard that cry above the shouts of the onlookers. He gritted his teeth. Nancy had changed her tune. He suspected that she had found the body of her father. Now she wanted revenge. Well, he wouldn't give her that satisfaction! He would deliver the gunman to her alive, but badly mauled and ready for trial. Stepping swiftly, arms driving in and out like pile drivers, his fists beat a relentless tattoo on the bully's face, driving him slowly backward.

Puff was getting groggy under the incessant hammering. One eye was completely closed. His lips were bruised and bleeding. His cheeks were swollen and his tongue was dry. A stark fear had risen in his gorge that this was the end.

He made one last valiant effort to deliver a telling blow. He missed. Cliff's fist connected with his chin as he sagged forward, sending a thousand bright lights dancing before his eyes. He fell to his knees, his hand darting into his waistband. Into his palm flashed a derringer, a deadly little instrument of death at close quarters.

Cliff saw it too, but too late. There came a sudden bark and flash of fire from the gunman's hand. For just an instant the medico rocked uncertainly on his heels. He had lost after all. A searing pain was gnawing at his vitals. He wouldn't be able to deliver the killer to Nancy as he promised.

Then the mist cleared from his eyes. He saw the gunman's swollen face and leering lips, saw him stagger to his feet. The medico's fist shot out with all the beef of his big frame behind it. It caught the sheepman behind the ear, snapped his head back as if a mule had kicked him, knocked him backward into a lifeless mass of bruised bone and muscle.

Cliff's hand went to his side once and came away covered with blood. A hush had fallen over the citizens of Brant county. They saw the medico take hold of his opponent's shirt collar, saw him look quickly around. Suddenly, his bloodshot eyes found Nancy sitting by the huddled form of her father, and gritting his teeth, he dragged the unconscious form of Puff to her feet.

"Here's your killer alive, as I promised," he growled.

"Cliff! You're wounded!" She struggled to her feet, forgetful for the moment that her father too was close to death.

But the medico only laughed harshly, avoided her outstretched and pleading hands, and pushing his way through the crowd, reached the steps that led upward to his office. Here for just an instant he turned and faced the men of Brant County. One hand clutched grimly at the railing. His face was now as gray as his eyes.

"You'll have to elect a new sheriff, men," he said at last, staring at them out of eyes that could now see only their outlines. "I saw Puff Gordon shoot Burke Starweather. Dorr 'ud like to have him brought to trial properly. I hope you'll do that much for your law officer." His voice hesitated, but he pulled himself together, fighting off the nausea that threatened to engulf him. "You had better get yourselves a new physician too. I'm leaving tonight for good."

But the medico was in no shape to leave that night nor for many nights to come. As he turned to stagger up the steps, his foot missed the first board and his eyes glassed over. He stumbled and fell headlong.

CHAPTER TWENTY-TWO PEACE COMES TO PAINTED SPRINGS

The sudden collapse of the medico brought the onlookers to life. Seeing Cliff pick up his assailant and drag him to a spot close to Nancy, they had surmised that the physician was not seriously wounded by the slug from the derringer. Jim Croll and Kentucky were the first to reach the doctor's inert form and to carry him inside the Mansion House.

The battered gunhawk was unceremoniously and roughly pulled into the jail, while other willing hands helped the girl to carry her father into the hotel. An icy hand had gripped Nancy's heart. She walked behind the unconscious form of her father seemingly incapable of realizing that the two men she loved were both close to death's door.

There wasn't an individual now in that crowded hotel who didn't realize what a physician meant to the community. The ranchers and punchers were all familiar with gun shot wounds but knew only the faintest rudiments of a surgeon's trade. Burke Starweather and Cliff were carried into the same room that held the other two patients. Jim Croll rolled up his sleeves and grim of jaw and with Maw's help tried to do what he could.

The essential thing for the moment was to bring the medico back to consciousness. Starweather was too far gone. So while Nancy, tight-lipped, and gray with remorse and fear, sat by her father, Maw and the rancher worked over the doctor. The medico's gaping wound in his side was stanched and whiskey was forced between his teeth.

Finally his eyes opened. He managed a grin although the searing pain in his side was almost unbearable. Then he saw Nancy sitting by her father. The grin left his face and his eyes came back to rest on the worn face of the mistress of the Mansion House.

"Hello, Maw!" His voice was wracked with pain.

The woman's eyes became filled with unshed tears. She mumbled, "You ain't goin' to fail us now, are you, Doc? The whole of Brant county is dependin' on you. Yo're the only medico within fifty miles."

Cliff seemed to stiffen. His hands clenched and his eyes became a deeper shade of gray. Maw was right. This was no time to quit. If he could get on his feet perhaps he could save Nancy's father. What difference did it make if she loved the gunman?

But Maw saw him try to get up and with quick hands forced him back. "Yo're just the general, Doc. Jim and I 'll do the surgery if you'll just show us the way. Jim thinks the slug is back of yore third rib."

Ignoring the pleading eyes of Nancy, Cliff looked towards Starweather. "Carry him over close to me, Maw. The sheepman has first call on my services. He looks pretty far gone."

Cliff knew that there was no hope for the sheepman. The pallor of death was already on his withered face. But in spite of his willing helper's arguments that his own life was of more importance, he sat pain wracked and directed the fight. Not once did his eyes meet those of the girl he loved.

And while the doctor and his assistants strove to save a life, a party of grim-lipped punchers and sheepmen rounded up the drugged and sleeping gunhawks and much against their own desires, lodged them in the jail with their chief.

Later the sheepmen and the cattlemen held a meeting in the dining room of the hotel. The information that the medico had imparted and the further testimony they had gleaned from him, had convinced them of its truth. Once and for all the hatchet was buried and peace declared in Brant county. The range war was ended.

At the close of that meeting, a posse of men, fully armed rode north across the mesa and through the foothills to the sleeping town of Bonita. The sheriff of that county was not disturbed. These men knew what they wanted. Before sun up they were on their way back with two badly frightened men. The trial they held in the early hours of dawn was short. The bruised and pulpy-faced Puff was their accuser. The gunman wanted to save his own skin if he could. He knew that the game was up. He gave all the details of his hiring, even to the promise of his employers of a thousand head of sheep and the Starweather ranch, with Nancy thrown in if he could win her.

Later the gunman was returned to his cell, but not before he had witnessed the untimely demise of his two employers. He still had hope that through some trick of fate his own life would be spared, and cunningly he had accused one of his employers as the real murderer of Pim. This didn't cut much ice with the cattlemen and sheepmen. The two greedy individuals from Bonita had had enough crimes laid at their door to warrant the merciless justice that was dealt to them. They had promised the medico that Puff Gordon would be brought to trial in the constituted way, but nothing had been promised relating to his employers.

Within a week, the sheriff was again hobbling about, Manuel Geosta had been buried, and the other two wounded were still in bed. Jim Croll's surgery on the medico and the sheepman had not been expert, but both of them were still very much alive.

Nancy had taken up her abode in the Mansion House to be near her father. The sheepman was hanging on to life with a tenacity that astonished Cliff. In spite of his over-taxed heart, in spite of the super-abundance of uric acid in his system, in spite of the horrible wound in his lung that made breathing almost impossible, Starweather was putting up a game fight.

Cliff had hardly spoken to Nancy. He kept his eyes averted when she was near, yet he was deeply conscious of her close proximity. Whenever her back was turned his eyes were on her with a hopelessness that would have torn her heart out if she could have but seen.

The girl was proud ; too proud to break down the wall of reserve she had put up about herself. Cliff had accused her of being in love with a criminal. The thought that he had misconstrued her pleas to such an extent had rankled until she was bitter in the extreme.

But such a condition couldn't continue indefinitely. Maw had seen it and her heart bled for both of them, but wisely she refrained from interfering. She knew that sooner or later, either the girl or Cliff would break under the strain.

Cliff, Starweather, and the girl were alone in the sick room one afternoon. Starweather had been dosing fitfully, his breathing becoming more difficult and spasmodic. Quite suddenly the old sheepman's eyes opened.

"Come here, Nancy," he whispered.

Something in the tone of her father's voice brought the girl to his bedside instantly. Cliff sensed it too, raised himself from a prone position, and looked at the man. He knew the signs. He had seen death before. Weak and nauseated from his illness, he forced himself to get out of bed to try and reach the sheepman's side. He was too late to be of help. Burke Starweather had reached the end of his career.

Nancy had knelt by her father's side, holding tight to his hand. Cliff swayed weakly to the bedside, gently disengaged her hand, and closed the staring eyes of the sheepman.

"It's the end, honey," he whispered.

His arm went about her shoulders. He stooped over to lift her to her feet. The terrible wound from the slug of the gunman's derringer had sapped more of his strength than he realized. He found he hadn't the strength to raise her. His face went gray. His knees crumpled and he pitched headlong to the floor.

Nancy let out a cry for help. Maw Blane came running. Between the two of them they managed to get Cliff back into bed. When he came back to consciousness, Nancy was clinging tight to his hand, stark fear in her eyes.

"You're not going to fail me now, Cliff. Not when I need you the most."

He thought he had never seen eyes as blue. They were like deep pools of crystal mountain water, mirroring the reflection of the tattoo-beating heart beneath her breast. Even a fool could have read correctly the light that shone from them. It wasn't the gunman she loved. Why had he ever imagined that it could be?

But as he stared at her, drinking deeply of the joy that radiated to him, she suddenly veiled those windows, and said tremulously, "You frightened me terribly, Cliff. I was afraid I was going to lose you, too."

His hand tightened over hers. "I've been a fool, Nancy, a blundering fool. Forgive me?"

Again she lifted the curtains that hid the happiness in her eyes. With a glad little cry, she leaned closer and pressed her lips to his. Maw fluttered out, her wrinkled face beaming with gladness and understanding.

And so peace and happiness came to the little cow town of Painted Springs. The spring itself even took on new vigor, for from some hidden subterranean source, a gush of crystal clear water burst forth, making the mesa and the range country lush with vegetation.

THE END

www.ingramcontent.com/pod-product-compliance
Lightning Source LLC
LaVergne TN
LVHW091135080826
845145LV00008B/2169

* 9 7 8 1 9 5 7 8 6 8 8 3 7 *